TOM GALLACHER

Tom Gallacher was best known as a playwright until
the publication of his short stories, APPRENTICE
which also featured Bill Thompson, and which won a
1983 Scottish Arts Council award. His greatest
achievements in the theatre were the three plays, MR
JOYCE IS LEAVING PARIS, SCHELLENBRACK
and REVIVAL! Apart from London, Tom Gallacher
has worked in Denmark, Germany, New York, Edin-
burgh and Dublin. Now returned to Scotland and living
in Glasgow, he has turned to writing fiction full-time.

Tom Gallacher's previous book about Bill Thompson,
JOURNEYMAN, is also published by Sceptre Books.
His latest novel, THE JEWEL MAKER, has recently
won a Scottish Arts Council award.

sceptre

Tom Gallacher

SURVIVOR

sceptre

Copyright © 1985 by Tom Gallacher

First published in Great Britain in 1985 by Hamish Hamilton Ltd

Sceptre edition 1988

Sceptre is an imprint of Hodder and Stoughton Paperbacks, a division of Hodder and Stoughton Ltd.

British Library C.I.P.

Gallacher, Tom
  Survivor.
  I. Title
  823′.914[F]   PR6057.A388

  ISBN 0-340-41354-9

Printed and bound in Great Britain for Hodder and Stoughton Paperbacks, a division of Hodder and Stoughton Ltd, Mill Road, Dunton Green, Sevenoaks, Kent TN13 2YA (Editorial Office: 47 Bedford Square, London, WC1 3DP) by Richard Clay Ltd, Bungay, Suffolk. Photoset by Rowland Phototypesetting Ltd, Bury St Edmunds, Suffolk.

For Barbara

ONE

Sixteen hours after the *Niome* went down I was drooping with fatigue, still dressed in the same clothes, smelling of oily sea water and on a plane for London.

As chief engineer, my first duty was to report to the owner's agent. To save the time a taxi would waste going right across the city, I went by airport bus and tube. The agent's office was in the Minories. Since that was quite near my father's office in Leadenhall Street, however, I went there first. The evening rush hour had just started and I met the first wave of home-bound workers as I emerged from the Aldgate station. It was a cold, squally evening and my frame of mind was not improved by the constant need to dodge the onslaught of other people's umbrella spokes. As I bent and weaved, the salt which formed a gritty ring around my shirt collar chafed my neck. Even my underwear seemed to have been impregnated with salt and I felt very uncomfortable.

My father, I knew, had received a telex message early that morning so there was no need to reassure him of my safety. However, I felt in great need of guidance on how to deal with the shipping agent. The prestigious engineering consultancy of Colin Thompson Partners at the upper end of Leadenhall Street was housed in one of the old, ornate buildings which had resisted all attempts at modernisation. The junior staff had all gone home but my father's secretary worked on and, with some ceremony, ushered me into the front suite where Colin Thompson himself was having an amiable discussion with his right-hand man, Sam Hanson. I'd seen Hanson two or three times since our less than successful first meeting in Montreal seven years earlier. And whereas I didn't like him any more now than I'd liked him then, both my father and I had readily admitted that he did his job much better than I would have done it. Surprised by my earlier than expected arrival, both men got up and the secretary, Mrs Schuster, hovered at the door, anxious to discover what I might need – apart from desalination and twelve hours' sleep.

When I'd related the main events of the *Niome's* sinking, including the odd circumstances in which I nearly lost my voyage notes, my father asked, 'Have you got them with you?'

'Yes. They're in my coat pocket. I suppose the owner's man will want to see them.'

'Why?' Hanson wanted to know.

'Well, as far as I know there's no other record of the trip.'

My father was doubtful. 'Even though there's no log, some of the deck officers may have kept notes – just as you did.'

'Yes, but as my second pointed out, there was no sign of anything wrong with the running of the ship.'

'What about tank cleaning after they discharged the crude?' Hanson asked. 'Ballasting? Ventilation? There must have been a whole lot of gas in those tanks to blast the bow off.'

'She was fitted with an inert gas system,' I told him.

'On engine room control?'

I nodded. 'So you see, considering what happened it looks as though it was a sheer accident or that what went wrong originated in the engine room.'

'In that case,' my father mused, 'it might be better to hang on to your notes for a while. Better still, let me hang on to them. While you're recuperating, Sam could go through them with a fresh mind.'

'Sure,' said Hanson. 'Glad to.' He strode at once to my coat and removed the crumpled folder.

'Meanwhile,' his principal continued, 'I'll get on to the certification office. Norske Veritas, you said?'

'Yes. The ship was built at the Lindø yard in Denmark.'

My father made a note. 'That's A.P. Moller. When?'

'In 1963. Originally she was the *Katia Maersk*.'

'That's an old ship,' Hanson observed. 'When did your owner buy her?'

'Five or six years ago.'

My father must have detected the extreme weariness in my voice. He immediately came round the desk and grasped my arm. 'You'd better put in your appearance for the agent,' he said steering me to the door. 'Don't give him any guesses on what isn't your business. I'll bring the car round in about half an hour.' He paused in the outer office. 'Mrs Schuster, will you call my wife and tell her I'll be home . . . *we'll* be home . . . for dinner after all.'

If I'd known how important it was going to be, I would have given a lot more attention to the access and layout of the agent's premises in the Minories. My first impression of the building was of a fairly standard old office block. In the tiled entrance hall an entire wall was faced in brass plates, which made it look as though there were about twice as many tenants as could possibly be found accommodation.

The shipping agent had three rooms on the second floor and each of them was overrun by filing cabinets. One of these contained my accumulated mail and I was astonished at the size of the bundle which was placed before me. I was also given the most recent news from Denmark. The total of those dead or missing presumed dead was now five, including the master, Captain Nils Meisling. The first officer had regained consciousness, though he was still in a critical condition. Injuries to the survivors were a number of broken arms and broken legs – sustained in abandoning ship. And there were one or two cases of fairly serious burns. It was evident that the agent had already received a full report, though I was asked to confirm that prior to the explosion the ship was under full power and – as far as I knew – free of hazards and on course.

Then the agent asked me for my file on the voyage. But he did not do it directly. He asked if, by any chance, I'd managed to rescue some 'documentation'. Someone must have told him about that. Yet whoever had told him could not know whether or not I'd managed to save the papers. The recent meeting in my father's office prompted me to caution. I told the agent that I had managed to save some private papers. He seemed content to leave it at that; for the moment.

I shifted irritably on the hard office chair and longed to sink into a warm bath. 'Am I the first to get back?' I asked, knowing that some crew members had left Copenhagen several flights before mine.

'Oh no.' The agent glanced at a list on his desk. 'The first back was Mr Foster. He was the most senior deck officer fit enough to travel.'

'Do they think the mate will recover?'

'We're hopeful. Eventually. Not before the preliminary inquiry, though.'

'When will that be?'

'The sooner the better,' the agent said grimly. 'This is a terrible loss, you know. Five lives, the entire cargo. And the ship.'

'Not the entire cargo, surely. We'd already discharged the crude in Poland before the explosion.'

He quickly corrected himself. 'Oh, yes. Yes, of course. That was fortunate.'

'No. Very unfortunate.' He looked at me sharply. Obviously we were thinking of different aspects of the same event. I went on, 'It must have been gas in the empty tanks which caused the explosion.'

'Empty?' He pounced on it. 'Mr Foster says the tanks were in ballast.'

'In ballast, of course. Some ballast.' I cursed myself for ignoring my father's advice not to offer an opinion on what was not my business.

And at that point the receptionist called to say that Mr Colin Thompson was waiting in his car. So grateful was I to escape that I did not wait then to be paid off with the money due to me. I clattered downstairs and out onto the now dark wet street, where the big Daimler gleamed by the kerb.

As we drove through the lessening traffic towards the South Downs I said nothing and gave myself up to dozing and overtired reflection. The most surprising aspect of what had happened was that so little attention was given to the fact that I could have been killed but had managed to survive. Surviving, it seemed, was a very dubious course of action which would be punished. The threat of retribution hovered over all the conversations I'd had since I got into the lifeboat. The fears of my colleagues, the warning of the salvage master, the pained reticence of the Trade attaché, the worried sympathy of my father and his chief aide and then the eager ferreting of the shipping agent. Behind all of these conversations was the signal unspoken charge of negligence. Negligence, if it could be proved, would somehow make the loss of the *Niome* comprehensible and therefore acceptable to others.

Although I was as sure as I could be that there had been no negligence on my part, that was a different thing from proving myself blameless. The worrying fact was that my knowledge of the ship and its systems was far from complete. The voyage which ended in disaster had been my first trip on the *Niome*. Fortunately Clifford Sandys, my second, had been with the ship since it was bought by the new owner. He would be able to advise me on any of the finer points which might occur to the inquiry as fruitful areas of investigation. Indeed, they might well enquire why Clifford, who'd been standing-by as chief, was not given the job I took.

I woke from a troubled doze as the car surged through Pyecombe. I stammered involuntarily, '*Niobe*. It should have been *Niobe*.'

'What was that?' my father asked.

'When the owner picked a new name, the character he was thinking of was *Niobe*. In the Greek legend, you know?'

'Uh huh.' My driver obviously thought I was rambling.

'Then he confused it with the name, Naomi.'

'I'm not sure I'm following this,' my father said.

I was beginning to lose the thread of it myself and wondered why I was mentioning it. 'Anyway, he put down the word *Niome* and everybody thought he couldn't have made a mistake about anything as simple as that.'

'Mmm,' my father chuckled. 'Owners never make mistakes. That's what they pay other people to do.'

'People like me?'

He ignored that and asked, 'Who is the owner?'

'Sir Hubert Cattenix.'

'Ah!' my father sighed knowingly, 'then he's the exception because he's made a number of mistakes. But I didn't know he was in shipping.'

'It's a fairly new company,' I yawned. 'North Cape Shipping.'

'Why did you sign up with them?'

'Short trips. More money,' I said. 'I have to earn a living, you know.'

He didn't respond to that, so I sat and watched the headlights search the narrowing leaf-strewn road ahead for the turn which would bring us home to South Lancing.

As soon as it was possible, I did sleep for more than the twelve hours I'd promised myself. Wisely, my mother decided that sleeping was more important than breakfast and she would probably have let lunch go by as well had not my body insisted that I deal with other necessities. That done, I bathed, dressed and went downstairs. Since I'd been in no condition to pay much attention to the house the previous night, it was with some surprise that I emerged onto the broad semi-circular landing in day-light. There was so much space. Conditioned as I was to narrow alleyways and over-equipped cabins with little headroom it struck me as odd that, once more, I could move in whichever direction I chose and not bump into anything. The silence too was very refreshing. And of course it had been completely done over since my last visit. Perhaps more than once. Marianne Thompson had a reputation among her friends as a tireless re-decorator of her home. She denied this and pointed out that the effect was always the same – only a different colour.

As we ate she questioned me about the voyage. Apparently, my father had mentioned to her that there had been some trouble on the ship for which I might be held responsible. Since she knew that her total lack of technical knowledge easily exasperated him, she turned to me for clarification of the event. I explained that the *Niome* had been carrying a cargo of crude oil and benzine in separate tanks for delivery at different ports. In the low temperatures of the Baltic, crude oil thickens to the consistency of tar, and it has to be heated until it is thin enough to be pumped ashore.

'How is it heated?' my mother asked.

'By low-pressure steam through coils of pipes set in the tank. We have to start heating it several days before we arrive in the port.'

My mother nodded. 'But if you heat it too much it explodes?'

'It could, yes. But it didn't.'

She spread her hands in bewilderment. 'Then what exploded, darling?'

'Empty tanks. You see, we heated up the thick oil and pumped it ashore in Poland. Then we went on to deliver the thin oil to Sweden. But the tanks which had held the thick oil were still coated with the stuff and that gives off an explosive gas.'

'"Inert gas",' she quoted triumphantly from my father's remarks.

'Oh, no! Inert gas is what you blow into the tanks to stop the other gas exploding. Inert gas is exhaust – from the funnel – which has practically no oxygen in it. You draw that off from the uptakes, treat it, and blow it down into the cargo tanks by fans.' I could see from her expression that she was about to abandon this arcane maze and quickly introduced a more homely analogy. 'Take an ashtray,' I said. 'Like an ashtray in a car which has a tight lid. If you put a lighted cigarette end into it and close the lid, the ashtray fills up with smoke and the cigarette goes out. That's because the smoke fills all the space where the oxygen was. The smoke is an inert gas.'

My mother beamed with pleasure, not only at suddenly understanding the system but knowing that it worked. 'Ah! You blow *smoke* into the tank.'

'Yes. More or less. Smoke that's heavier than air.'

'And that should have prevented the explosion?'

'It should have, but it didn't.'

This did not surprise my mother, who expected mechanical things to go wrong, but it was to prove a very worrying fact for me. As chief engineer my responsibility was to see that mechanical things did *not* go wrong.

When we'd had lunch the whole fanciful business of smoke-blowing was forgotten as she led the way into the drawing room and settled to continue reading a biography of Saint-Saëns. Music was her main interest. She'd given up a promising career as a concert pianist to marry and since then had built up a formidable knowledge and expertise on all aspects of musical history and performance. Not content with that, she was a tireless fund-raiser for any new venture which could meet her own stringent standards of ability or talent.

I collected the bundle of mail from my coat in the hallway and joined her. Among my letters was an absurdly early Christmas card from Isa Mulvenny. Mrs Mulvenny had been my landlady when I was an apprentice in Scotland. She was now in a nursing home. No doubt the staff there seized upon every opportunity to engage the attention of their charges upon pleasant and time-filling duties. Unfortunately there could be very few people on Isa's list and the pleasant duty was too soon accomplished. I sighed and got up to place this first card of the season on the piano. My mother glanced up from her book.

'Isa Mulvenny,' I explained.

'How thoughtful of her.'

I smiled as I carefully placed the card clear of the piano lid. 'It would be nice to believe it was her idea.'

'You said she had improved a lot. She obviously does know who you are now,' my mother said – alluding to the fact that when Isa had been rescued from the crumbling tenement she was not entirely sane and had failed to recognise me.

'Yes, but that's only because she remembers what she's been told. I don't think she remembers at first hand.'

My mother nodded sympathetically. 'Perhaps, now that you'll be ashore, you could visit her at Christmas.'

The possibility came as a pleasant surprise. 'Yes! I think I shall.' And it was only then I realised the extent of the free time I'd been so abruptly granted. Suddenly there were no obligations to any ship or management. After the preliminary inquiry, months would elapse before the inquiry proper. And during all that time it was doubtful whether I'd be expected or allowed to sign on with another company; certainly not as a chief engineer.

It was just at that moment, however – as though to deny the

possibility that my time was my own – there was a telephone call from Sam Hanson. He asked me to come to the office immediately. He wouldn't explain why, except to say that he couldn't discuss it on the telephone and anyway there was someone he wanted me to meet. I took my mother's car and drove back to London.

My father's young partner occupied the office that could have been mine. Indeed, he occupied the position which had been designed for me and which I had refused when, during my critical year for such considerations, the illusion of becoming a novelist was stronger than an assured partnership as a consultant engineer. My father had immediately advertised for an outsider and brought Hanson over from the United States to work in the London office. Moreover, he showed every sign of being well satisfied with the choice he'd made.

The choice *I'd* made came to nothing.

Hanson was alone when I went in.

'Bill! You made pretty good time.'

'You said it was important.'

He waved me over to a long side-table on which my log readings and notes were carefully laid out. 'Have a look at this.'

'Is there anything wrong?' I went over to the table, noting that although he was leaning forward, the jacket of Hanson's excellently cut suit did not bunch at the collar and the sleeve on his extended arm maintained an even margin of starched shirt cuff. The repatriated Scotsman was not only a snappy dresser; he was an expensively snappy dresser. He was pointing to an entry registering that steam had been applied to the heating coils. 'That's right. We put them on early.'

'Why was that?'

'Because even in the southern Baltic the sea is very cold in November.'

His finger moved sharply to an entry. 'Yet within a couple of days the crude was already above the normal temperature for discharge.'

'Yes. We couldn't understand that.'

He straightened his back to gaze at me sceptically. 'You couldn't understand it – then, or now?'

'At all. We assumed there was a fault in the temperature gauge. I reported that ashore.'

'You didn't cut the steam, though, before you reached the port.'

'But I did.'

'Show me.' He stepped back from the table to allow me free access to the available evidence.

I shook my head. 'There's no record of it there because the gauge kept showing a high temperature.'

'But you personally cut the steam to the heating coils after only two days?'

'Not personally, no. It was young Dolby who reported the apparent overheating and I told him to shut off those coils.'

'Not all the coils?'

'No. It was only the forward tanks that were showing high.'

'So – the crude in the forward tanks was high, you had the steam shut off, but the gauge still showed high, so you put the steam on again.'

'That's right.'

'Personally?'

'No, my second and I agreed that it must be a gauge fault and he put the steam on again. Otherwise there was a danger that the real temperature in the tanks would be too low and we wouldn't be able to discharge as soon as we got to port.'

Hanson gave a very tentative smile and nodded. 'And the discharge went okay?'

'There was no trouble with it.'

'And you checked the actual temperature *at* discharge?'

'No, I didn't,' I told him as evenly as I could, well aware that my devil's advocate had found a lapse in the argument.

Hanson gave the impression that he was trying not to show his dismay. He looked quickly away from me, then directly at the notes on the table. After a moment or two of accusing silence he abruptly changed the subject. 'Mr Thompson called the Norske Veritas office in Copenhagen. The surveyor on the *Katia Maersk* was a Dane called Aage Jensen.'

'What did my father want to find out from him?'

Hanson shrugged. 'Just to check on the manufacturing codes,

the regulations at that time and if there had been any problems during construction. That kind of thing.'

'And were there any problems?'

My interrogator looked at his watch. 'We're about to find out. When Mr Thompson called yesterday, Jensen was already on his way to London. This morning *he* called *us*, asking to arrange a meeting with you. Apparently he tried to reach you before you left Copenhagen.'

Both of us stared at the array of papers on the table for a moment, then Hanson asked, 'How about some coffee?'

'Yes. Thank you.'

He went away to instruct Mrs Schuster and left me very puzzled indeed. I just could not imagine why the Danish surveyor would be so interested in work he'd completed more than ten years before. And since, as far as I knew, the *Katia Maersk* had provided long and trouble-free service for the original owners, he could have no further responsibility in the matter. As for his wish to see me, that was so unusual it was alarming. No possible purpose could be served by such a meeting, yet – with an instinctive wish to defend myself – I quickly gathered the papers from the table and laid them in a pile, face down.

I put it to Hanson. 'Don't you think it's strange that the same surveyor is still available after all this time?'

'It seems he made himself available. He asked to be put on this job, though he's quite a senior man in their outfit now.'

When he arrived in time to share our coffee, Aage Jensen proved to be a tall, thin man who looked quite young until you got close to him. Then you were struck by the age and the weariness of his heavy-lidded eyes. Across the room, he looked thirty; at arm's length, I guessed he was around fifty. He shook hands with both of us, then sank gratefully into the chair which Hanson indicated. He seemed to fold himself in order to sink deeper into the cushions. Without any preamble he asked me, 'Hr Ingenior, will you tell me why you did join this ship?'

'Yes. If you will tell me why you want to know.'

He gave a faint, wan smile but let the weight of his eyelids mask any other expression. 'Tell me something else then. Was there ill-feeling between you and the master of the vessel?'

Before I could reply his quiet, lazy voice continued, 'Or you thought that he expected too much of the old *Katia Maersk*?'

'I've no idea what he expected of the ship. And all he required of the engine room was perfectly within the capabilities of the machinery.'

'And the men?'

Hanson quickly interrupted. 'Bill can only speak for the people in the engine room.'

Jensen turned his head slowly, but completely, in the direction of the desk before he murmured, 'It is the people in the engine room who are of interest to me. For, of course, I knew that ship very well.'

'That's why we wanted to get in touch with you,' Hanson told him.

'Naturally. Everybody is looking for someone to blame.'

I spoke up. 'And who do you blame, Hr Jensen?'

He swivelled his head slowly, as though it were a precious and heavy object unworthily attached to the rest of the body. 'That,' he said suavely, 'depends on the stage at which you look at it – five years ago, one year ago, one week ago or yesterday.'

To Hanson that reply seemed evasive, to me fanciful. It did not convey anything of practical value to either of us. Yet, a long time later, I had cause to remember it and to marvel at the Dane's intuitive grasp of a whole intricate series of events. Right there in Hanson's office, though, we let the observation pass unchallenged.

Jensen returned to what seemed to be the purpose of his visit – and now more directly. 'I would like to know, Hr Ingenior, if your second is already qualified as a chief.'

'Yes, I believe he is.'

Jensen gave a fractional grimace of irritation. 'Do you know that he is?'

'He is,' I asserted.

'And he has been with that ship for some years now?'

'Yes, but not as chief.'

Hanson grew impatient. 'I don't see how all this gets us away from where we are now.'

The Dane smiled. 'No. But perhaps it helps us to understand

how we got to where we are now.' He leaned forward a little.
'If a man is employed by the agent or the new owner of this ship
for many years then they must be satisfied with his work. During
that time he has qualified as chief. But then, when a new chief
is required, they did not appoint him to the job.' He uncoiled a
long finger and allowed it to point languidly in my direction.
'Instead, they bring in a stranger whose ability they do not
know.'

'That's quite simple,' Hanson told him. 'They wanted a man
who'd already had experience sailing as chief. People are willing
to pay for experience.'

Jensen kept his eyes fixed on me. 'I believe your experience
was on more modern ships.'

'Of course,' I replied sharply. 'There are very few antique
ships being built nowadays.' It annoyed me that, evidently, he'd
checked up on me in some detail. Also, he seemed to be implying
that my unfamiliarity with the specific machinery in my charge
could have contributed to some failure. Curiously, though, my
response seemed to please him. Or maybe he was just amused
at my identifying him as an antique surveyor. In any case, he
turned his attention from questioning me to answering the
questions which Hanson put to him about the rules and standards
in force at the time the ship was built.

When all that had been established Hanson tried to turn the
meeting along more sociable lines. He smiled. 'I believe you
were the surveyor on the old ship, Hr Jensen.'

'Yes, I was.'

'You must have a sentimental attachment to her.'

'Not particularly.' The Dane smiled but his eyes scanning
Hanson's face were busy on other calculations. 'I have some
attachment to the place however. The yard at Lindø, where she
was built. That is where I did much of my training when I was
a student. My family had a small farm quite near Lindø.'

I could well understand his attachment to a shipyard and
remarked, 'Hanson and I both trained on Clydeside.'

The Dane was surprised. 'So! I thought Hr Hanson was an
American and you, Hr Ingenior, an Englishman.'

'Bill *is* an Englishman,' my father's partner confirmed. 'But

why have you taken such an interest in the *Niome*? And in the
second engineer, for that matter.'

'Because I find it particularly strange,' Jensen stated blandly.
'And I have a personal reason.'

As soon as he'd gone, Hanson raised his eyes gratefully to
the ceiling and made a supplicating gesture. 'God! Norske Veritas must be easy to please if that's the kind of bum they send
out.'

'What do you mean?'

'Bill, you heard him. The man's a dozy, cloth-eared clown.'

I was amazed that Hanson could be so mistaken. Even though
I had not understood all the Dane had said I was aware of a
formidable intelligence behind his lazy exterior. And I knew he'd
gone away knowing a great deal more about us than we knew
about him. At the time that seemed to me a worrying disadvantage. It proved to be nothing of the sort.

Meanwhile, Hanson and I were drawn into uneasy collabor-
ation. He was, as I'd told Jensen, a Clydeside engineer but he
was also a native Glaswegian – a fact which was equally well
disguised. I'd learned a lot about him from a boyhood friend of
his. Indeed, that friend and I, and other friends of mine, had
spent a lot of time during the World Fair in Montreal searching
for Sam Hanson. That was in 1967. When we found him it was
clear we'd been wasting our time. He completely ignored his
former buddy. All these years later, it was the coldness and
disappointment of that rejection which still coloured my attitude
to him. Many times I'd conceded to myself that I was being
unreasonable. After all, Hanson had not rejected me. He didn't
know me. And when I met him later in London he went out of
his way to be agreeable. But I chose to interpret that as currying
favour with the boss's son.

Now, seated behind his large hi-tech desk which clashed with
the sober panelling of the room, *he* was in the superior position.
Everything about his behaviour this afternoon indicated that he
would do his best to rescue me from whatever folly had placed
me in the position of surviving a disaster at sea.

TWO

Now that I was being held very strictly to account for my actions, I thought more and more about what had actually happened. It was possible that in the jumble of recollections and occasional nightmares some clue might be found which would explain the loss of the ship. As I walked over long stretches of the Sussex countryside in early winter my effort to reconstruct the events was hampered by my being too much involved to see clearly. I began to marvel at reports of other such disasters I'd read. In them the chronicle always begins with a detailed and accurate array of facts which is no use to anyone after the event and of no significance to anyone before it. Such facts are discovered by researchers, not participants. The name of the vessel and her port of registration is always given, then the full date, the exact time of day on a twenty-four-hour clock, the precise co-ordinates of latitude and longitude and – not infrequently – a complete weather report. Then comes a series of thumbnail sketches stating who was where immediately before the event – presumably to illustrate that the victims didn't know what was going to happen to them. But of *course* they don't know! If victims knew what was going to happen to them before it happened they'd stand a fair chance of not being victims at all. And survivors would have little to survive. And any officer coming before a formal inquiry would come well prepared.

I didn't know what everybody else was doing before the explosion, but I was in charge of the engines and the first blast threw me to the deck of the control room. As I lay there dazed, the whole ship heaved with the second and third explosions that followed in quick succession. Then everything was flung violently

forward and I was pitched through the open control-room door
and down several grating steps to the alleyway on the generator
flat. My first thought was that we must have hit something; and
something big to cause such a jarring loss of momentum. But
we had not. There was no one near us. The bow had sheared
off exposing a square bulkhead. It was the immediate build-up
of water pressure against that which imposed the enormous
braking force.

Subjected to an overload beyond all limits, the first things to
go were the bearings of the main shaft. As I struggled to my
feet against the increasing aft pitch of the deck, I could hear a
grinding roar from the shaft tunnel. Before I could regain the
control room to shut off the engine, one or more blades of the
'built' propeller stripped and at once the main shaft, which had
been rearing and grinding, started to race. There were alarms
sounding in every part of the engine room, and on all levels of
the machinery spaces red warning lights blazed and flashed. I
stopped the main engine and was about to shut off all fuel and
high pressure steam lines when I was caught in a spasm of
indecision. At that moment I did not know what had happened
to the ship and therefore could not be sure what power would
be needed to cope with the situation. I tried to ring the bridge
but the line was dead. So, it was up to me to choose between
cutting all the main auxiliaries except lighting to prevent danger
of further explosion or to maintain power where it might be
essential. The main generators were turbo-drive and the main
pumps were steam-driven. Cargo handling, transfer and ballast
with their maze of cross-linking and emergency lines might all
be needed in this crisis.

The feeling of panic and inability to move came back to me
several times as I stood on the hill behind the house, and on
each occasion the duration of that indecision stretched longer.
Yet increasingly, too, I began to doubt that I'd ever been in
the situation which I so clearly remembered. It just did not
seem possible that the person straining to remain upright in the
fierce clangour of machinery and alarms and flashing lights,
trapped in a tilting steel box, could be the same person who

now moved without effort over the wet grass safe at home, or stood on the firm earth in the unconfined quietness of such a familiar hill.

But really the stricken indecision had lasted only a few seconds before it occurred to me that I was not alone in the engine room. I heard shouting and looked up to see two motor-men climbing the ladder to the upper flat, apparently under the impression that the further away from the noise they went the safer they would be. Dolby, the third engineer who'd been sharing the watch with me, lay moaning behind a gauge board where he'd been thrown. I moved towards him, then froze again at what sounded like a volley of rifle shots. It was the seams and joints of metal plates snapping under pressure. A new klaxon started up and I could not decide which way to move.

It was the second engineer, Clifford Sandys, who settled the matter for me. He'd been off duty, but now came slamming into the control room shouting, 'Out! Out! On deck. Get on deck!' He shoved me towards the ladder then rushed across to pull Dolby to his feet. The young engineer was able to stand and, after a moment, was able to move. Clifford supported him as they moved towards me – still groggy and stupidly blocking the doorway.

Finally it got through that this was not an emergency but a disaster, for Clifford was fully dressed in deck clothes and wearing his life-jacket. He turned me round and continued pushing me and supporting Dolby as we climbed out of the engine room. As we ascended through the dry-store rooms and the changing rooms the aftward tilt of the ship increased. Below us everything that was loose or lightly fixed became detached and fell with whining ricochet against the grating edges. I looked back and down into the receding cavern of the engine room and at all the stabbing red warning lights. Adding to the din I could hear the shriek and whistle of safety valves blowing off. The escaping steam from the high-pressure lines was invisible for several feet then materialised into rapidly expanding cones of fierce white energy.

When we reached the crew accommodation we were caught

up in a frantic bustle of activity. Everyone was scrambling to collect some possessions or to find life-jackets. Whereas the younger men were donning the life-jackets over briefs or singlets or pyjamas, the older men took time to dress as fully and warmly as they could manage with their own or other people's clothes. As I stumbled against the steep incline towards the upper decks, Clifford pulled at my arm. 'Where the hell are you going?'

'The bridge. There was no answer and I want to . . .'

'No time!' he shouted. 'Put on your gear and go!'

He tried to push me into my own cabin but I pulled away from him and started to climb a vertical ladder which was now tilted backward at an impossible angle. Even so, I pulled myself up to the next deck – and the next one. And it was there I got some idea of the scale of the event. The deck-head was folded in so that there was a space of only three or four feet between floor and ceiling. The access ways were completely blocked with crumpled metal. As I made my way back to the crew accommodation the ship lurched sideways. Apart from settling by the stern she was developing a heavy list to starboard. I managed to get back to my cabin and to prepare myself for whatever lay outside.

My father questioned me about those several changes in the ship's trim after the explosions. We frequently discussed the matter after dinner at home; and in the office, too, Hanson took several opportunities to test my recollection of events. It was their intention to prepare me for questions that would be asked. And I had to concede that they would be relevant questions. If the ship had moved through a series of positions – listing then settling by the stern – that indicated a progression of tanks being flooded. They wanted to know what might have happened if the extremely powerful pumps had been set to work. Was it possible that the ship could have been saved? Whereas, in my opinion, nothing could have saved the ship, it could not be denied that I did not start the pumps either to combat flooding or to stabilise a worsening condition. My father was concerned, also, about my part in abandoning the ship. He foresaw possibilities of conflict in the evidence which would have to be considered by the inquiry. Of course he himself approved of my actions but it was a prickly area in which any presumption on my part would be criticised. Again I conceded the point. But the way things were that night, presumption was simply common sense.

By the time I reached the outer deck everyone else who could make it was already there. They were all staring up and forward and their faces were bathed in a bright orange light. I joined them. But only gradually did I become aware of the enormous damage we had suffered. The midship tanks of benzine were ablaze and forward of them there was nothing. By the roaring light of the fires, though, I could see what I thought was an impossibly early rescue ship approaching. But the name I could make out was the name of *our* ship. Our entire bow section was still afloat and drifting back towards us. Aft of the blazing tanks the scene was of even greater devastation. The flying bridge – that raised central walkway which runs the whole length of the deck – had been blasted up and backwards so that it curved in a great angular sweep, smashing deep into the bridge front. Deck machinery, samson posts, derricks and support structure had all been hurled back by the explosions. The master and whoever had been on the bridge with him were certainly dead. Nor was there much hope for some others of the crew. Though horrified by the evidence, I had to acknowledge that the safest place to be that night was in the engine room.

But many others besides the engineers had survived the destruction of the ship. The next danger was getting away from it. The third officer marshalled what forces were available for lowering the boats. When he saw me he immediately claimed my support for the action he proposed to take. Yet even in this crisis the inbuilt deck-versus-engineers bias asserted itself. He felt he had to explain in elementary terms the problem which I could plainly see for myself. The ship was sinking by the stern because the bow had been ripped off. She was also listing to starboard because the benzine cargo on the port side was lost or already burned. That meant it would be increasingly difficult to lower the lifeboats on the port side because the davits would

not swing the boats clear. But the boats on the starboard side
– where we were standing – would swing away from the ship
when lowered and the remaining benzine could go up at any
moment catching us in a tide of burning fuel.

I shouted, 'Christ, man! I'd rather jump than be burned alive.'

He gave me a startled look then took several paces towards
the rail to see that two of the starboard boats had already been
lowered. 'We've time to get away,' he called.

Vehemently I shook my head and pointed to the port side.
'Have you tried them?' I knew he hadn't. I also knew that if the
starboard tanks did go we'd have some protection from the deck
housing. And as the starboard tanks spilled and burned the list
could be corrected. Some others apparently made the same
calculation because I found there was a general movement to
follow me. And Clifford Sandys did his best to argue the case
that even if we had to cut the port side boats free and drop them
on the water that was better than imminent incineration.

In fact we did not have to cut them free. The davits swung
out enough to cope with the list. The difficulty was the fore and
aft alignment. The boats hung from their bow attachments while
the stern lines were slack. They could not be loaded at deck
level. The boats were lowered onto the water empty, then lad-
ders were thrown over the side of the ship for the men to climb
down and scramble into them.

The radio and electrical officers were to go in the first of the
large diesel-powered boats. Since the new owner had greatly
reduced the manning on the ship there was no danger of over-
loading even the two boats that were available to us. The crew
were assigned places and I gathered the other officers together.
After the master of the ship I had senior rank, though no training
for the procedures of abandoning ship. The third officer assured
me that a *m'aider* call had been sent out and that the radio man
had also set the automatic repeater distress signal, which would
last as long as the ship remained afloat. In each of the lifeboats,
I knew, was a radio beacon. Whether they were in working
order or not was another matter. The ship's logs and papers
were buried in the tangled debris of the navigating bridge and
the deck immediately below it. There was nothing we could do

about that and it was my view that as soon as we were able we should quit the vessel. To my amazement and anger the third officer baulked at this. He stared into my face, his eyes red and streaming with water from the effects of the sickly acrid smoke which engulfed us. And his first lunatic point was the question of salvage. Regardless of the inferno still raging and eating its way the length of the ship; the fact that we were slowly but certainly sinking by the stern; the fact that a quarter of our bulk was completely detached and threatening to ram us; and that what was left of our cargo was making a widening slick on the black swelling waters of the Baltic – he worried that we were making a gift to salvage. The sheer incredulity on the faces of the rest of us then drove him to another point which seemed to me even more absurd, though in this one he had the support of the remaining deck officers. He wanted to know how we were going to prove the ship had been lost if she were lost.

Clifford and I turned to each other with identical expressions. Involuntary amusement battled with disbelief. The third officer went on to assert that without the log books and official papers we were legal nonentities and the status of the ship could not be determined by our evidence alone. He said we must make an effort to take with us some intrinsic part of the ship as proof of the whole. We didn't bother to argue about it because the starboard tanks suddenly blew out and, though protected in the lea of the superstructure, we were all thrown to the deck by the shuddering force of the blast.

The second lifeboat was now in the water and the only available rope ladder had been dragged aft to the new position. I told everyone to keep down and crawl out over the exposed area of the main deck. Very slowly and under threat of another explosion the second party began to descend to the waiting boat. The third officer and I were the last to reach the ship side. To my relief, I noted that the first lifeboat was already under power and a fair distance away; though still within the huge area illuminated by the inexhaustible blaze of the ruptured tanks.

We'd almost reached the bottom of the ladder when we were forcibly shaken off by yet another violent lurch. This time it was not an explosion but the grinding collision of the bow section with the starboard beam. The impact threw us bodily into the lifeboat and snapped the line which tethered us to the sinking ship. Then the sudden surge of water lifted and bore the lifeboat sideways as lightly as a surfboard on a breaker.

When I'd regained my breath and more or less convinced myself that my ribs were not fractured I pulled myself up and looked back at the last of the *Niome*. Now the stern was much deeper in the water and the flaming, ragged, square forward section was tilted much higher. On the far side, the bow must have imbedded itself amidships for it was hidden from us by the wildly tilted superstructure and the massive peeled-back scroll of the flying bridge. Yet the deck and accommodation lights were still on. That incongruous fact gave me the impression that the aft end was just lying back for a rest, unaware that at the forward end all hell had broken loose.

As we chugged away into the icy wind and the swell to evade the massive oil spillage we all looked back and waited for the end. Before long the funnel housing touched the level of the sea and a few minutes later the whole ship disappeared in a shroud of smoke. But she left the sea burning and, for a long time, those flames were fed by huge bubbles of air rising from the wreck to the surface.

If there was any good fortune at all in the loss of the *Niome* it was in our position when the disaster came. The southern Baltic is busy with shipping and we were on the main route to Stockholm. Even without the distress call from the ship and the beacons in our lifeboats other ships would have been aware of the disaster. The flames from our burning tanks made a spectacular glow on the horizon for other vessels in all directions. Some even heard the sound of the explosions. Also, the over-cautious Swedish navy had helicopters in almost constant patrol and we were not far outside their territorial waters. All things considered, if the *Niome* was going to explode she couldn't have chosen a better place to do it. Nor did we have to wait long for rescue. Naturally the first to reach us were the salvage tugs. They too maintain a regular patrol, though they tend to run down the lifeboats in their eagerness to fasten on the abandoned hulk. Indeed, one of the tugs did steam past us to the position of the distress call – just to make sure we hadn't left anything valuable lying about. We were picked up by his patrol partner. Since both tugs were on their way to the richer pastures of the North Sea, they did not take us to Stockholm but chose the course of least diversion by landing us in Copenhagen.

It was during that trip that I got the first warning of how deeply I was going to be involved at the reckoning on the loss of the *Niome*. The salvage master on the tug, however courteous, came briskly to the point. Of course he waited until I'd had a drink and something to eat – but he did not wait long. First he wanted to know about the cargo and then he made the same bizarre point that the third officer had been making. When he found we didn't have the official log in our possession he asked how we were going to prove the likely cause and certain loss of the ship. Clifford Sandys, who was sharing the borrowed cabin with me, exclaimed with indignant irritation, 'Captain, you intercepted the distress call. You noted the position.'

'But she was not there when we reached that position.'

'We were, though,' I said. 'And you've got one of the *Niome*'s lifeboats in tow.'

The big jovial man smiled broadly. 'Ah! A lifeboat is not a 30,000 ton tanker.'

'But surely it's obvious that she sank?'

'What is obvious is that we do not see her afloat.'

'So where do you think we're hiding her?' Clifford demanded.

The salvage master ignored that, and went on in a gentle, musing way which managed to suggest that we need not take him seriously, yet warned us that we'd better. 'There will be trouble, you see. There is no log of the vessel, the master and many of the crew are missing, there is no apparent reason for the explosions.' He shrugged, 'Nothing, you understand, the inquiry can look at to inquire into. And if they do not have anything to read they do not like it.'

'They will have the evidence of the survivors,' I reminded him.

He pursed his lips and leaned back in the little chair. 'I know for sure that all survivors see different things. It is always so. Inquiry men are suspicious of survivors – for somebody must be blamed.'

Clifford tried once more to assert the obvious. 'If there's no evidence of negligence, how can they blame anyone?'

The captain smiled broadly. 'Then they blame you for not having the evidence – *or* the ship.' He eased himself out of the chair and spoke directly to me. 'I think you should look for some very good evidence in your own records.' He paused before going out. 'You have that? Your own notes and papers?'

'Yes, I have.'

'Good. Look there for signs of troubles that you have already reported ashore.' He snorted with amusement. 'Inquiries believe *every*thing that is known ashore.'

When he had gone, Clifford immediately turned to me with an expression of surprise and relief. 'That's a stroke of luck. Have you really got your watch notes?'

'Yes, of course.'

'What made you think of saving them?'

'Because I was on watch when it happened.'

'Oh, it's just the one set of readings you've got, then.'

'No. I've got my folder for the whole voyage.' I reached across the narrow cabin for my torn and oil-stained topcoat to reveal the doubled-up folder thrust deep in the inside pocket.

'And is there anything there you've reported ashore?' Clifford wanted to know.

'Just the trouble we had with the heating coils.'

'That didn't do any harm.' He seemed depressed that there was so little we could blame on the ship. 'What we need is a good reason why she blew up. And preferably a good fault you'd warned the owner about.'

I nodded wearily. That was a question I knew I'd have to spend a lot of time on. But clearly my second engineer wanted immediate reassurance.

'What do *you* think caused it?' he demanded.

'I don't know.'

'They'll tell you it was your business to know. I mean, *our* business. And they'll have our tickets for it.' He lay back in the bunk and with irritating composure began cutting out all other options. 'Apart from getting killed, you see, the master did nothing wrong. He was on time, on course, in good trim and he didn't hit anything. In fact, dead or alive, all the deck boys are in the clear. Young Foster's going to make sure that comes out.'

'Foster! If we'd listened to him we would have been grilled on the starboard side.'

Clifford suddenly raised himself on one elbow. 'And that's a good card we'll have to keep in reserve.'

'What do you mean?'

'Aw, chief!' He swung his legs off the bunk and hunched towards me. 'Do you honestly think we'll get through this if we play *fair*?'

For a moment both of us seemed hypnotised by the enveloping sound of the engine in that low-decked cabin of the ocean-going tug as we surged at full power towards the Danish coast. And the smell of over-ripe fruit which is always apparent in small diesel vessels seemed particularly strong in the cramped quarters we temporarily shared. I looked very carefully at Clifford Sandys. His lean, sallow-complexioned face had an expression of contempt which I had not seen before. His voice, too, had taken on a quite surprising edge. No doubt it was just the effect of the crisis we'd been through but it made me aware of how little I knew my colleague. Whereas we'd never got on very well together, he'd always been efficient, polite and uncomplaining. I was the chief and he was the second. But now the only thing which had held us in those positions was at the bottom of the Baltic. We were merely survivors, and equals; and – he seemed to suggest – unwilling partners.

Before I could give an opinion on the virtue of blackmailing the third officer, we were interrupted by that officer himself. And he was a newly defined person too. Just a young, though fairly haggard-looking man called Foster. He said, 'Chief! The captain's got our Trade attaché on the radio. He wants you to set up our arrangements ashore.'

'Right. I'll see to it.'

'Do you mind if I have some of your coffee?'

'Help yourself.'

As I left the cabin to go forward I noted that Sandys was genially pouring for the man he saw as a threat.

On the ship-to-shore radio the Trade attaché at the British embassy gave no hint that he'd been roused from his bed in the dark hours of the morning to cope with a catastrophe. He was calm, sympathetic and helpful, even though I could not answer many of the questions essential to his duties. Very tactfully he outlined what I should already have found out about the surviving crew and those lost or missing. To my shame, I knew more about the cargo than the men I'd been sailing with. And the cargo was certainly lost. As the protracted, line-by-line interrogation went on I was glad to be joined by Sandys. While I went on talking, I handed him the sheet of paper on which I'd scribbled the outstanding questions. He immediately started filling in the answers and I relayed this new information to the office in Copenhagen. The tug's radio man grew increasingly restive as the transmission continued. Apart from the fact that we were crushed against each other in the tidy radio office, he had the possible loss of business to consider. By blocking his receiver we deprived him of the opportunity to hear of other more lucrative founderings elsewhere. And *our* business could as well be done ashore.

When we got back to the cabin we found it dark and its rightful occupant asleep in one of the bunks. We tried not to disturb him as we gathered up our belongings then went to join the others crowding the galley/mess. I was preoccupied with my failure to deal adequately with the embassy. It seemed to me that I'd given the impression of being inept, if not callous. Yet, as I listened to the others talking and recalled all the bits and pieces of conversation that had occurred since the *Niome* went down, it became clear that, if callous, I was not alone. Expressions of sadness or regret were totally absent. To our rescuers it was just a matter of hauling in and transporting survivors. And now that nothing could be done to alter the fact of those who were lost, we survivors thought only of ourselves. It was not callousness because there was no one there to interpret it as such. No doubt we would modify our behaviour when we got ashore and we were subject to a more hypocritical, never-endangered society.

And before long we were going ashore. When the pitch of the engine noise altered and we felt ourselves riding on the waves instead of ploughing through them, everyone was eager to get on deck. We emerged into a misty raw cold and I pulled my topcoat tighter to button it at the collar. Immediately, I knew the folder had gone. I opened the coat and plunged my hand into the deep pocket. The folder with my notes and readings of the voyage was missing. As the tug nudged gently against the quay I scrambled below. It seemed unlikely that such a bulky folder would have fallen out of the pocket and certainly I hadn't put it anywhere else. First I searched around on the benches and on the floor of the mess under the feet of the crew who were settling to breakfast. I asked them if they'd seen it and described it to them. Some of them didn't understand and those who understood couldn't help. Then I retraced my steps back to the cabin where I'd last been sure I had the documents. The man was still asleep in the bunk. I decided I'd poke about everywhere else before I woke him to search his bedclothes. In a fever of impatience I tried to recall where I'd thrown the coat, where I'd been sitting, where I'd moved the coat and where anyone else could have moved it in my absence.

I got down onto my hands and knees then sprawled on my stomach to make sure the file hadn't been kicked under any of the few pieces of furniture. And that is where I found it. There was a clearance of about an inch between the deck and the base of an old-style mariner's chest. The file lay under the chest. I could extricate it only by lying at full stretch and poking two fingers into the aperture. I pulled it out then got to my feet to see the man in the bunk staring at me in amazement. I smiled and indicated to him that this was my property before bolting into the narrow passage and up onto the deck.

As I went ashore it was perfectly obvious to me that the file had not fallen from my pocket, unfolded itself to lie flat – and then been mistakenly kicked under the chest. Someone had taken it from my pocket and hidden it. No doubt Sandys had been right. We were *not* going to get through this by playing fair; especially with deck officers. And, as it turned out, we were not going to get through it for quite a long while.

THREE

I'd first met my second engineer when I joined the ship at Tripoli in Lebanon. During our first and last voyage together Clifford and I didn't get to know each other very well, mainly because we didn't like each other much and saw no good reason to find out why that should be so. He was a lean, energetic man of about thirty; not tall, with dark hair and intense brown eyes. He gave the impression of being more of a pale Spaniard than an Englishman. The crew seemed to like him; perhaps because he responded to any lapses in their work with cynical amusement rather than annoyance. Few took advantage of the fact. Realising he knew all the dodges they were less inclined to dodge. They also felt some sympathy for him, I suppose, at the injustice of my appointment. Yet I could not detect any feeling of resentment on his part that I'd been appointed as chief over him and over whatever just claims he might have to the job.

In the period immediately after the ship was lost my estimation of him went up quite a bit because I realised that, potentially at least, he had saved my life and young Dolby's too. He got us out of there because he knew that the instructions I could have waited a long time to receive from the bridge would never come. Jumping all the rules and text-book procedures he took the initiative. My gratitude for that, however, did not lead me to suppose that he'd become a different person. We did not exchange addresses or telephone numbers before we said good-bye to each other in Copenhagen and I did not expect to see him again until we were called to the formal inquiry.

However, about a week after that parting he came down to see me in Sussex. Startled to find him there at all, I was also taken aback by his looking so unfamiliar. He wore a greenish duffelcoat over a jerkin and a pair of jeans. His dark hair was wet from the steady drizzle that was falling and he looked much younger even in lowering daylight than he had under the unvarying artificial glare which illuminated most of our lives aboard ship.

He arrived as I was about to go out for my ritual walk, and although apparently he had already walked some distance from the nearest bus stop, he insisted on joining me out of doors. As we moved through the woods which rose onto the hill behind the house, I was grateful to have some activity to disguise the long silences with which the meeting began. We had practically nothing in common except the *Niome*; and even that was over. But he had his mind on what was just beginning – and in two quite separate directions. Looking back on it, I can see both of the aims he hoped to advance. At the time, though, I thought there was only one plot afoot and stupidly congratulated myself on spotting that. It was when I mentioned my conversation with the Norske Veritas man, Aage Jensen, that my companion suddenly became fascinated with what I was saying.

There was a small urgent surge in his voice as he asked, 'When did you go to see him?'

'I didn't. He came to see me. In London.'

'But this is none of his business. What did he want to see you about?'

'Do you know him?' I glanced at the sharp-featured face which plodded along by my side.

Clifford nodded, took a few more paces, then asked, 'Did he ask you about the cargo?'

'No. He seemed mainly interested in why you weren't appointed chief.'

Having waited for a response and received none, I prompted him. 'It does seem odd. Why weren't you?'

But what was of great interest to the Dane and now to me was evidently of little importance to my second. The boyish brightness with which he'd greeted me now lapsed into the withdrawn, moody, expression with which I was more familiar. Eventually he said, 'Jensen's a man worth keeping your eye on.

He has a lot of pull.' He glanced sideways at me. 'And in some very awkward directions.'

'Apart from being a Norske Veritas surveyor?'

'Huh,' my colleague grunted, 'that's what he *used* to be.'

'How did you come to know of him?'

'Oh, friends of mine have run up against him.' Clifford ducked under a rain-laden branch protruding from a hedge. 'He's a ruthless bastard, you know.'

It occurred to me that anyone who found Jensen ruthless probably deserved it, but I phrased the thought in a less accusing way. 'In what circumstances? I mean, it wasn't just a matter of insisting on regulations.'

He gave a contemptuous grunt of amusement. 'No, no. Jensen makes his own regulations if he gets his knife into anybody.'

It now struck me that I'd been unwise to mention the Dane's interest in Clifford, and again became aware that there was no one I could really talk to about any part of the business without encountering doubts, suspicions or implied threat. A change of subject would be safer. 'How are you coping with all this free time?' I asked.

He brightened. 'No trouble at all. Barbara and I have plenty to do.' He gave me a questioning smile. 'You know about Barbara, don't you?'

'Oh, yes.' I said, and made it sound as though I knew a whole lot more than was actually the case. It was only her name which was familiar.

'She would have liked to come down to see you but she has a costume fitting.'

'Oh,' I said, deeply puzzled by both these pieces of information. 'What a pity.'

Clifford increased my bewilderment by adding, 'I've told her a lot about you.' This struck me as odd since he didn't know a lot about me. 'And we've thought once or twice about paying you a visit.'

'Where did you get my address?' I asked.

He looked surprised. 'From the ship's agent – where else?'

'Yes, of course!' That much was obvious. But what was still not obvious was why he'd taken the trouble to travel down from

London by train and bus to see me. He now came to that point.

'Bill, I thought you managed to save your log and notes.'

'Yes.' And now, contaminated by innuendo and the suspicion of others, I decided to lie. 'I saved them from the ship but they must have got lost on the tug that rescued us.'

'So you've no record at all?'

'Not at the moment. But I'm hoping to get the papers back.'

'Oh, sure. When the salvageman comes off patrol.'

We emerged onto open ground above the wood and I noticed that my companion's lightweight city shoes were coated with wet mud and there was a tidemark of darker blue almost up to the knees of his jeans.

'We'd better find a dry way home,' I said. 'You'll stay for dinner, I hope.'

'No. No, I can't. Thanks, but I'd better get back to town.'

I wondered if he'd be so anxious to leave if my answers to his questions had been different. Plainly it was ridiculous to have travelled all that way for no more than a brief muddy walk in the rain. Something of what I'd said worried him. As he looked around over the gently rising hillside for a quick escape route his manner was impatient and preoccupied.

I made an expansive gesture in an easterly direction. 'We can get back to the main road over that way. I'd run you to the station but my only transport is my mother's car and she's away all day today.'

As we moved off along the flank of the hill Clifford resumed some of his initial heartiness. 'Bill, what I wanted to ask you was if you'd like to come and spend Christmas with us. In London.'

'With you and . . . ?'

'Barbara. She'd very much like to meet you and I'm sure you'd find it more enjoyable than all these trees.'

Desperately I flogged my memory in an effort to recall if she was his wife or just a girl he was living with. But probably he'd never told me. I said, 'Yes, I'd like that very much, but I've already arranged to spend Christmas in Scotland.'

'Oh, I see. Some other time then.'

'I look forward to it.'

As I waited with him at the bus stop, the oddness of his unheralded arrival and the brevity of his stay reclaimed my attention. The vague idea presented itself that our rescue tug might that very day be docking in Stockholm. So what? I asked myself. Even if he searched it, would that prove I had lied? But even such idle speculation increased my feelings of unease. Alternatively, now that the intervention of the formidable Dane had been revealed, there might be urgent consultation which Clifford was anxious to pursue in the very proper defence of his own actions on the *Niome*. And, of course, I knew that if I'd been able to tell him that I had my notes there in the house he certainly would have stayed for dinner; and insisted on seeing them.

The main purpose of a preliminary inquiry into the loss of a ship is to determine whether or not a formal inquiry should be held and, if so, where and by whom. Since there had never been any doubt that the loss of the *Niome* cried out for full investigation, the preliminary was a fairly perfunctory affair held in a committee room at the Institution in Upper Belgrave Street. Those who were in a position to do so stated their recollection of the actual events. The insured value of the ship and the value of the cargo being carried was established. The identity of those who had died was registered and notification given by those of their dependants who intended to seek compensation. My part in these proceedings occupied no more than a couple of hours on the morning of 18th December. I saw a couple of the other survivors whom I recognised but we had no opportunity – or, for that matter, inclination – to talk to each other. And that was another aspect of the situation which would become even more pronounced. Contrary to popular belief, we survivors of a sunken ship felt absolutely no bond of brotherhood as a result of our shared peril. It was every man for himself in the event, and ever after. While waiting to cross into Victoria Station I saw Clifford and a woman I took to be Barbara. They were in a car. Probably he was on his way to the Institution and he was dropping her off to do some shopping. They didn't see me but I noticed that the car was flashy and new; also, if it was Barbara, she seemed quite a bit older than Clifford.

Just before Christmas I saw my parents off to their usual Florida break, then I flew to Glasgow. As always, I was struck by the thought that the tourist trade would be helped a great deal if it could be arranged that all flights would approach Abbotsinch from a north-westerly direction. As it is, when you finally get below the cloud, what you see is the ugly scarring of Clydebank and the lumpy grey mass of Paisley. Everything looks cramped and drab and old. The airport itself is very modern of course, but always dirty. So – it certainly wasn't the sight of the place again which aroused the warmth and pleasure I undoubtedly felt when I got there. It was the irrational certainty that I was coming back to a place where I belonged. And I belonged with total fealty because it had claimed me when I was young.

Between the ages of sixteen and twenty-one I'd been a lodger in the Mulvennys' house at Greenock while I served my apprenticeship. To begin with, Isa Mulvenny had been a tall, easy-going, resilient woman who was full of fun. By the time I went to sea she'd already been forced to abandon much of her own personality. Now she was in a nursing home gradually recovering a sanity which was not her own but which everyone thought was better than nothing.

As I prepared myself for my first visit I wondered what we could talk about. There were plenty of memorable events that we'd shared, but even those which had started happy would inevitably lead to sad conclusions. In the event my worries proved unnecessary. She didn't want to talk about anything in particular. It was enough for her that she had a visitor. The fussing and attention needed to get ready for that had taken a delightfully long time. It was a pleasure to have someone – anyone – that you must look your best for. And indeed she did look well. Of course, she couldn't move without a wheelchair now and her hair which had been long and glossy and auburn was short and brittle-looking and white. But her eyes still had something of the mixed amusement and naivety which gave an eagerness to her expression. And her voice, though softer and

stumbling a bit, had lost none of its warmth 'Aw, Billy, son! Ye
shouldnae hiv grew a beard. It's put years on ye. An' it's the
wrang colour.'

By this she meant that it wasn't the same colour as the
fair-to-greying thatch on my head. 'I thought you'd like it,' I told
her. 'What have you done with *your* hair?'

She knew this must be a compliment and raised thin mottled
fingers to touch it. 'The lassies keep it awful nice, don't they?'
She leaned forward to me while keeping a lookout for eavesdrop-
pers. 'Dae you know, they wash it and set it *every Thursday*!'
She smothered a little chuckle and added, 'It's a wonder A'm
no' baldy.'

Having found a topic of such great mutual interest we continued to discuss it through variation and fugue. But not once
did we allude to the disastrous occasion when she'd cut her own
hair and abandoned the style once favoured by Mrs Simpson,
who married the King.

I'd booked at an hotel which was within walking distance of
the nursing home but several miles from the centre of Greenock,
so I had to take a taxi when nostalgia for my old haunts overcame
the reasoned certainty that I'd be disappointed. Many shipyards
had closed since I worked there and others had amalgamated.
But even in them there was little work building ships. All the
talk was about the prospect of constructing drilling rigs and the
bonanza that was sure to bring. The local paper carried an
artist's impressions of the new skyline which would dominate
the river front.

It was not until I got back to the rural fastness of Kilmacolm
that I noticed in the same paper an item which totally transported
me to the vivid time when I was eighteen. It was the photograph
of a man who had once robbed me of four hundred carefully
saved pounds. Tony Liddle: there he was, smiling to the camera
and confiding in the caption that his club-disco would soon
re-open, now that he had proved to everyone's satisfaction that
it was not, nor had it ever been, a cover for illegal gambling.
Although I knew nothing of the circumstances I was absolutely
sure that illegal gambling was the whole purpose of the venture.
I smiled and wondered when Tony had got out of prison. For

whereas there had been no charge or conviction attached to robbing me, he had been brought to trial on a much more serious matter. His fifteen-year sentence had started in 1962, so he must have given a sustained performance of good behaviour to get out and set himself up in business already. It didn't really surprise me. I knew from experience what a convincing performance he was capable of when the occasion looked auspicious.

I got up and swung my arms a few times to improve circulation. It was a damp and cold little hotel in which the only effort to maintain warmth was concentrated in the public rooms. At the window I looked out on a short avenue of over-pollarded wintry trees. No doubt that had been done to improve the view but it seemed to me characteristic of the area which insisted on stunting anything which threatened to grow tall enough for its own good. There was no sign of life whatever in the avenue or on the minor road which served the staid dormitory settlement of Kilmacolm. It had been built to house rich men beyond the sight and sound of the hectic bustle of industry on the river bank where they made their money. Now it was as redundant as the thousands who no longer worked on the Clyde; and protected its new inhabitants only from signs of decay.

I'd hoped that it would have been possible to take Mrs Mulvenny out for a celebratory meal and perhaps a visit to the theatre in Glasgow. Since she was now in a wheelchair, that would have proved difficult for her, so I accepted the Matron's invitation to join patients and staff for their Christmas dinner. It proved a rather strained event for me and the only other visitor. She was a middle-aged woman who seemed to be in pressing need of a good meal. But both of us became like prize crackers to be circulated among *all* the patients and acknowledged as the generous donations of the individuals we'd come to visit. I had expected that sometime during the day Mrs Mulvenny's son, Andrew, would put in an appearance but he didn't. One of the nurses told me that Andrew did come to see his mother on the first Tuesday of every month. But of course Christmas falls at the end of December; and, that year, on a Wednesday.

When I returned to Sussex I found waiting for me a telegram
from Aage Jensen. Mrs Benstead, the wife of the couple who
looked after us in the house, told me that it had arrived the day
after my departure for Scotland. Since she considered telegrams
to be the word of God which shall not be denied she was plainly
offended by the fact that I had not left an address where I could
be reached. She hovered while I read the telegram, hoping no
doubt to see evidence that my blasphemy had served me right.
I told her, 'I'm going to Copenhagen in the morning. I should be
back by Saturday.'

When I telephoned the number Jensen had provided to confirm
that I would come to see him, he gave the impression of being
more than a little irritated that I had not called earlier. My
explanation did nothing to improve his manner. Visiting the
elderly sick did not seem to him a good excuse. Then, to my
surprise, he gave me his home address as my destination and,
just before he hung up, added, 'The weather has changed. It
has started snowing here.' Presumably he'd mentioned it either
to complain that I'd let the clear weather slip or to ensure that
I came properly dressed. It amused me to think he was running
out of warm clothing to comfort his feckless guests. Or those,
anyway, whose native air blew off the Gulf Stream and not the
Baltic.

And, of course, it was still snowing when I got there. His
apartment was in a modern block on the Fredericksberg Alle.
Jensen greeted me amiably enough, possibly heartened by the
layers of outer clothing I took off before he led me through to
meet his wife. And it was fortunate that he specified his relationship with the girl who shook my hand because Fru Jensen could
well have been his daughter. When she went off to prepare
coffee for us – moving with no obvious sign of trepidation over
the mirror-polished wood floor of the living room – Jensen
intercepted my admiring glance and I promptly switched my
attention to the room in general. Several carefully placed lamps
gave a cosy glow to the spare good taste of the furniture. For
although it was only late in the morning the density of the falling
snow greatly reduced the daylight.

The Norske Veritas man came immediately to the point.

'Now, I think, I must be very honest with you, Hr Thompson. The reason . . .'

'Could you make it, "*Mr* Thompson" or "Bill"?'

To my astonishment, he seemed to give that request a lot of thought. He stared at me with polite, if rather weary, interest. When I knew him better I was able to interpret that look more accurately. He wasn't thinking about my request at all. He was signalling annoyance that I'd interrupted him. People who knew him well never interrupted him.

'Bill,' he said at last. 'It seems to me that you could help us in this business of the *Niome*. Also, I think, you can benefit from our help.'

'I'm sure I can – benefit, I mean. But I don't see how I can help Norske Veritas. To be honest, I don't understand why you should be involved.'

But his pursuit of honesty did not stretch to a clarification of that point right away. 'I have seen the preliminary inquiry report which says there was nothing wrong with the ship, her equipment, her loading or the way she was handled.' He made a leisurely gesture with a long, pale hand. 'Yet five men are dead, the cargo is lost and the ship is sunk. One set of facts cannot produce the other.'

'Unless it was a freak accident.'

Jensen lowered his eyelids to inspect the corner of an orange-coloured rug spotlit by his reading lamp. 'Even freak accidents have causes,' he said.

'If there was negligence the formal inquiry will say who was responsible.'

'You are confident that you will keep your Chief's ticket?'

'No, I'm not. But I hope so.'

He looked up, not by moving his eyes but by raising his head. And he smiled as though he had forced me to let slip exactly what he wanted to hear. 'I have asked you to come quickly here because there is something which I want you to see before changes are made.'

'What is it?'

'The entire bow section of the *Niome* has been salvaged.' I stared at him in amazement. The hairs on the back of my neck prickled and I saw again the macabre vision of our own bow, like a huge disembodied hand, forging upon us to ram against the ship. And still it was not done. 'But it was sunk! One of the tugs searched the area and found nothing.'

He shook his head impatiently. 'They *saw* nothing. On the surface. And it was dark, of course. But the bow was floating still – just below the surface.'

Apparently, when the bow ran into the main hull the force of the collision toppled it so that the broad surface of the sundered bulkhead came uppermost and stable just below the surface, though jagged edges of the side plating jutted above the waves. In the weeks that followed, this bulky remnant of the ship drifted many miles westward. Before long it came near Swedish coastal waters and was promptly identified by several helicopter patrols as a submarine. *Any* peculiar object in Swedish coastal waters is identified as a submarine, but near the naval base of Karlskrona panic sets in.

'We are lucky they did not bomb it,' Jensen said. 'There could be as much as five thousand tons of benzine floating free.'

'That is incredible.'

'And quite valuable,' he murmured drily. 'Luckily it started to drift south towards Bornholm and the Danish tugs went out. I sent you the telegram as soon as I heard the news. It was not possible to judge how long they would take negotiating, then bringing it to harbour. There have been many difficulties and the movement has been very slow. Last night, though, they brought it in.'

'And you want me to inspect it. Why?'

'Because I know only the hull. You know the piping and pumping systems and the machinery connections.'

'When can we go down there?'

'Today. It is important that we are first.'

Before I could ask why we should be first the conversation was interrupted by the arrival of fresh, strong coffee together with a wide assortment of what we call Danish pastry but the Danes themselves call Vienna bread. Jensen's wife – Irene as I now learned – must have been used to her husband's conversations stopping abruptly whenever she came into the room because she brought her own topics with her and pursued them with great vivacity. And, to his credit, Jensen showed every sign of being quite captivated by the change her presence imposed.

As we relaxed I began idly to take in more details of the Jensens' living room. There were a great many books whose bindings glowed in the cunningly placed and subtle lighting. This also caught the sparkle from a great many crystal ornaments and gleamed on the silver frames of photographs.

That photograph. The chilling prickly sensation returned for, prominent at the end of a long sideboard, there was a photograph of Captain Meisling, the dead master of the *Niome*. I stared at it and Fru Jensen paused in what she was saying to find the focus of my enthralled attention. She said something to her husband in Danish and he shook his head. To me she said, 'Aage should have told you. That is my father. I am Irene Meisling.' Now I could begin to see why Jensen had particularly requested the duty which brought us together. There was much more to it than I'd supposed.

Later, as we drove south through the city in his ancient Volvo, it occurred to me that the salvors must have had trouble striking a profitable bargain with the owner. The cost of securing, towing and beaching the wreck would be considerable and nobody could be anxious to regain what was now just scrap metal. Certainly, the remaining cargo could be sold by those who'd saved it but if they were wise there might be greater gain from invoking the anti-pollution laws to make the owner buy the whole pig *and* the poke. Whatever the deal it would have been settled when the salvors had secured the wreck, yet could easily set it adrift again as a hazard to shipping, a danger of pollution, a threat to Swedish national security and a direct liability upon the owner. There is no trade more ruthless than the salvage trade.

The beaching which had been arranged was an old graving-dock now owned by a shipbreaking company. It was to be flooded for the wreck to be floated in and then gradually drained when the sea gates were closed behind it. Thus, the sheared section of the deck and bulkhead which were of interest to us were ideally situated for inspection.

When we arrived on the dockside the draining had not yet
started. Work was still in progress shoring-up so that as the
water level dropped the prow would rest on the bottom but the
wreck would not topple. And still the snow fell, thick and steady.
Jensen and I clambered over ice-coated debris and trudged
through slush to reach the edge of the dock and looked down
on what was left of the *Niome*. The rupture had split the deck
around the centre of No. 3 tank so that a reservoir of sea water
was still held in the forward half of that tank. The 'bottom' of
this reservoir was the watertight bulkhead. Under that were
cargo tanks Nos. 2 and 1 and the wedge-shaped forepeak tank
which held permanent ballast. On the visible remnant of the
main deck – now rising vertically – I could see that the plating
was remarkably unbuckled and almost all of the deck fittings
were intact. The forepart of the flying bridge, though, the
samson posts and all superstructure had been swept away.
Jensen reasoned that the damage forward was not caused by
the explosion but almost certainly by shearing as the bow
section grated against the main hull after they collided. The first
explosion, we reckoned, had been in the completely lost No. 4
tank which had generated further explosions fore and aft of it.

As soon as the shoring-up was completed, the salvage master
rigged pumps to empty the reservoir of sea water which
brimmed in the ragged half-shell of No. 3 tank. If the tanks had
not been so efficiently battened down and sealed there would
have been less of a problem for his men. Jensen told me, 'As
soon as they finish the draining we must get on there.'

That seemed to me unnecessary, and very dangerous. 'I think
we can see all that's to be seen from here.'

'Not the interior pipe lines and fittings.'

That was true but it did not outweigh the hazards of crossing
a narrow swaying gangway from the dockside to the edge of the
shell plate then descending a rope-ladder inside the greasy hull
– and all of this in fading light and a snow storm. 'I think we'd
better wait until tomorrow,' I said.

'Tomorrow the owner's men have possession and it will not
be allowed,' he told me.

And that, of course, was the reason behind his urgency in

summoning me. Whatever his eventual aim in the matter, his freedom to operate lay with the salvors and not with the owner. So – we had only that day to work in and by the time the pumps had reduced the water sufficiently we would be working by floodlight.

Getting aboard the wreck was an even more frightening experience than I'd anticipated. The gangway was secure enough on the lip of the dock but sprang immediately over a black void which seemed to gape even wider and deeper in the great shadows cast by the lights. The handrails were just ropes looped through stanchions and, underfoot, the planks not only swayed with the movement of the wreck but sprang up and down at each footfall the further one edged along it. On reaching the far end there was nothing to hold onto. The rope ladder dropped a shifting and dizzying sixty feet to the ribbed surface of the bulkhead. The most stomach-churning moment of all was the operation to transfer from the end of the gangway to the first few rungs of the ladder. Jensen had gone first and, watching him, I'd wondered why he took so long. When I reached the same point I marvelled that he'd done it at all. Every sense and instinct screamed a warning that the manoeuvre was impossible. If I hadn't seen the pale oval of Jensen's face staring up at me from the depth of the dripping cavern I would certainly have obeyed my instincts and shuffled back to the safety of the dockside. Eventually, though, I did get on the ladder and started to lower myself – getting both feet on each spar before I essayed the next one. It was then I noticed a ridge of blood across my knuckles. Probably I'd grazed them in the scramble but just as probably they'd simply burst from gripping so tight.

Nor was it easy to stay upright when I reached the bottom. Water still surged between the bulkhead stiffeners and we had to move about by stepping on the narrow flanges of these angle bars and climbing over and between a lattice-work of frames and girders which make up so much of the interior structure of a tanker. However, at Jensen's insistence, I did satisfy myself that I'd seen every pipeline and fitting which encroached upon that tank or led from it through the cofferdam. Jensen himself inspected not only that part of the hull which was available from the surface of the bulkhead, but insisted upon having an inspection cage rigged so that he could view the intervening spaces as well. And this thoroughness ensured that neither of us had to get out the way we got in. Instead we were lifted by a crane in the inspection cage and deposited on the grimy but marvellously firm dockside. When that delightful moment came, the time was almost midnight.

There were no showering or drying facilities in the breaker's yard but Jensen did manage to borrow waterproof capes for us to wear on the way home so that our soaked, oily boiler suits did not ruin the upholstery of the car. We got back to the flat cold and exhausted, but we were not done yet. While Irene prepared food for us, we cleaned up. Then we set about converting our rough sodden notes into detailed sketches which would illustrate as accurately as it was possible to remember the layout, fittings, pipes and plating of the wreck. By the time we'd finished that it was after three o'clock in the morning but each of us felt, I think, that a difficult job was successfully accomplished.

Naturally, at the time we had no idea how crucial that inspection was going to be. And perhaps it was the implicit danger in the situation which sharpened our powers of observation. For my part, the memory of being isolated in an upended world was fixed in vivid detail because it had been viewed in that slow-motion which fear and intense concentration always impose. In retrospect, it was ironic that the most significant factor had been apparent in our first view of the wreck, before they'd pumped the seawater out for us to go aboard. If only we'd known what to look for, we could have seen it from a safe position on the dockside. At the time, though, we had only looked at it while waiting for the water to be pumped out of the half-shell of No. 3 tank. That difference between looking and seeing was one I have never forgotten.

Next day I was aching in every muscle as Irene drove me out to Kastrup airport. I asked her about Jensen's dedication to the task we'd been pursuing. She told me, 'It is not really for my sake he is so angry. My father and Aage were great friends, you see.' She gave me a shy smile and I noted that the steering wheel of the old Volvo seemed to stretch her arms. And she had to tilt her chin up to get a clear view over the bonnet. In fact she looked endearingly like a child driving a bus. 'They were friends before my father married. And of course before I was born.'

'What is it that he wants to prove?' I asked.

'Why . . . the *cause* of it.'

'Oh, yes. But there's more than that.'

'And so that those who were to blame are punished,' she added, obviously unaware that, arguably at least, I could be one of those persons.

'It's possible that mistakes were made which couldn't be avoided,' I suggested.

From her puzzled look I deduced that we were not thinking along the same lines. After a sudden flurry of activity with the long, cranked gear-stick she took up the point. 'Mistakes is not it. Aage is not looking for mistakes.'

I flew back to London not greatly enlightened, but with black oil deeply ingrained under my fingernails, severely grazed knuckles, heavy bruising on both my shins and in urgent need of a masseur.

Over the New Year holiday period I recovered from the energetic scrambling over the salvaged bow. Then I was ready to deal with any further developments. However, the Department of Trade had no intention of rushing into its obligations. Early in 1975 we were told that the formal inquiry would not begin until August of that year. I had about seven months in which to do nothing. It passed pleasantly enough, but it did confirm my suspicion that I'd become an alien in Sussex. Of course I had not lived there for any length of time since I was sixteen, and so I had no close friends and even the acquaintances tended to think of me as a crypto-Scotsman. For a few months in the early summer, my mother deployed all her forces to reclaim me for England – and, more specifically, for any one of the many daughters of her friends. There were parties and outings and a number of more intimate meetings but the well meant effort was not successful. I found the girls pleasant enough and usually very pretty. But they seemed to me too young – and somewhat pointless.

'Pointless?' My mother arched her brows in bewilderment. 'Darling, what *do* you mean?'

'Yes. There are so many of them who seem to be exactly the same person. They have the same likes and dislikes and no opinions about anything. Nor are they doing anything. One wonders what they're all *for.*'

'What do you want them to do?'

'I don't know. Perhaps they are like that because they have no *need* to do anything.'

'Bill, the fault may be yours. They find you rather strange.'

'I dare say.'

But only gradually did it occur to me in what way I was strange to the affluent middle-class milieu where I should have belonged. The trouble was that for a long time I'd been exposed to working-class reality and had accepted it as a valid standard. From my acquired vantage point it was plain to me that middle-class crises are usually so trivial. Often the people are secure enough to *choose* what they're going to worry about. And usually – to provide further insulation – they choose something which is none of their business. Thus, if it goes wrong or they lose, they can regretfully wash their hands of the whole affair and retreat to a neutral position which was never in danger.

FOUR

About a week before the date set for the opening of the formal inquiry I received a baffling letter from Clifford Sandys. The tone of the letter alone was surprising enough – revealing a marked discrepancy between what I knew to be our rather cool professional relationship and what he evidently saw as just the latest instalment of a long and very friendly correspondence with an old buddy. For a moment I thought he must have put a letter written to someone else in an envelope addressed to me. But the substance of it clearly applied to me. He suggested that I should stay with him in London during the proceedings. He had a flat in Lower Sloane Street. Corroded as I was by recent experiences, it seemed plain that there must be an ulterior motive and I spent a lot of time trying to work out what it might be. The invitation just did not fit the circumstances. However, free lodgings in London would certainly be more convenient than hotels and commuting, so I accepted the offer.

I arrived there on Saturday for lunch. Fortunately, a line in his letter clarified what might have proved a rather uneasy meeting. He'd written: '. . . delighted to put you up in the flat which Barbara and I share.' From this one could reasonably assume that Clifford and Barbara Cree were not married. Within a few hours I was – however obscurely – glad of that.

It is difficult now to be sure of that first impression of Barbara. So much has been added to it which could not have been seen then. She was a slim, rather angular woman in her mid-thirties with long unruly-looking chestnut hair. She wore absolutely no make-up and that made her eyes seem small and naked, though undoubtedly alert and friendly. What impressed me most, however, was the raucous warmth of her voice. It was she who had come to the door and she took my arm to lead me along the narrow hallway into the living room. 'Cliff promised you'd be very tall,' she complained. 'Of course he thinks everybody is very tall, including me.' She paused at a door to wheel me round. 'He's in there. I'm in the kitchen.'

The flat was a modern one and fairly roomy by modern standards. There was a large living room, the outer wall of which was almost entirely glass and overlooked the grounds of the Royal Hospital. At the other end was a dining area with a serving hatch and a door to the kitchen. Two bedrooms and the bathroom led off the hallway. All the furniture was glossy Habitat and – I guessed – the choice of the owner rather than the tenant.

Clifford was lying full-length on the couch reading, and fairly bounded up to welcome me. He certainly looked a lot better than the time I'd seen him in Sussex. He wore stylish casual clothes and, during the intervening months, he'd put on some weight which showed more in the improving fullness of his face than on his compact and wiry body. 'Bill!' He took my hand in both of his and shook heartily. 'I'm so glad you could get here before the actual inquisition.' He indicated an armchair, then asked, 'Drink?'

'Thank you. Whisky straight.'

'I mean, we've never really had a chance to talk over what happened.' He busied himself at the table where the drinks were set out and gave the impression that he was preoccupied with that as he added, 'Though I'm told you've been discussing things with . . .' he laughed carelessly, 'a third party, as it were.'

'My father?'

'No, no.' He handed me the drink with one hand and tapped me lightly on the shoulder with the other. He smiled broadly, 'Your father is a party of the first part as far as you're concerned. I'm thinking of outsiders.'

'Aage Jensen, perhaps?' I said, trying to match his bright throwaway tone. But really I was thinking that Clifford was angry about something. There was that feeling in the air and I suspected that I'd walked in at the end of a domestic quarrel.

'I did warn you about Jensen.'

'Yes. You didn't forbid me to see him, though.'

'Forbid?' Clifford threw himself back on the couch where, I noticed, he already had a well-filled glass close at hand. 'I was just trying to save you some hassle.'

'I don't think any of us can get through this without *some* hassle.'

Clifford altered his tone. 'True enough.' He sighed, took a sip of his drink and tried earnestness. 'But we can prepare things to go as smoothly as possible in the circumstances. That's why it's important for *us* to have some time to talk.'

What we were to talk about had to wait until after lunch. During the meal I learned that Barbara was an actress.

Since she seemed to me a particularly *un*-actressy person I said, 'Oh, a character actress?'

She allowed me a brief, comprehensive, stare then let out a whoop of laughter. 'My God! Does it show?'

'What? Have I used the wrong term?'

'Depends on what you mean. "Character actress" is often a euphemism for an *old* actress, or a *plain* actress – and, of course, a plain old actress; particularly if she's a difficult bitch.' She grinned mischievously. 'Was that what you had in mind?'

I was heartily grateful that my beard concealed most of the fierce blush I felt spreading from my neck to my scalp. 'No! No, not at all!'

Clifford said, 'All actresses are difficult.'

In trying to make amends I began woofling, 'I meant the sort of actress who actually . . .'

'Acts?' Barbara suggested.

'. . . assumes the full character she is playing instead of . . . of just being herself and . . . behaving agreeably.'

But she wouldn't let me off the hook. With raised eyebrows she enquired, 'Don't you think *I* could behave agreeably?'

'Oh, yes! Yes, of course.'

'But you're not,' Clifford declared. 'Now stop embarrassing him.'

She patted my hand in apology. 'Sorry.' And we went on to talk about other things.

As soon as Barbara had left for her matineé Clifford and I started on a detailed examination of events on the *Niome*.

Despite the attention I was giving to our recollection of the voyage during the afternoon, I could not help noticing how much my colleague was drinking. And it came to me that *that* was the subject of the quarrel I'd sensed when I arrived. I was puzzled because it was quite contrary to what I knew of him. Probably I should not have been surprised that anyone facing a tribunal required something to ease the tension. On the other hand, perhaps I'd been mistaken about his former habits. It could be that the reason he didn't get the post as chief was the company's awareness that Clifford was secretly a heavy drinker.

However, the whisky did not noticeably impair his grasp of the subject and he moved from one point to the next as though he had rehearsed not only his questions but my responses. By the early evening he suddenly remembered, 'Oh! Barbara thought you might want to see the play she's in so she . . . But really we've still got an awful lot to get through.'

'We don't have to get through all of it tonight, though.'

'Well – if you fancy going out – she left tickets, somewhere.' He lurched to his feet but just stood there gazing aimlessly around him. The fact that Barbara herself had not mentioned this was easily explained. She wanted to give me the opportunity of having something better to do without fear of giving offence. Clifford went on, 'The thing is, I've already seen the play.'

'I would like to see her,' I said. 'And I'd quite happily go by myself.'

He waved his hand and shook his head simultaneously. 'No, no, no. Can't have that. She'd skewer me.' He moved rather lopsidedly towards the door. 'Just let me have a shower and we'll have something to eat.'

There was time only for a very hurried dinner in a place devoted to hurried diners in the King's Road. As I picked at the reheated food my companion remarked, 'Barbara seems to have taken a liking to you.'

'Why do you think so?'

'Well – you've got a lot in common, I suppose. Books, music; stuff like that.'

'She's a very interesting woman.'

He nodded. 'And very loyal.'

'I'm sure she is,' I asserted, but could not see any immediate relevance.

Barbara was playing the lead in a successful revival of *What Every Woman Knows*. It was a play I'd never seen before and one which affected me a good deal. The character Barbara played – in a very convincing Scots accent – was that of a plain spinster whose family virtually bribe a man to marry her. And she is the making of him. He becomes a very powerful and moderately contemptible politician while the wife feigns submission and docility. What every woman knows, apparently, is that men are blinkered fools. I was completely entranced by Barbara's strength conflicting with her own vulnerability. But above all I was amazed at how she could let an interior light and grace shine through the awkward plainness of the woman. And she had energy to spare.

Clifford, who knew the lady much better than I – and had already seen the performance – was evidently not impressed. In fact he slept through most of it. This meant he was sober and refreshed when we got back to the flat and determined that we should continue our *Niome* post-mortem. So, when Barbara got back from the theatre I had no opportunity to tell her how entrancing she had been. She poked her head around the door but, seeing us deep in seawater and exploding benzine, just waved and went off to bed.

About three o'clock in the morning I got to bed as well. I lay for a while reflecting on what Clifford was up to. It was natural that he should want to make sure that we agreed on the relevant events in the engine room. But, insistently, during the hours of talk, I'd become aware of a more precise intention. Over and over again he'd alluded to and even listed the watch-keeping sequence at the time of the trouble with the heating coils. In particular, he seemed confused about exactly when the steam was applied to the coils and when it was turned off, then on again. His recollection was that all of these actions were taken during *my* watches. Since I'd had the opportunity to consult my notes – and he had not – the correct sequence was clear in my mind. But I did not tell him why I knew he was wrong. And really I could not see that it mattered. The explosions had

occurred long after we'd discharged the tanks with the troublesome heating coils. It was not a material factor.

It may be that after a night's sleep he saw the pointlessness
of his watch-keeping argument, because during Sunday he did
not once refer to it. Instead we quickly agreed on the sequence
following the discharge of the crude at the Polish terminal when
he had supervised the stripping and ballasting of the empty tanks
and I had operated the inert gas system which forced practically
all the oxygen out of the potentially lethal spaces. We agreed,
too, on what had happened after the explosions, and upon the
fact that I was in charge of the engine room when they occurred.

With all that settled Clifford decided he was very tired and
took a whisky bottle into the bedroom with him. I immediately
asked Barbara if she'd like to go out for some fresh air. It was
a fine and fairly warm summer's afternoon as we strolled up
through the quiet squares and crescents of Belgravia towards
Hyde Park. She accepted my renewed congratulations on her
performance but did not seem eager to discuss it at any length.
So I got on to my next burning topic – how on earth had she
managed to get tied up with Clifford. Of course I phrased this
with less partisan amazement than I felt and began by asking
whether she and Clifford had been together long.

'Several years,' she said. 'Four or five, I think.'

'How did you meet him? Actresses and engineers don't usually
mix.'

'They do on ships.' She gave a deep chuckle, 'Especially
freighters.'

That was even more puzzling. 'What were you doing on a
freighter?'

'Enjoying a cruise. They're much cheaper than passenger
ships and you meet a more interesting sort.'

'In what way, interesting?'

'Well – *younger*, for a start,' she said and laughed. 'Also,
they're men actually working at something which matters,
instead of working so that a bunch of geriatrics do nothing.'

We reached Knightsbridge and crossed over into the park,
following the edge of the sand track. The smell of horse dung
was heavy in the air. What I wanted to know, of course, was

not how or where Barbara and Clifford had met but *why* she'd chosen him as a lover.

'I don't know Clifford very well.'

'And you don't like him at all,' she said, smiling as she watched her feet advance through the coarse grass.

'Why do you say that?'

She shrugged. 'If you did, you wouldn't need to *act* being pleasant with him.'

I gasped. This was very accurate but I was not at all sure whether to acknowledge it, deny it or keep my mouth shut. After about half a dozen paces I said, 'I'd no idea it was so obvious.'

'Oh, not to anyone else, Bill! Certainly not to him. But I know where the strain lines show when people are acting.'

I stopped and confronted her. 'Where do they show?'

She lifted her hand and with two fingers stroked a long muscle in my neck behind my ear. 'There,' she said, moving her fingers to the corner of my jaw, 'there,' to a spot between and slightly above my eyebrows, 'and there.'

'Thank you,' I said, seizing the opportunity. 'They're not showing now, are they?'

'Not in the slightest.'

'So you know that being pleasant with you is not an act.'

She looked straight at me and smiled. 'I know that.'

'Good. Because I really am enjoying this.'

'Yes. So am I. Rotten Row is a favourite beat of mine.' As we continued walking she inhaled deeply, 'Of course it helps if you like horses, too. A *lot*.'

'Did you have a pony, as a child?'

She didn't look at me but I could see her smile subside. 'No,' she said gravely, 'I had very little as a child.' As she turned her head and looked towards the Lido she added, 'And certainly a pony wasn't what I wanted most.'

The inquiry was due to start at 11 a.m. in the ballroom of the Prince George hotel just off Queen Anne's Gate. Before then I called at my father's office again to accept a final briefing and to pick up the original copy of my notes in case that was deemed a material document by the board. My father was still on his way up from the coast but Sam Hanson was there with a couple of other staff engineers. He asked Mrs Schuster to bring the file and we waited in Hanson's office. We waited a long while. Finally Mrs Schuster reappeared and stated that the file could not be found. It was obvious that never before in her life had she made such a disgraceful statement. She was practically beside herself with embarrassment. The poor woman was sure it must be her fault and Hanson, though amazed, seemed to agree with that. But I was perfectly sure the file had been stolen and said so. 'Stolen!' echoed Mrs Schuster, her manner brightening perceptibly. She prompted me eagerly, 'Do you really think it could have been stolen?'

'Yes. And they probably took other things as well just to confuse the issue.'

'Who?' asked Hanson. Mrs Schuster didn't care who and scurried away to find further proof that her filing system could still be considered infallible.

I said, 'My first guess would be Clifford Sandys.'

'But you're staying with him, aren't you?'

'Only so that I can be nobbled, apparently.' The overnight change in Clifford's attack occurred to me. 'It might be useful to know *when* the file was taken. When was the last time you saw it? The original, I mean.'

'Oh, months ago. We took four copies right away and I've been using one of them.' He went to his desk and unlocked a drawer. 'That's my copy. We delivered one to your solicitor, your father has one and he gave you the fourth.'

'Maybe Mrs Schuster will be able to work out when the original could have been taken.'

'I'll get her on it,' said Hanson and went through to the outer office.

While he was gone, I ran over in my mind the argument I'd had with Clifford about the watch-keeping schedule and tried to isolate any assertion he'd made which he could have made only with knowledge of the stolen file. There was none I could think of. Indeed, if he'd had the file there would have been no point in his pursuing the argument. On the other hand, it could be that my certainty in recalling the disputed events persuaded him that the file *had* been saved and now it was crucial to his evidence at the inquiry. Hanson came back to report that apparently nothing else had been taken – so there seemed little point in calling the police upon the loss of a document which had no intrinsic value.

When my father got in he quickly demolished my theory but gave credence to my line of reasoning. On Saturday morning he'd had a call from the solicitor asking for another copy.

'Whose solicitor?' I asked.

'Yours, of course. Keeble.'

'Did he say why he wanted it?'

'No. But presumably because he needed it.' His tone indicated the displeasure he felt at having any action of his questioned. 'They sent a messenger round.'

I persisted. 'My point is that he may have needed another copy because his own copy had been stolen.'

'And where did you put the original document, sir?' Mrs Schuster enquired sweetly.

My father just glowered at her. 'It must be in my office,' he said and strode through, closely followed by the now blameless secretary. When she had reclaimed the original folder, Hanson and I went in. We discussed the likely rules of procedure for the inquiry and I was given firm and clear advice on how to say what I was obliged to say and, above all, to say no more than I was asked. Although listening carefully to all of this, I was aware that something had changed in my attitude to what lay ahead. The very serious and proper apprehension had definitely lifted. Fatalism with a light touch had replaced tension. Occasionally my attention jumped entirely away from the issue and I thought of Barbara.

Despite the hiatus there was quarter of an hour to spare when the taxi turned the corner of Petty France. Several years had elapsed since I'd been in that part of Westminster and I was astonished to discover the smoke-blackened, mountain-with-windows called Queen Anne Mansions had been demolished and, apparently, they were building a modernistic museum in its place. The taxi driver said no, that was the new Home Office.

He could not as readily identify the Prince George Hotel however, and I got out to cover the final stretch on foot.

The odd-seeming venue for the inquiry had been chosen to
meet several circumstances. Many of the people summoned
to attend were to come from abroad and had to be found
accommodation. Also, the normal inquiry venues at the engineers' institute and the naval architects' institution were not
available for the length of time our inquiry would take. But the
overriding factor was that Sir Iain Selby, QC – who was the
chairman – had held a planning inquiry at the Prince George and
liked it there. The ballroom was an addition to the original
building and projected into the garden. It was sound-proofed,
had extensive toilet facilities and though fairly self-contained was
convenient to restaurant and bars. The Department of Trade
was more than willing to hire these amenities for a couple of
months knowing that 'condemnation in costs' could be one of
the main penalties on any one of the other participants. It was
rather as though the Department was determined to throw a
huge compulsory party, knowing that eventually it must be paid
for by whichever of the guests was caught holding the parcel.

In the ballroom the tribunal sat behind a table which had been
set up on the shallow dais where the band would normally be.
Sir Iain was in the middle with a master mariner on his right
and a distinguished marine engineer on his left. Ranged in a
semi-circle behind them were various officials and advisers. On
the wide expanse of polished floor several blocks of seats had
been set out and all of them were occupied by the interested
parties, their counsel, assistants to their counsel, their solicitors
and sundry accredited observers. In all, there were some eighty
people assembled and none of them was a member of the public.
I marvelled that it took so many to determine what caused the
loss of a small-to-medium tanker valued at fifteen million pounds.
If the *Niome* had been a super-tanker it might have been
necessary to hire the Albert Hall.

I found my place in the appropriate block of seats and looked
around for Clifford. He was some distance away with the other
officers who were all being represented by the same counsel.
The recovered first officer, Pedersen, and I shared another

counsel. The remainder of the surviving crew were also represented separately. Clifford gave me a cheery wave as the
proceedings began. I whispered to Pedersen, 'Mr Sandys seems
to be very confident.'

'Of course,' Pedersen nodded. 'He has the confidence of the
owner.'

'What did the master think of him?'

'The master could see no good reason for it,' said the Norweg-
ian second-in-command slowly. His face and head were still
badly scarred and the inflamed areas of skin grafting stood out
in vivid patches. Indeed, most of the surviving deck officers and
crew showed some signs of injury from the explosions and the
terrible fire. In contrast, those of us whose work was in the
engine room bore no trace at all of having lived through a
disaster. It seemed to me an apt, if cruel, illustration of the deep
traditional difference between deck-men and engine-men. On
board ship the enmity is almost tangible but even in official
reports, in membership of societies and in the whole literature
of the sea the conflict is sustained. It is insisted that deck officers
are top dogs and engineers are lucky to get stowage space.
Even the agenda and procedure of this inquiry reflected the
conflict. As chief engineer I was, theoretically, senior to
Pedersen in rank, but in all the documentation his name came
first and certainly his evidence would have the greater weight.

Not until late in the afternoon was I questioned by my own
counsel. Really, he just led me through the statement I'd given
at the preliminary hearing and prompted me to expand on some
detail. As we'd anticipated, the engineer member of the board
pursued the matter of the apparent overheating in the tank coils
but, to my relief, did not pursue the question of checking the
temperature of the oil at the point of discharge – the oversight
which had alarmed Sam Hanson. As I was about to sit down
everyone was surprised when Clifford's counsel decided to
continue the questioning. He wanted to relate the various engine
room decisions to the watch-keeping schedule. As I'd practically
memorised my notes on that aspect the strategy didn't alarm
me. However, it soon became clear that his questions were
directed at information which was *not* in my notes. It was

uncanny how he was able to locate and exploit the gaps in my necessarily incomplete record of events.

There was a rustle and a murmur of surprise which spread over the rows of seats in the ballroom. To many it seemed astonishing that the expected unified front among the officers was being fractured. Also, they were interested to observe that my assured delivery began to falter. The counsel seemed unaware of the reactions he was causing. He then came to the sequence of events after the discharge of crude in Poland, which Clifford and I had had no difficulty agreeing about on Sunday. With restored certainty I recited what we had agreed and I was allowed to resume my seat away from the microphone.

It was then Clifford's turn. At first I just could not believe that I was hearing him say what he was saying. It was as though I'd been held up as a negative and now, holding his client in full view, the counsel developed the print before our eyes. What I'd been sure about wasn't mentioned. Where I'd been unsure, Clifford was certain. But, most damning of all, he contradicted much of what we'd previously agreed upon. What was more, in an open friendly way, he went outside the area of agreement or disagreement to report as fact things which had not happened at all.

So the substance of our opening examination established a conflict of interest which was much deeper and more damaging than I'd had any reason to anticipate. Of course I'd suspected Clifford of trying to gain an advantage by conniving, by theft and by attempted brow-beating. All of that was, I thought, no more than a sustained effort to defend himself which, though not exactly endearing, was natural enough. But after that first day before the tribunal a drastic reappraisal became necessary. There was something else going on, and whatever it was Clifford seemed more intent on undermining confidence than sustaining it. For a moment during his testimony I had a clear impression of revenge at work, yet if he had any such feelings surely they would be directed against the owner, not me.

At the close of the first session I saw Clifford make for the bar and I waited to talk to Aage Jensen who'd been an alert observer in one of the back rows of seats. When most of the people had filed out I went over and sat beside him. 'What did you think of that?'

'I think you are in trouble,' said the Dane. Then, dismissing the whole subject of the tribunal, he turned to me and asked with polite interest, 'Would you like to work for us?'

I was startled. 'Pardon?'

He tilted is head back to inspect the large glass panels in the ceiling which tinted the daylight pink. 'You have no work to do and we think you would suit the bureau in London very well.'

'Which bureau?'

He puffed a little gasp of surprise. 'Norske Veritas, of course. We need another engineer surveyor.'

'A temporary job, you mean?'

He lowered his head and turned to face me in the same unhurried movement. His expression betrayed some amusement. 'No. A permanent job.'

'But when this is over I'll be going back to sea.'

'I do not think so,' Jensen said. And that was the same as saying that after only one day he thought me seriously at fault and that after two months the tribunal would come to the same conclusion of negligence and find me unfit to sail in the merchant fleet. So amazed was I at this arbitrary decision I did not pay proper attention to his next remark. He added, 'And from what I've heard today, you would be very useful on our side.'

'You think they'll sack me?'

'At the moment that is not the important point.'

'It's important to me!'

But he had no aptitude for calming or cajoling and merely shrugged at my inability to listen intently enough to what he'd said. Foolishly, I compounded my error by responding with a great show of wounded integrity. I just got up and walked out on him.

When Clifford got back to the flat Barbara had departed for the evening performance and I'd eaten my share of the dinner she'd left us.

'What the hell were you playing at today?'

He seemed surprised by my tone. 'I thought it went quite well.'

'You called *me* a liar and you made up some fancy lies of your own.'

His frown suggested an earnest effort to recall what might have upset me.

'Well? What are you up to?'

He gave me a worried smile. 'Take it easy, Bill.' Then he set about serving himself from the dishes on the hotplate. While he did so he gave a soothing commentary on his blameless behaviour. 'All we did today was go over the statements we made at the preliminary, right?' He paused with spoon at the ready to encourage my agreement, but did not pause long. 'Naturally, with two lawyers there's going to be two ways of looking at it. My lawyer asked you questions, your lawyer asked me questions. For clarification.' He grinned as he settled himself at the table. 'There's nothing wrong with that, is there?'

'Are you telling me that what you said today was in your original statement?'

'Sure!'

'Lucky I didn't see that.'

'Well, I didn't see yours.' He glanced up at me with the fork to his mouth and added softly, 'I didn't see your private log either, or your notes.'

'Until this weekend, you mean?' He didn't deny or confess that the document had mysteriously come into his possession. He just smiled regretfully and went on eating.

I took a chair at the cleared space opposite him and tried another tack. 'You do remember what we discussed on Saturday and most of Sunday? And you remember what we agreed upon?'

'Didn't we *dis*agree quite a lot?'

'Yes. But we did agree on a lot of things that you flatly denied today. And I want to know why.'

He rested his knife and fork for a moment. 'Bill, I'm sorry if anything that came out today worried you, but . . .'

'What worries me is the fact that you contradicted the very things that you'd asked me to say.' I leaned across the table in an effort to shake his puzzled blandness. 'And you did it when there was no way I could withdraw my testimony.'

'It's not my fault they called you before me,' he said. 'And whatever we discussed or agreed on Saturday is pretty hazy.' He grinned. 'Bill, I was drunk! How can I remember? We had so much to talk about.'

I leaned back, baffled by the sheer effrontery with which he defended the indefensible. For a moment I considered the obvious and immediate response of packing my bags and getting out of the flat. But, again, the thought of Barbara intervened to make a fraught situation somehow less than a matter of life and death. And the man was somehow so calm and apparently unaware of the enormous damage he had done to my credibility. In silence I watched until he'd finished his meal, then pursued what seemed to be the only point of contention on which he might be drawn. 'You did manage to get a copy of my log, didn't you?'

'You shouldn't have tried to hold on to that, Bill.'

'But you have seen it?'

Not looking at me, he nodded. 'Sure.'

'How did you manage that?'

'Easy. My lawyer asked your lawyer to get another copy – from your father's office.' Seeing my look of astonishment he smiled, 'They talk to each other, you know. Lawyers talk to each other.' He stacked the used crockery and rose to clear the table. 'It's just an inquiry, after all. It's not a *trial*.'

Just for a moment as he walked into the kitchen I wondered if my attitude had been wrong and somewhat paranoid. Clifford was a very convincing man. And no doubt he had convinced the tribunal that I was a liar.

FIVE

Two weeks into the inquiry found me far from its exhaustive pavane in the Prince George ballroom. I was sitting in a narrow, cramped private plane skimming, it seemed, far too low over the North Sea towards an island in the Kattegat. Behind me in the roaring cabin crouched Aage Jensen. My opinion of him had changed, because I now knew exactly how and why he was involved in the *Niome* investigation. Moreover, he had convinced me that I had a part to play in it which could not be pursued as effectively by anyone else. As we bounced and lurched in the small plane – which obviously required more than its single propeller to keep us in the air – I considered the events which had dictated this urgent journey.

On the day after Clifford's remarkable turnabout, the third engineer, Dolby, effectively backed up all that he'd said. So it was necessary to revise the illusion that Clifford had dashed into the engine room immediately after the explosion to save my life. Obviously it was Dolby he'd come to rescue. For the first time I mentioned these events to Jensen and described the scene.

'He was fully dressed,' the Dane repeated. There was a hint of excitement in his voice.

'Who?'

'The second engineer, Sandys.'

'Yes. And wearing his life-jacket.'

Jensen smiled. We were seated in the lounge bar of the hotel after lunch. He lifted his drink using the very tips of his long fingers and asked, 'Did you not think that was strange? Immediately after the explosion he is ready to abandon ship!'

'I assumed he'd seen the state of things on deck.'

'Why would he be on deck? He should have been resting in his cabin.'

But even then I was not prepared to take in the significance. 'Maybe he was in his cabin at the first explosion, then rushed on deck to see what had happened, then . . .'

'Then rushed below to put on all his outdoor clothes and his life-jacket, then rushed down into the engine room to save you.'

'To save Dolby,' I corrected.

Jensen shook his head. 'There was not *time* to do all this.'

He was right. 'No,' I conceded, 'there certainly wouldn't have been time.' Which, on the face of it, left only one conclusion. 'You think he knew there was going to be an explosion.'

Jensen nodded.

I threw myself back in the armchair. 'But that's impossible! Surely it's much more likely that for some reason he was going on deck and put on the heavy clothes for that?'

'Possible.' The Dane gave a slight shrug as he replaced his glass precisely in the centre of the square coaster. 'Possible – but not likely. He has just come off duty, it is dark outside and very cold, there is absolutely nothing wrong with the way the ship is sailing.' He leaned across the table. 'How likely is it?'

'Not very. Not at all, in fact.'

'So, consider what has been his behaviour since then.'

I called a waiter to bring another round of drinks and the Dane went on to marshal the events in that soft unemotional voice which, even with less contentious subjects, always implied more than it betrayed.

He began: 'In the salvage tug you tell him that you have saved your log of the voyage. Those documents are taken from your pocket and hidden on the tug. When you are talking on the telephone to the Trade attaché – Sandys knows the entire disposition of the ship and crew.'

'I don't see what's wrong with *that*.'

Jensen grunted and, involuntarily, delivered an axiom in Danish which he quickly translated as, 'What is wrong is that it is too right.' His quick glance detected that this was less than clear to me. He explained, 'Why would he be so well-informed about matters which are not his business unless all these things entered into his calculations?'

The waiter brought the drinks, assessed the denominations of coins in my change, took the tip he'd anticipated, lifted the empties and departed. I smiled and raised my glass to Jensen. 'Please go on.'

'When you see the ship's agent he knows about your log.'

'The young deck officer, Foster, could have told him.'

'How would Foster know about it?'

'Because Clifford told him.' Again the obvious struck me only when I declared it. I continued lamely, 'At least that's what Clifford said. Foster was alone in the cabin while Clifford and I were in the radio office.'

Jensen knew that was nothing to the purpose and waved it aside. 'Next, Sandys comes to see you. And even you . . .' he bowed mockingly across the table, 'even you suspect that he wants to find out what happened about your log and – not before time – *you* lie.'

'Yes. But all this about the log could be just Clifford making sure he's got a strong case.'

'Indeed. And as soon as he gets a copy of the log, suddenly he *has* a strong case. And a case that is strong because it has nothing to do with the log and avoids everything in it.'

'That's true. But even so . . .'

'Bill!' Jensen grew a little impatient. 'Surely it is clear that Sandys did not want your log. What he wanted was to deprive you of it, and everyone else.'

'Why?'

'Because a clear record of events in the engine room posed a threat to his calculations. The threat of losing his ticket means nothing to him, so he must be involved in something more than that. And it must have started in the engine room.'

'It's all very strange,' I said.

'It is more than "strange" that the master of the ship is dead.'

'Considering what happened it's astonishing so many survived.'

'Not at all. She went down in a very convenient place. And the explosions were well away from the accommodation.'

It was with great difficulty that I tried to assimilate all the points which Jensen made. Obviously he'd reasoned the whole thing through before our conversation in the bar. His remark about the master did not seem to fit, though. I prompted him, 'Why are you surprised that the master died?'

'I am shocked that the master died.'

'Yes, of course. I'm sorry.' It was difficult keeping in mind the personal connection. 'I shouldn't have mentioned that.'

Jensen gave me an even, amiable stare. 'Even if it had not been Nils Meisling the fact would be surprising. You see, normally when a ship is scuttled the master is *always* among the survivors.'

I gulped and a lump of ice went into my mouth.

My companion continued urbanely, 'Of course even an experienced master could not have foreseen that the flying bridge would be blasted against the superstructure.'

We sat in silence for a few moments while I came to terms with these new and unavoidable facts. In my mind I saw again the *Niome* – ablaze across a stretch of swelling, flame-burnished water, with the flying bridge peeled back like a segment of banana skin and only the jagged, chopped end of a tank where the bow had been. There had been no possibility at all of saving the ship. And Clifford Sandys was to blame for all that. It was directly due to him that five men had died. 'And I'm his *guest*,' I said aloud.

'Pardon me?'

'I'm living in the same flat with the man who has caused all this.'

The Dane nodded. 'Yes. No doubt there was a purpose in having you there.'

'Well, I can't stay there now.'

'But you *must*,' Jensen asserted with surprising vigour. 'Until we are ready to trap him, you must remain there. And do not give him the least hint of what we know.'

'That would be very difficult.'

'It is essential. If he knows he is suspected, everyone involved will make it impossible for us to proceed further.'

I took another sip of my drink and looked around the quiet,

rather sombre lounge. Quite a number of the people earnestly talking together at the low oak tables were participants at the inquiry. They would spend weeks together arguing about what had caused the loss of the ship. Eventually, after deliberation over several months, the tribunal would apportion blame. And all of that time would be wasted and all the conclusions wrong because they could not forestall the real object of the enterprise. Yet here on the second day – sprawled in the chair opposite me – was a man who already knew the real answer; who had probably known it before the inquiry began.

Seeing me look directly at him once more, Jensen said, 'As you will guess, my business is to represent the underwriters of the insurance. It stands at two hundred and seventy million Danish kroner. That's about a hundred million kroner more than the ship was worth.' He went on to explain that, in the fanciful world of marine insurance, owners are allowed to place whatever value they like on their ships. Insurers do not object to this because the higher the value set, the higher the premiums will be. So, what was really at stake was not the negligence or competence of someone on the ship but the prize of over fifteen million pounds for its loss.

The little plane reared and twisted in a thermal shift as we crossed the western shore of Jutland. My knees scraped against the seat in front and I tried vainly to wedge myself into a more comfortable position. Jensen, seated immediately behind me, was making exactly the same adjustments. It certainly would have been less wearing to go the long way round by commercial flight, train and ferry. But we did not have the time to do that; nor did we wish to advertise the chance we were taking.

The chance was that the yard which had built the *Katia Maersk*, later the *Niome*, would still have the original piping diagrams. Of course all documentation, drawings and diagrams should have been passed on to the new operations when the vessel was sold. It was those drawings and the amendments to them which the tribunal had requested be put up for examination by the expert advisors. And that request to the owner was what triggered our flight. For Jensen had worked at the Lindø shipyard

and knew that when the ship was being built the records department had just introduced microfilm to its archive. And whereas
microfilm is an excellent form for storage, it is absolutely no use
to operators of the vessel who require full-scale prints and
velographs.

The urgency of our flight to Lindø was dictated by Jensen's
all-embracing suspicion of the owner, his agent and whatever
evidence they would present next day. He reasoned that if this
possible loose end could occur to him then it could occur to
those who might wish to prevent its discovery. He acted quickly.
The request for drawings had been made at the opening of
the hearing that morning. Possessing *carte blanche* from his
employers, Jensen immediately chartered a small plane to leave
from Gatwick. Then he phoned me at the flat to tell me how I'd
be spending the rest of the day. And it was up to me. Jensen
himself was basically a naval architect and, as he'd pointed out
before, his specialist knowledge was confined to the hulls of
ships. But however the scuttling of the *Niome* had been achieved
it had been done through the engine-room systems and control.
That was my area.

Below us – and now we were over land I could see we were
flying at a respectable height – the intricate pattern of fields and
the fretwork of small roads on the Danish mainland ended in a
sharp and visible line where they met the border with the more
sparsely populated landscape of the north German spur; which
the Danes continue to think of as their own Schleswig-Holstein.
Our pilot made sure he kept to the north of that border. Before
long the plane dropped again as we cleared the peninsula and
banked north over the Kattegat. We were nearing our destination.

I wondered where Clifford was at that moment. After our
initial appearance at the inquiry we'd been told that we need not
attend again until requested, though our respective solicitors
were obliged to be there all the time. But in the ten days which
had elapsed since then Clifford had left the flat every morning
and returned again only occasionally for dinner. Barbara didn't
seem to mind these unexplained absences and I was glad of
them. It gave Barbara and me a lot of time together during the

day and we did indeed have much in common – as Clifford had predicted. The same things made us laugh and we had remarkably similar tastes in books, paintings and music. Clifford, though, was still a very strong presence in his absence and when he came back in the evenings he seemed to take sardonic pleasure in making it clear that whatever we'd been doing during the day meant little. Barbara would go to bed with him.

It was that damnable fact – and a vivid illustration of the fact – which was in my mind as the plane jolted down on a grass-strip runway at Beldringe. A car was waiting by the little airfield office which looked like a cricket pavilion. With the minimum of formality we were allowed to drive off across the island to the shipyard. Jensen sat in front with the driver and they chatted in Danish as the many white-walled, red-roofed farm buildings whisked by – always at least a field away from the road. Then suddenly before us were the tall cranes. The huge building docks had been excavated from the flat land and at a distance only the high-rise superstructure and funnels of the ships could be seen. I laughed at the sight and Jensen turned to give me a puzzled look. The whole thing just seemed so incongruous. All around the complex there was nothing but a chain-link fence and, running right up to that, acres of freshly harvested fields.

It was our intention to examine the originals using the shipyard's equipment. Then we would be able to compare what we'd seen with what the owner's counsel would put on display. In the main administration building Jensen asked to see an old colleague in charge of the archive. As soon as he came into the room I knew we were too late. And, indeed, he immediately confirmed that the microfilm record of the *Katia Maersk* had been sent to London that morning. Jensen's friend was apologetic but he could not deny the urgent request of the owner's agent.

'What reason did he give?' I asked.

'He said the court had ordered him to produce the material.' The man shrugged, 'It seemed strange after all this time. When I asked him if the court had a microfilm projector he said he didn't know.'

'There is no projector,' stated Jensen flatly, 'and the tribunal did not ask for the microfilm.'

'Nevertheless,' his friend declared, 'the material does belong to the new owner.'

As we drove back to the airstrip through the crisp and apparently deserted countryside I could not avoid thinking that this had been a very extravagant mission. And the extravagance wasn't just in money. It bothered me that I was engaged in something as bizarre as industrial espionage and a search for vital microfilm. Probably, it was just the word 'microfilm' which caused me embarrassment. Though, certainly, that is the system used to store bulky drawings. There was also the fairly embarrassing fact that this sudden adventurous mission produced no result. Yet my companion did not seem unduly depressed and I wanted to know why.

'Because this proves that we are right.'

I smiled. 'That *you* are right. I'm just agreeing with you as far as I can understand it.'

'And what do you understand about the microfilm?'

'That something important has been changed which they don't want anyone to know about.'

'Ja, sure! What else?'

'Before they show the microfilm to the board they want to make the same alteration on that.'

'No,' the Dane shook his head decisively. 'They cannot do it. They cannot alter the original microfilm. Perhaps, if they had a lot of time and all the necessary drawings they could make a *new* microfilm but that would be unconvincing, even if it could be projected.'

At a loss, I asked, 'So? Why do they want it?'

'For the same reason that Sandys wanted your notes. Not to use it but to prevent its use against them.' He grinned, 'And that tells us something else. Or *me* it tells.'

'What?'

'That they know how it *could* be used against them. That is reassuring.'

'But not much help unless we know *how*.'

He looked at me carefully and I could see that he was genuinely amazed that my powers of reasoning were so much less efficient than his own. Before he could instruct me further the car swerved and bumped over the grass around the airstrip and we got out. The pilot had not expected us back so soon and had just started refuelling for our return journey. We went into the tiny waiting-room and Jensen described the state of play as he saw it. Gradually all my scepticism of our actions began to evaporate. The game was worth the candle if only because there was a very large amount of money at stake. Beyond that, lives had been lost and reputations could be ruined. I tried to shake myself out of selfish preoccupation to see what Jensen so clearly saw. First, the vessel had been purposely sunk. She had been bought in order to be sunk and wildly over-insured to make it extremely profitable. A new chief engineer was hired as scape-goat in case the plan miscarried. The plan for sinking was calculated to destroy all evidence – and yet ensure the speedy rescue of those involved. The method was directly connected with the engines or engine-operated systems. I agreed with all of these conclusions before Jensen asked me, 'Now, which of these things did not work out as they planned?'

'All the evidence was not destroyed. I saved my notes.'

'Your notes, yes. Also, the Lindø shipyard saved the original microfilm . . .' he grasped my arm with suppressed glee, '. . . *and* the bow section did not sink! The bow came back to haunt them. You see?' It must have been clear from my expression that I didn't for he went on very slowly and carefully to state, 'They must know that it is possible for us to reach the truth of this matter by comparing what was available before the explosion with what is available *now*. So? What is there to compare with?

'I don't know.'

'Just one of these things became available only *after* the explosion.'

'The bow!'

Jensen nodded with satisfaction, and some relief, that I'd finally reached the point he had started at. 'That is it. They have pointed a finger to where the truth is.'

'But the bow has been broken up now, surely.'

'Yes. That was done very quickly. The owner paid the salvors, sold the benzine and *paid* to have the wreck broken up.'

'Then it's no longer available as evidence.'

'No, but the photographs are available,' he sighed, 'at a price.'
I was astonished. 'Who would have photographs of it?'
'The salvors, of course!' He chuckled at my expression.
'Salvors treat every wreck as though it is a fabulous monster
they alone could capture from the sea. They photograph it from
every angle. It is essential to their bargaining with owners.'

The pilot tapped on the window of the waiting-room. Jensen
waved to acknowledge that we too were ready – but for different
journeys. To me he said, 'You will go back to London. I must
now go to Copenhagen and start my bargaining.'

When I got back to London I enquired if my father was at
home or away then phoned him at home to say I was coming
down to have a talk with him. The whole new situation which
Jensen had revealed needed some clear advice based on experience. Before leaving the city, though, I called in at the flat just
as Barbara was leaving for the theatre. When I told her I wouldn't
be back that night she said, 'How odd! Clifford phoned to say
that he wouldn't be back tonight either.'

'Did he say why?'

'Business, apparently.'

'Business where?'

'In Copenhagen.'

'Ah!' I said, but knew that was quite an inadequate expression
of the excited, rather queasy feeling in my stomach.

Barbara paused at the open door of the taxi. 'What's wrong?'

'Clifford is much smarter than I thought he was.'

'And what's wrong with that?'

I put my hands on her shoulders and gave her a quick kiss on
the cheek. 'We'll see,' I said as I helped her into the cab.
'Tonight, you just give John Shand hell.'

She laughed and the taxi moved off to execute a leisurely
U-turn in the face of the early evening traffic heading for the
Embankment.

By the time I got to Lancing I was too late for dinner but Mrs
Benstead saw that I more than made up for it before I went
through to my father's study. He poured me a drink and with
admirable reticence waited for me to raise the purpose of this

unexpected visit. I outlined what Jensen had told me and no doubt indicated that I fully believed all of it. To my relief, so did my father. He nodded, 'So! The vessel was cast away.'

'Scuttled,' I said.

'No. These words have precise meanings. "Scuttling" means providing holes to let in water.' He gave a rather prim smile and added, 'Usually by opening valves which ought to be closed.'

His calm response to my news and the amused cynicism with which he identified the nature of the events reflected exactly the attitude which had amazed me in the salvage skipper, the Trade attaché, then Aage Jensen himself. All of them were very familiar with the ways of the merchant marine as a business. Possibly they would have been more surprised if the sinking of the ship had been a genuine accident. Now, comfortably settled in my father's study I learned some of the background which informed the opinions they shared.

Trying to tune myself to a more detached point of view I said, 'Yes. Well, the *Niome* wasn't so much cast away as blown away.'

'Not an easy thing to arrange,' said my father, 'but in the circumstances well worth the effort.'

'What circumstances?' I asked.

He pointed out that in 1973 when the oil states practically doubled the price of crude the very first people to be affected were the tanker owners and charterers. Faced with an exorbitant price rise, oil importers immediately reduced the volume they would buy. That meant fewer carriers were needed. But the nature of the carriers also changed. With fears of another Suez Canal blockade preference of hire went to the very large tankers which did not use the canal and which were much more economical in the handling costs of the volume carried. Thus, many small to medium-sized tankers became redundant.

But there was a further crushing liability for the owner running a steam-powered tanker. Steam turbines burn fuel oil to make the steam. Diesel-powered vessels are much cheaper to run. Indeed, according to my father, the probable reason why A.P. Moller sold the *Katia Maersk* five years before the oil crisis was that the running cost of steam was already too high. After the jump in fuel prices the vessel could not have been *given* away.

But by then the medium-sized, oil-burning, practically useless tanker had a new owner. And still the crude oil trade continued to drop and the fuel oil price continued to rise. 'I'll say this for them,' my father concluded, 'they didn't hold on to their liability for long.'

When I'd heard even this brief exposition of the background, it occurred to me that every crewman on the *Niome* had unknowingly signed on for a kamikaze run at the behest of the owner. 'Surely the board of inquiry must know it was sunk on purpose.'

My father nodded and got up to prod the large slab of coal in the fire to a more efficient angle of burning. 'Oh, yes. They certainly know that.'

'Then why are they looking for negligence?'

He laid down the poker and rubbed his fingers briskly together, 'Because – all things considered – negligence is better for morale.'

I gurgled, 'What?'

'Oh, yes. If it gets out that owners are casting away their tankers like old boots the people who spend their lives keeping ships afloat get depressed.'

'I see.'

My father spread his hands equably. 'So the inquiry's first choice is negligence, but they'll keep their eyes open for diligence, too.'

'Diligence? You mean competence.'

'No.' And he quoted another of the precise terms of which he was fond, '"Destructive diligence" is a recognised pattern of behaviour aboard vessels which are cast away. It means whoever sunk it had to work at sinking it.'

I shook my head in wonder. 'So I shouldn't bother trying to prove that I was not culpably negligent . . .'

My father interrupted to correct this sloppy statement. 'It's impossible to prove you were *not* something.'

But it had been a long day and I could not immediately follow that. I twisted in the soft leather folds of the armchair and reached out to finish off my drink. He immediately took my glass and poured another. It always pleased me to note that, for a portly man, my father moved with such lightness and ease.

'Okay,' I said, 'I cannot prove I was not negligent. But it seems scarcely worthwhile proving I was competent either. What I have to watch out for, apparently, is somebody else proving my destructive diligence.'

He gave me an expansive smile, 'That is the point, exactly.'

'Clifford wants me to get the blame for what he did.'

'If the inquiry cannot blink the facts, yes.'

'And the best defence is attack.' The whisky was getting to me and it was only with stern concentration that I was holding onto this arcane and detached line of argument. 'So . . .' I took a sip of my third drink.

'Yes?' He waited patiently for the point of my remark to surface.

'. . . what I have to do is forget about me and prove Clifford did it.'

'To do that you first have to know *how* he did it.'

'How would *you* do it?'

Settled again in his chair, my father let his head tilt back so that his chin pointed at the ceiling. I could tell he was enjoying the conversation. 'Well, it's practically impossible to scuttle a tanker. And of course if I were serving on the ship as an engineer I wouldn't want to flood the engine room, or blow the boiler. Very uncomfortable – and bound to arouse suspicion.'

'How about a straightforward fire?'

'Firefighting provision too good – except in the accommodation.' He brought his head forward to look directly at me and negotiate a concession. 'Am I allowed the collusion of the master?'

'Depends on what you want to do.'

'What they normally do – drive the vessel ashore or onto rocks.'

I denied him the collusion of the master. 'No. We could have frozen to death on Baltic rocks. We've got to be able to get away comfortably and be rescued quickly.'

'In that case,' my father had to agree, 'the vessel should be near several well-used shipping lanes and suffer an extremely damaging explosion well away from the accommodation.'

My voice took on a markedly querulous tone, 'I know that.

Clifford knows too. That's exactly what *happened*.' Sustained by
a deep breath I went on, 'The question is, how in God's name
was he *able* to do it exactly when and where and how he wanted
it – unless he planted a bloody time-bomb.'

The relaxed figure opposite me did not seem at all put out by
my vehemence. He was silent for a moment then decided,
'Undependable. Too many unforeseen delays – through the
Denmark strait, at the discharge ports, bad weather, mechanical
breakdown.' He sighed. 'No. If it was a bomb it wasn't a time
bomb.'

Many months later I had occasion to recall that observation
and note how pertinent it had been.

Next day in the Prince George ballroom I waited anxiously for
Jensen to make his appearance. He was punctual. As he threaded
his way through the ranks of chairs I tried to guess from his
expression whether or not his impulsive detour to Copenhagen
had been successful. His face was blank. Then I saw that Clifford
was just behind him and watching our meeting. For a moment I
thought of moving away to avoid any apparent complicity, then
remembered my new role as investigator rather than defendant.
It no longer mattered in the least that what Clifford knew for a
fact should also be obvious. Jensen told me he had managed to
buy the photographs. But that was all we had time for before
the chairman opened the session.

As requested, the owner's counsel produced and made available for inspection all the drawings, diagrams and documents
pertaining to the building and running of the ship. He also
circulated a complete list of these with reference numbers. But
there was no mention of the microfilm.

Over lunch I told Jensen about my visit home and complete
conversion to his own attitude. He seemed pleased that my
father had endorsed it. Then I asked if there had been any
mention of Clifford in bargaining with the salvors.

'No. Of course they would not say who else was bidding.'

'But Clifford was there yesterday.'

'What makes you think so?'

His girl told me she'd had a call from him. From Copenhagen.'

'And you believed her?'

The simple question, mildly expressed, quite floored me. 'Well . . . yes! Of course.'

Seeing my reaction he paused a moment as though wondering if he was wise to trust *me*. Keeping his eyes on his plate, he continued, 'It would be unlikely, or very foolish, for Sandys to involve himself directly in the matter at this stage. As to what the girl told you . . .' he cleared a fragment of food from the corner of his mouth with his thumbnail, '. . . it seems to me that *if* Sandys called, he could be anywhere and say he was in Copenhagen. Or – he did not call but she wanted you to know he would not be home last night.'

'Why would she tell me that?'

Jensen was blunt, not because my apparent obtuseness irritated him but only to express what seemed to him a fairly obvious deduction. 'Perhaps she wanted you to sleep with her.'

I seized upon it. 'That is possible, I suppose.'

'More than possible – if you have not slept with her before.' Jensen, thus informed that I had not, smiled. 'So – you do not mind so *very* much that you must stay at the flat.'

'Oh, yes. I mind sharing it . . . er, the flat . . .'

'Of course.'

'. . . with Clifford. But Barbara does make it easier.'

The sly Dane nodded with every appearance of gravity. 'I'm sure that is true,' he said, managing to disguise a smile in swallowing his food. 'Sex has few scruples.'

SIX

While the inquiry went grinding on, considering matters which were not my concern – loading, ullage, tank division, permeability, pumping patterns and even several hundred photostats of welding certificates – life outside of the Prince George ballroom continued. I became familiar with the area around the flat in Lower Sloane Street, went shopping, tried cooking, visited galleries with Barbara and slept alone, cursing the traffic which roared well into the early hours of the morning. Clifford maintained his amused and contemptuous manner towards me, no doubt biding his time until he got his cut of the insurance. I wondered if he intended to share it with Barbara. And if he did, would she be willing to share it? Despite our many pleasant excursions I knew very little about her. And whereas I was perfectly content gradually to find out about her, the process was strikingly condensed one Saturday afternoon in a wine bar. That morning at breakfast I'd been complaining of how boring London is at weekends. Indeed, how self-centred and tiresome it always is unless you have a job to keep your mind off it.

'Well, if you're doing nothing this afternoon, you can give me some moral support,' Barbara said. 'Cliff refuses to have anything to do with theatre people.'

Clifford, without raising his head from the newspaper spread on the table before him, said, 'Theatre people are not real people.'

'What about me?' his lady demanded.

'You're an imposter,' he said.

I asked, 'What theatre people do you want me to meet?'

'One person is all. A playwright. My agent's talked him into writing a play for me. Or we think he has.'

'Wonderful,' I said.

Barbara took a long drag of her cigarette and forced the smoke out through gritted teeth. 'Perhaps. If it happens. Unfortunately *this* playwright is everybody's idea of a cantankerous bastard. We must have a personal meeting and it's your job to make sure he doesn't go as far as a biopsy.' She stretched her rather large mouth in a grin. 'You can also hold my hand if you like,' and offered me some practice, 'under the table.'

Clifford gave a growl of mock jealousy and ground his teeth. And that was indicative of his attitude to the friendly relationship between Barbara and me. It seemed that whenever he bothered to think about it at all, he had to remember to show concern or even curiosity.

The meeting with the playwright had been arranged for that period of limbo in an actor's week – the free time between matinée and evening performance. I waited for Barbara at the stage door and, when she eventually emerged, I was again struck by how *un*theatrical she looked off stage. As Clifford had remarked, she was something of an imposter. She wore a headscarf, a long, loose-woven coat and flat shoes. A keen observer of all expressions, she noted mine and laughed. 'This is my peasant-who-got-lucky look. Got to make the right impression. Do you like the coat?'

'It looks very . . . comfortable,' I said, but thought it looked as though essential padding and stiffening had been very roughly torn out of it. The brown lining showed at the cuffs and, here and there, below the hem too. As we walked the short distance from the theatre to the chosen wine bar she kept pulling the collar up around her neck as though affected by a chill wind on the still, fairly mild September day. Later I would be able to identify those gestures as nervousness.

Knowing that I would not be able to hold the information at the introduction I asked, 'What's his name?'

'Howard Murray.'

'And why do you think he'd like you to look . . . dowdy?'

'Because he's very shy. Vicious, but shy.' She squeezed my arm reassuringly, 'Believe me, I know just how to play it.'

And quickly her manner did take on an air of calculation and studied pretence, so that by the time we went into the wine bar, which mistook gloom for subtle lighting, she was markedly different from the person I'd started to know. The short, grey-haired man was sitting alone at a corner table, leaning back in his chair and facing a wall. With me following very much in her wake Barbara swept up to the table. 'Good afternoon. Mr Murray?'

'Yes.' The man gave both of us a careful look before he stood up. 'Miss Cree?'

'Can you possibly forgive me. For being so late.'

'It's fortunate you were. I've only just got here myself.'

Barbara pointedly took her eyes off his face and looked at the well-filled ashtray and the uncleared empty glass. 'Oh?' she smiled. 'Oh, that is fortunate.' She brought his attention to me. 'I'd like you to meet Bill Thompson. Bill – Howard Murray.' We shook hands and as I cast around for another chair Barbara, settling herself and her sling-bag in the corner so that she directly faced the playwright, continued to explain why she was late – imperturbably brushing over Murray's interruptions. 'There were so many . . .'

'Is Mr Thompson an agent?'

'. . . visitors. No.'

'I'm just a friend,' I told him.

'I see. Well, what would you like?'

'After the matinée,' Barbara continued.

'Not that there's much choice.'

'I really couldn't eat much but . . .'

Murray tapped the table to secure her attention. 'What would you like to eat and drink?' he enunciated intensely.

Barbara came immediately to the point. 'Roast beef, a light salad and whatever wine they are trying to get rid of today.'

'Mr Thompson?'

'I'll just have some wine, thank you.'

'That they're getting rid of, or that you prefer?' To my startled amusement he made absolutely no effort to disguise the hostility in his voice.

'I prefer what they're getting rid of. It's bound to be cheaper,'

I said and felt Barbara give my knee a congratulatory nudge under the table.

'Bound to be,' he murmured drily and called the waiter over. While he was giving our order I looked at him more carefully. He had a pale, washed-out face on which the rigid straight lines of his dark eyebrows contrasted with his carefully brushed grey hair and his grey eyes. His moustache was neatly clipped. He came nowhere near my idea of what a playwright should look like. But he did have in abundance the theatrical attribute of 'presence'. And he was not striving for it.

Barbara asked, 'Did you say you'd seen this thing I'm in at the moment?'

'I haven't, no. I don't go to the theatre.'

'That's odd, isn't it? For a playwright.'

'You only go to your own plays,' I suggested.

'Not to them, either.'

'Hell!' Barbara exclaimed. 'Why ever not?'

'I try to avoid disappointment in circumstances where it can, very easily, be avoided.'

'Then you haven't seen me in anything?'

'Does that matter? I know the Barrie play you are in and I know the part you are playing.'

'Yes, but . . . you won't know what I can do.'

'I don't know what you have *done*. At least, I haven't seen what you've done; though I've heard very good reports of it.' Barbara gripped my hand as she fought her mounting annoyance, and Murray went on, 'What you can *do* is what I hope to find out. Today.'

Feeling Barbara's tension I tried to introduce a more relaxed note. 'Well, as a person who doesn't know very much about the theatre . . .'

'You shouldn't say much about it, Mr Thompson.' He looked straight at me as he delivered this snub and again I was both startled and amused that he made absolutely no effort to observe social graces or even to acknowledge that they existed.

Barbara came to my rescue, demonstrating that she was able to separate what her voice and face did from the way she was feeling. All gracious charm she said, 'I'll tell you anything you want to know, and hope it will be enough.'

The playwright gave her a sceptical look and then we paused while the food and wine were delivered. The actress extended her effusive manner to her reception of the meal. 'Just how I like it, quite rare.' But only one plate had been laid on the table. 'What are you having?'

'I don't like eating in public,' he said.

'How strange. Then I wonder if you can bear to watch *me* eating in public?'

'Depends on how well you do it.'

We both stared at him, incredulous. Barbara, very deliberately, picked up her knife and fork and started to eat. It occurred to me that it was Murray's intention to make her lose her temper. No doubt that would give him readier access to the sort of information he needed for the very complex job he had contracted to do. Piercing the pretence was probably essential but, in my view, dangerous.

'The beef does look very tempting,' I murmured inanely.

Murray ignored me. 'Miss Cree, you would like me to write a play for you. Since I have not seen any of your performances, it would help me to decide if you could tell me what you're good at.'

'Eating,' she declared flatly.

'Before you answer that, however, I should tell you I already have a play in mind which . . .'

'Have you really!'

'That's not unusual. I always have – at some point of growth. They grow like geraniums; flowering at decent intervals. And there is one budding at the moment. If you'll forgive the metaphor.'

Barbara paused in slicing to shrug off the metaphor.

Undaunted and helpfully, I mentioned, 'Eliot had something in a poem about geraniums.'

'Yes. He spoke of a madman shaking a dead one,' said the playwright bleakly.

'Why? I mean, why a geranium particularly?'

'I imagine, because he wanted the name of a common plant

which had four syllables, rhythmically stressed – ending in "um".'

I nodded, for that did seem likely.

Barbara, who'd been chewing with great relish, swallowed and asked, 'What sort of play is it?'

'That would depend on you,' Murray told her. 'So – to start with, perhaps you'll tell me what you're good at.'

'I don't know. I really don't. Sometimes I'm not very good at all.'

'You get good parts.'

'Just luck. I've been very lucky. There hasn't been a time since College when I've been out of work for more than a couple of months.' She took two quick sips of wine. 'God knows what they see in me.'

'But whatever it is, they want it.'

'They seem to.'

'Maybe they think they're just lucky as well – getting you.'

Barbara laid her glass down very carefully and watched it all the way. For a moment she seemed to be listening to the subdued murmur of other voices in the bar, or to the piped music which filled the background. At last she suggested, 'I expect they try plenty of others before they get to me.'

'Do you really think so?'

'Well, yes. It must happen sometimes.'

'But not as often as you'd lead me to suppose,' Murray completed lighting a cigarette and tucked the slim lighter into the breast pocket of his jacket. 'Unless your agent doesn't try very hard.'

'Of course he does! I was lucky there, too. My agent, bless him, works wonders for me.'

'On the off-chance *he* might just get lucky?'

'Oh, no! He believes in me,' Barbara protested.

'That is refreshing,' Murray sighed. 'You were beginning to stretch luck beyond the point of credibility.'

'What?' She glanced between the slight smile on Murray's face to the undisguised dismay on mine. It seemed to me she had walked right into a trap. But now she made some effort to extricate herself. 'You ask me what I do well. I don't know. Everything I get I try to do as well as possible. And I *have* been lucky; taking what comes and trying to fit in. No big star ambitions. In fact I often think I'd be better doing something else.'

'So, there is something else! Something you're actually good at – apart from being lucky in?'

'Plenty of people could do what I'm playing at the moment.'

'If only they'd been offered the job.'

'What are you getting at?'

Murray raised his straight black eyebrows, 'This attitude of yours . . . is very endearing.'

'"Endearing"! You think I...?' Barbara scraped her chair back from the table a few inches.

'Yes, I do.' He tapped his cigarette on the edge of the ashtray. 'And it might work if you were talking to an actor. At least he'd let you go on believing that he believed you.'

I chuckled and Barbara glared at me.

The playwright continued, 'Particularly, it would go down a treat with any of the actresses who auditioned for the part you got.'

'Just a minute, Mr Murray!'

'However, it fills *me* with disquiet. The only reassuring thing you've mentioned is that your agent knows a good actress when he gets one on his books. That makes your agent credible.'

Barbara's face flushed with anger. 'And I am incredible, you mean!'

'No, no. You are merely lying.'

'And why do you imagine . . .' the gritty raucous quality was back in her voice, '. . . I'd want to lie to you?'

'Perhaps because you think I'm a fool.'

Barbara shook her head with vigour. 'Not a fool, no! I think you are an ill-mannered, arrogant bastard, Mr Murray, but no fool.'

Murray laughed. And his laugh was quite out of keeping with everything else about him. It was a loud, hearty, genuine laugh which bubbled up from his stomach and belted into the air. When he got his breath back there was a delighted smile still on his face. 'Ha! That's much better.'

Barbara was not so easily mollified. 'It could have got better

sooner if you'd asked the right questions.' And now it was her
own voice and manner at last. Murray had known what he was
doing, and he'd been right. She went full-bloodedly on with no
pretence whatsoever. 'What the hell's the use asking me what
kind of actress I am? I don't see it. I'm inside, working blind.
With me. But if it's *me* you want to know about, forget all that
shit. Window dressing. I'll give you the raw material. Can you
make use of that?'

'I'd rather use raw material than shit,' Murray primly allowed.

'Right!' She pushed her empty plate away and laid her arms
squarely on the table; her fingers coiled into fists. 'Story of my
life, short version. Predictable as hell, but still hurting – okay?'

Murray nodded and refilled her glass. 'It's what hurts I can
use,' he said with surprising gentleness.

What had astonished me about the meeting up to that point,
and more in what followed, was the tacit acceptance by these
theatre people that their only importance lay in their talent.
Murray, apparently, had given up any wish to be seen as an
acceptable person. He knew that he was no more than what he
could do. And although Barbara had tried to sell him short by
pretence, when she was caught out, she quickly made amends,
'Orphan. Uh huh!' She mimed playing. 'Violins? Orphan at the
age of nine – which is leaving it a bit late, if you plan to become
an orphan. The adoption market runs on infants. Infants aren't
anything definite, or anybody's – yet! Which made it easy for
my young brother to be snatched up. He was ten months old.
Practically that year's model. Great condition. Low mileage.'

I couldn't take my eyes off her – now awkward, somewhat
red in the face and vulnerable. And her compelling voice went
on with such honesty that it seemed bent on leading her to
defeat. She must have been aware of such a danger because
she kept making defensive asides which would have been humor-
ous in other circumstances. She leaned forward to pull a tissue
out of the bag at her feet and in doing so looked up into Murray's
face. 'Aren't you going to ask how my parents got killed?'

He shook his head.

'I do a great description of the car crash.' She blew her nose.
'People usually ask me that. But nobody came near adopting

me. Well . . . a fat nine-year-old who was, frankly, messy; given to tantrums and, on the face of it . . . God, yes! On the *face* of it . . . hadn't much hope of even turning out pretty? Tough trading situation. Buyer resistance. No takers.'

'Where is he? Your young brother?' I asked.

'In the States. They emigrated with him. Suddenly he was not my brother. He was an "only child" and emigrating with his "parents". To the States.' She made a wide but fragile gesture which disintegrated in midair. 'Years ago.'

Murray prompted, 'While you went on living at the orphanage.'

'And loving it. Plenty of authority to fight and absolutely no danger of hurting the bastards.' She tried a grin. 'No matter how hard you tried.' Having lifted her wine glass for a couple of sips she kept it in her hand and ran a finger around the rim. 'Mr Murray, while barely in my teens, I was making escapes that would have earned a standing ovation at Colditz. Unsuccessful escapes, naturally. All I wanted to be was a whore. But when they finally put me out to work it was . . .' she laughed and finished the wine, '. . . it was in a nursery. A nursery! For kids that had twice as many parents as I had. Parents who couldn't be bothered – except in the evening. Every one of those kids had a *mother* who was spending the day fulfilling herself.'

'You resented them?'

'No. But that's why I gave up my ambition to be a whore. Too much of a public service. Instead, I won a scholarship to train as an actress. The hours are better.'

'Do you remember your father?'

'Certainly. And my mother. And my brother. I was *nine*.'

'But your father . . .' Murray persisted.

'That I'm "looking for", you mean?'

'No. That you almost closely *are* – was what I meant. If you're looking for anyone, I imagine it would be your brother.'

And that provided me with a valuable clue to the puzzling relationship between Barbara and Clifford. Before he became her lover he might have seemed a likely younger brother.

'And I hope to find him, Mr Murray,' Barbara replied. 'He'll be twenty-seven years old now.'

'Twenty-seven!' I exclaimed.

'Well, I'm the same age as you,' she asserted defiantly.

'Yes, I know that. You told me. I was thinking of another connection with the age of twenty-seven.'

Murray turned with the first sign of interest he'd shown in me. 'What connection?' he asked.

'It's a theory of a friend of mine.'

'Oh, I see.' The playwright lost interest in something as tenuous as that. To Barbara he explained, 'I hope you understand, it's important that I should be able to put myself in your place.'

'To create the character?'

'Yes, of course.'

Barbara expressed surprise. 'Are you always one of the characters in your plays?'

'I am always *all* of the characters. There's no other way it can be done.'

'That is ridiculous,' Barbara said.

'Very often.'

'So – what do you need me for?' There was no mistaking the angry note surging back into her voice but the playwright, unwisely, did not heed it.

'I don't need you in particular,' he said.

Barbara gasped. 'Then I'll go!' She signalled impatiently for me to clear her escape route. 'Bill!' I moved my chair clear of the table and stood up as she dived to pick up her bag in preparation for a stormy exit.

Murray was taken by surprise, 'No, Miss Cree, I..'

'Thanks for the *beef*,' Barbara declaimed, jolting to her feet and making the wine glasses and the bottle teeter and clink. Then Murray also got to his feet and their voices, loud and overlapping, drew the attention of the entire clientèle – much to my embarrassment.

'No. Please don't go yet.'

'If you don't want me in particular you could have a chat with my . . .'

'The point is . . .'

'. . . understudy. Or anybody else who can spare the time. If any passing . . .'

'Miss Cree, you are . . .'

'. . . actress would do, why not stand out there and *whistle*!'

'. . . jumping to conclusions!'

'And out again,' Barbara insisted, drawing her tatty old coat around her as though it might confer invulnerability. In doing so she swiped her own glass over.

'You asked if I need you,' Murray reminded her. Having got over his surprise he now regained his composure in the noisy squabble. Possibly he'd had experience in provoking such scenes. 'You did ask me that,' he insisted.

'Yes! I did.'

'And I don't need you . . .'

'Right!' She slung the strap of her bag over her shoulder and barged out of the corner.

'. . . as a character. But . . .'

'That's okay – I'll go!'

'But I want you . . .'

She was halted several paces away from him, facing the door. She turned and I stepped aside so that she could see him. 'What?'

'As a person. To write it *for*,' he said.

'How the hell can anybody make sense of that?'

'Stop! . . .' his voice dropped effectively after that word, '. . . this ridiculous *act* and I will try.'

She came back a pace or two and cut the volume of her voice to match his. 'I'm a fool to sit here spilling my guts to you.'

'It was your choice.'

'Choice!'

'To have raw material instead of talent. Or *luck*! It was all through luck, you said. You denied any talent whatsoever.'

They glared at each other for a moment in silence then Murray resumed his seat saying quietly, 'Why should I believe such a liar? Talent is something *nobody* should deny – and especially the person who has it.'

With one hand Barbara ground back the hair from her brow and with the other grabbed the back of my chair and banged it into a square position of defiance. 'All change then, Mr Murray.'

The playwright made an elegant gesture inviting her to sit,

and she did so while I squeezed round to take the chair in the corner.

Barbara asked, 'How hard do you think I've had to work so that I could afford to *say* I've been lucky?'

'Don't tell me about the efforts; just give me the results.'

She unslung her bag again and dropped it on the floor with a decisive thump. 'Results. Fine. Great results. Though if you gave a damn about my results you'd have been to *see* some of them!'

'As I said . . .'

'However – first result: sympathy. Onstage this is. I am very sympathetic. Combination of warmth, cultivated clumsiness and wide-open approach. Which leads to – vulnerable. Make a lot of that as well. Very low threshold of hurt. Hardly a doorstep, really. Great for second leads in Town, or taking over on tour. But that also needs something positive. Brashness is my answer – and no great threat to anybody. Just barge through it and carry the day. Damnable thing is . . . people take it for real.'

Again the painful honesty was showing through and I felt a little guilty to be observing it. For the qualities she described as merely her technique on the stage were – all too plainly – not technique at all. They were her own real qualities. And Murray, even at this short acquaintance with her, must have seen that too. Such a display of baffled hurt might be acceptable in private at night between two people but not in daylight, in public, in the middle of the afternoon.

And still she went on, 'Yes! Natural! Great compliment. They think I just naturally come on loud and strong. Naturally! Get no credit for it. Get no credit for the . . .' her voice and defiant expression crumpled but she managed to grind out the rest of the sentence. '. . . for the constant effort of keeping up the . . .' She lowered her head and made an abstracted holding gesture for our continued attention as the words became muffled. 'But . . . you don't want to *know* about the effort. Either.' She collected herself and raised her head with a grin already in place. 'And you're not even paying to see it – or not to see it, as the case may be.'

'Thank you, Miss Cree,' said Murray softly.

'Will you let me know?' she challenged him, straining to recapture briskness. 'What else? What other results can I offer? Taking all these things together – Comedy. If you were thinking of writing one. They value my sense of comedy. Why shouldn't you!'

'Thank you,' the playwright repeated.

'Is that all?'

He was puzzled. 'Mmm?'

'I mean, couldn't you squeeze out just a little more than, "thank you"? Fair do-es, Mr Murray. I'm all for writers being reticent, but how do I know you really have a geranium?'

I laughed, and this time she seemed to welcome my appreciation.

He retorted, 'I wouldn't have accepted the commission unless I had.'

'So now you know you're going to get paid anyway, what's your answer?'

'To what?'

'To *me*! Are you going to write this play for me?'

Murray smiled, 'Oh, yes! You seem to be exactly the person I want to write it for.'

As we walked back to the theatre, Barbara was in high spirits and that affected me almost by a direct link. I said, 'That was very stimulating.'

'I'm sorry you were embarrassed,' she said.

'It was worth it.'

'I hope so. I mean, I hope the play turns out to be worth it.'

'What if it isn't?'

She gave a deep and rather malicious chuckle. 'Then I won't do it. And the bastard will be stuck with it.'

At the stage door she persuaded me to go in and keep her company until the performance. And I was delighted to do so. Both of us felt, I think, that too much had been given away to lose any of the beneficial side-effects. It was a kind of 'high' which lasted while she changed and made up and put on her costume for the play. There was also a great deal of interest on my part about the backstage preparations and theatrical machinations in general. I could see that my questions pleased her. Clifford had no interest in such things. Aware of this difference between us I foolishly ventured a reference to the difference which Murray had put in my mind.

'I wonder if, in a way, you think of Clifford as a younger brother?'

With one hand holding the band on her brow she was pulling her wig back into position and did not answer until that was accomplished. 'If I do,' she said, 'then there's a strong possibility of incest. The fact is, Cliff is a marvellous lover.' She glanced at my face in the mirror and added in the arch accent of the character she was to play, 'Dear heart! Why do you think I'd go cruising around on freighters?'

Once or twice after the meeting with Murray the subject of the lost brother surfaced again. Apparently, Barbara had made many attempts to find him but had been frustrated by regulations and omniscient bureaucrats. 'I got the impression,' she told me, 'that it was my own stupid fault I didn't die in the car crash. All they wanted from the wreckage was the negotiable infant.' She hated bureaucrats. Indeed, she detested most agents of authority because they derived their power from a source which excluded her. 'The whole bloody State is geared to the family unit,' she protested. 'All the laws and benefits exist only for the married couple with two point whatever-it-is children. Honest to God, Bill, you don't know how lucky you are that you *fit*.'

'I don't, really. My parents only had one point zero children.'

She brushed that aside. 'Lucky there, too! You've got nothing to lose.'

'Not much to gain, either,' I said. And it occurred to me that though I might have started off as acceptable to the authorities I'd severely compromised my credentials by surviving shipwreck. And, now that I thought of it, I was no longer much of an asset to my parents either. My rejection of the plans my father had made for me, probably at my birth, had widened the cool gap between us. My mother, with so little practice of having a son at home, tended to treat me as an amiable younger cousin who happened to find himself at a loose end in Sussex.

Thus, I was very glad to spend all the time I could in London with Barbara. It proved fortunate that I'd overestimated my importance to the tribunal. Most days, all that was required was a brief attendance in the morning to check with my solicitor, then the rest of the day was free. After that I went back to the flat where Barbara was just thinking about getting up. Frequently, I had lunch and she had breakfast at the same sitting. Our afternoons were leisurely and quite often I spent the evening in her dressing room at the theatre. Gradually, I was accepted by her friends. They never enquired what my work was, where my home was or who my parents were. They took me as they found me and because they always found me with Barbara it was assumed that I must be vaguely connected 'with the arts.' That suited me fine, though I asked, 'Barbara, why do they never mention Clifford?'

She laughed, 'My dear, lover-turnover in the theatre is quite high. They have trouble enough keeping track of their *own* "ons" and "offs" without bothering about mine.'

This was encouraging. 'Am I an "on", then?'

'As far as they're concerned, yes.'

'And as far as you're concerned?'

She sighed. 'Bill, let *me* decide about what concerns *me*. And if you're looking for a declaration of rights, forget it.'

I quickly changed the subject. It worried me that I could so easily jeopardise a relationship which was becoming very important to me. The secret seemed to be not to plan ahead, not to anticipate and – above all – not to forget that, as a refugee from an institution, Barbara valued freedom at rather more than its fee.

SEVEN

About halfway through the inquiry – and shortly before we were due to testify again – Clifford announced to Barbara and me that he had accepted the offer of a job in west Africa. He held the news until a Sunday afternoon when the three of us would be at ease, working our way through an increasingly untidy pile of newspapers scattered on the floor between us. I waited for Barbara to make the first comment, since, clearly, the news had come as an unpleasant surprise to her. But she did not say anything right away. She was leaning forward and, after a moment's suspended animation, she gave great attention to shuffling the guts of the *Observer* back into place. No doubt he had chosen this way of telling her in order to avoid a more emotional reaction.

I asked him, 'When did this come up?'

'I've been discussing it off and on for a few weeks. They held interviews in Copenhagen.'

So that was the 'business' which he'd been engaged upon while Jensen was bargaining for the photographs. However, I still wanted to know – 'What sort of job?'

'Engineer supervisor.' He grinned, 'Good money. Nice climate.'

'But why are you leaving the sea?'

'I've decided it's too dangerous.'

Barbara asked, 'When would you go?'

'As soon as the inquiry's over.'

'Suppose they decide to take away your ticket?' I conjectured.

Clifford shrugged. 'That wouldn't bother anybody in Monrovia, or the Liberian government.'

'I think I'll make some more coffee,' Barbara said and, with admirable control, crossed between us and into the kitchen.

'What about Barbara?'

'I think she understands,' he said. 'Things have changed – as you know.'

'Whether she understands or not, it's obviously come as a shock for her.'

He shook his head complacently. 'No. It doesn't work like that with us.' He suddenly smiled and added with a kind of weary affection, 'In fact she'll probably be glad to get rid of the responsibility.'

It was impossible for me to guess what that might mean or, indeed, to imagine what sort of relationship there could be between a person I was close to loving and one for whom I felt nothing but contempt. Even so – 'It must be difficult for her to understand why you want to walk out on her,' I said.

He shook his head, again with that air of resignation. 'No. Barbara and I are very much alike.'

Surprise, if not vivid disbelief, must have registered on my face for he looked straight at me and laughed. 'Yes! We are! Both of us are takers of what we can get. Not like you, Bill.'

'Really.'

'Oh, no. You're a picker and chooser.'

'And this job? Are you taking it because it's the only one you're likely to get?'

He stared, daring me to go further. 'I've told you,' he said, 'working at sea is far too dangerous.'

'Not when you know where the danger's likely to come from.'

He shrugged doubtfully, 'Even then, things can go wrong.'

'Yes,' I told him, 'even when you think you're home and dry.'

This sparked a glint of annoyance in his eyes. He got up, was about to move away, then decided he could now afford direct hostility. He looked calmly down at me to declare, 'Bill, I could outsmart you the best day you ever saw. And I can see much further as well. That's why you're *here*.' He stabbed a finger at the floor.

Barbara came back with a freshly made pot of coffee. I declined to have any more and told them I was going out by myself for a walk. The day was cooler than it had looked from the window and I had to move briskly to stimulate circulation. At the square I turned left down the King's Road which seemed to be given over almost entirely to male boutiques. All were displaying, in russet colours, impossibly tight jackets and widely flared trousers laid over bulbous-toed surgical boots. It puzzled me that men's clothes should be designed for Indonesian maidens with bad feet. Yet many of the male strollers I passed had squeezed themselves into just such outfits.

Since I could be reasonably sure that the last thing Clifford had said to me was the only true thing he'd ever said, I found myself going over and over the exact terms of the statement. That he could outsmart me the best day I ever saw, there was no doubt. 'And I can see much further than you as well. That's why you're here.' By which he meant not alive and ashore but there, in the flat. And that was true, of course. He had invited me: twice. But what had that to do with his ability to see much further than I? Trying to organise my mind to work like Jensen's I connected the statements. I was living in the flat because he could see further ahead than I, and was a lot smarter. Knowing what I now knew about him it was clear that he foresaw collecting a large bounty for sinking the *Niome*. And he couldn't afford to be so suddenly rich at home. He'd have to get away from the flat and London.

My attention now turned to Barbara's reaction when told he was leaving for Africa. She was shocked and therefore I was very ready to conclude that she had never been part of his plans for the future. Thinking of Barbara my mind gave up the Jensen method and led me to consider my own future. With Clifford gone to Africa, and there being very few theatres in Africa where Barbara could pursue her career even if she wanted to follow him there, I was hopeful that I could remain with her in London, at least until the inquiry had cleared me and I was able to go back to sea. Of course there was a strong possibility that the inquiry would not clear me – Clifford had seen to that. Could I then find a suitable job ashore? It was a depressing prospect, particularly in the King's Road on a Sunday afternoon. The litter-strewn thoroughfare stretched broadly before me, popu- lated exclusively by persons left over from the sixties, clinging to fashion as though it were a lifeline which would prevent their being swept overboard into middle age.

It was during that walk I decided I wanted to marry Barbara. Quite why I wanted to go as far as marriage was not immediately clear, though some relevant factors were obvious. Certainly, it was about time I married *some*body. At thirty-six my stake in the market must surely be declining. But I was well prepared for middle age. I'd started rehearsing it when I was twenty-seven. It was then Hugh Gillespie had pointed out that marriage comes into its own when nothing else seems worth pursuing. On that depressing Sunday, with even the second-best career I'd settled for in the balance, there was nothing I wanted to pursue.

At no time during my walk did it occur to me that Barbara might decide she didn't want to be my wife. That was because I knew how self-assured, talented and successful she was. Having me as a husband would pose absolutely no threat to her. What had to be overcome was my uneasiness that having such a wife would be too unsettling to my well-entrenched habits of thoughts and behaviour. But was that not exactly what I needed? Although we were the same age in fact, she was much younger in reality. And much, much livelier. She had spirit and vitality to spare.

Events in the Prince George ballroom were now reaching a stage crucial to the determination of the issue. The tribunal was still pursuing matters which might be relevant to establishing negligence. The idea that the ship had been sunk on purpose had not been even breathed by anyone. That's how Jensen wanted it. His plan was to intervene at the last moment with incontrovertible evidence. However, we were having difficulty making the evidence hold together. It seemed we had all the pieces except the locking piece. And that was the original diagram of the engine systems which were on the microfilm we'd just missed capturing at the Lindø shipyard. The owner had, as requested, provided the tribunal with a complete set of full-scale drawings but they were not the 'approved' copies we could rely on. They were not stamped. Normally when a ship is being built there are three copies of every drawing which has to be approved by the certification authority; which in the case of the *Katia Maersk* was Norske Veritas. One copy would be held by them, one copy would go to the owner and the third would be retained by the shipyard. But that had happened more than ten years before – and Norske Veritas could not keep bulky stacks of drawings that long. Since the shipbuilders and the original owners were the same company they had passed their approved drawings on to the new owner when the vessel was sold.

The board of inquiry took a week's break before they began hearing the individual representations and I took the chance to accept a long-standing invitation from Hugh Gillespie in Scotland. It was eight years since I'd seen him. At that time we'd shared a bleak upper room in Montreal while he'd pursued his trade as a freelance journalist. Now he was a sub-editor on a city newspaper. And that was one reason, really, why I suddenly decided it would be good to see him again. His job gave him access to a whole range of information which could prove useful. Long established in Glasgow, his paper would have comprehensive records on ships, wrecks and shipping companies.

Hugh and his wife Moira lived with their two young daughters in Helensburgh – one of the city's 'dormitory' towns on the Clyde estuary. But when I arrived on the overnight sleeper he met me at Glasgow Central and took me immediately to his office where his night's work had just ended. Though I had no difficulty recognising him at the ticket barrier, it was by his stance more than anything else. For he certainly had changed a lot. He was now completely bald on top, his face drooped and he'd grown quite fat – which made him seem much shorter than I remembered. Most unsettling of all, perhaps, was the fact that he was smoking a pipe. My image of him always included a stabbing hand with a squashed cigarette clamped between the knuckles. Throughout the initial pleasantries most of my attention was fixed on his completely new gestures with the alien pipe.

When we got to the massive Victorian building whose interior was a wasp's nest of prefabricated-looking offices he asked, 'Now, Bill! What d'ye want tae look at first?'

I had, of course, told him of my ulterior motive when I'd

phoned him and now I referred to my notes. 'A. P. Moller's *Katia Maersk*, change of owner, 1969. Or change of name.'

'What was the new name?' Hugh asked as he reached for an index. We were in the basement Records Department surrounded by shelves of heavy books in thick, uniform bindings.

'*Niome*,' I told him, and spelled it. 'Owner, North Cape Shipping or Cattenix.'

As he thumped a book onto a well-scarred table and started fanning through the pages Hugh explained, 'This'll no' tell us much more than ye know already but it will give the date and we can tie that in wi' the nearest Friday list in the paper.'

'And will that give more?'

'It might – if there was anythin' in it for us. The yards here, A mean.'

'Why should there be?'

'Christ, Bill, even a second-hand car has tae be tarted up a bit. There's bound tae be a lot mair work on a thirty bloody thousand ton tanker.'

Obviously his mind had been working efficiently on my behalf, and he knew exactly where newspaper interest might lie. 'True,' I smiled. 'But I don't think any of the berths on the Clyde which were big enough to take it would have been interested in ship repair.'

He grunted, 'Even in 1969 they'd take anythin' they could get.'

In the relevant back number of the paper we found that the shipping correspondent had indeed commented on the sale of the ship but mainly to regret that the refit and conversion would be done by a west African yard. I smiled. 'Of course.'

'Does that help?' Hugh asked.

'In a way.' I was thinking of Clifford's sudden decision to accept a job in the very port where the *Niome* had been refurbished. Obviously the trail of destructive diligence started much further back than I'd thought possible. But Aage Jensen had seen it was likely at the outset. I recalled that at our first meeting in my father's office when asked who he thought was to blame for the loss of the ship he'd replied that it depended on the stage you looked at it – 'five years ago, one year ago, one week ago or

SURVIVOR 109

yesterday.' It was becoming obvious that the outside limit he'd set was the correct one. To Hugh I said, 'Can I use the phone?'

'Sure.'

'I've got to tell a man who's never wrong that he seems to be right again.'

Hugh led the way to a telephone. 'Then I expect he'll know what ye're gonnae tell him. Who is he, anyway?'

'A Dane like a tall thin Buddha.'

Hugh chuckled as he got me an outside line. Jensen lifted the phone as soon as the hotel receptionist got through to him and I reported the sequence of events and the details now in my possession. The listener at the other end of the line made none of the encouraging, commenting sounds which most people make when they are being given information by telephone. He simply listened until I stopped talking then said, 'Thank you. I'll get in touch with our agent in Monrovia,' and hung up.

On the way downriver to Helensburgh I outlined the nature and some of the specifics of my situation. Hugh, naturally, fastened on the specifics. 'Then ye'll just have tae get this microfilm ye mentioned.'

'How? The owner has reclaimed it and his agent will be keeping it safe.'

'Sure. But *where* is he keepin' it?'

'In his office, I suppose.'

'So this tribunal can get a search warrant.'

'Oh, no. They've no powers like that. In fact they don't even know the microfilm exists.'

Hugh concentrated on driving for a few minutes as he gauged the gaps between the clay-pigeon cars skimming up the slip road from the Erskine bridge. When we reached the top of the rise I looked down on the whole Clyde estuary, spread out in the crisp morning sunshine. Even Greenock, three or four miles distant on the other side of the river, was remarkably free from rolling fog, rising damp or rain. The driver, aware of my shift in attention, commented, 'Back tae yer old haunts, eh?'

'Yes. At a distance.'

'A've still got yer notebooks, y 'know.'

I grunted with amusement. He meant the notebooks I'd filled

while serving my time in Greenock and which, much later and for various reasons, he'd taken into custody.

By the time we got to Helensburgh, Moira had already taken the girls to school. She had also prepared a very good breakfast for us. Whereas my first impression of Hugh was that time had dealt unkindly with him, the reverse was true of Moira. She was slimmer, a little older, but much more vivacious than at our last meeting – perhaps because she was much happier. After breakfast, when Hugh went off to get some sleep, she suggested that I go shopping with her. I agreed, though shopping was not an activity I much enjoyed. But I did enjoy it in bright and spacious Helensburgh which seemed to have been designed for shoppers and where, astonishingly enough, all the shop assistants had excellent manners. I commented on this to my guide.

She smiled, 'Yes, that's true. But of course they charge extra for it.'

'In London,' I said, 'they charge extra for casual sadism.'

Gradually, as the sun rose higher and the air grew warmer I could feel myself relax in this pleasant strolling about with a very agreeable companion. Indeed, it was not until that morning I realised how tense I must have been for so long. Of course, being in Scotland was always a relief to me but this time it brought a new kind of ease. My only regret was that Barbara was not there with me. That thought was how Barbara got into my desultory conversation with Moira – who immediately suggested that I should bring her up to see them. I said I certainly would.

'Is she responsible for the change in you?' she asked.

Shrugging, I conceded, 'Perhaps. What change?'

Moira turned away from the shop window she was inspecting to give me a direct, appraising look. 'You seem a lot more human.'

I laughed as we continued slowly along the broad, clean pavement. 'Wasn't I human in Montreal?'

'In Montreal,' Moira asserted, 'you were humane.' Then, anxious not to be too critical, she added, 'And very kind.'

When we got back to the house Hugh was still asleep and so

it was not until late in the afternoon that he and I got down to the very satisfying business of catching up with Time. Contrary to my fears I did not find it difficult to avoid mentioning the fact that Sam Hanson now worked for my father. Others of our mutual acquaintance were sufficient matter for the conversation. He told me that he'd kept in touch with Emile, the young Frenchman who had brought sparkle to our days when time stood still in the long delightful summer of 1967.

'He was full of life,' I remembered.

'Full o' magic, more like,' Hugh suggested, meaning by that a condition of hilarious imagination and wild, impractical dreams. Even so, it had been wholly acceptable in the young dock labourer we knew.

'What's he doing now?'

'He's in a monastery in France.'

'*What*!' I was shocked.

Hugh nodded soberly. 'Aye. Three or four years ago when his father died he went back tae France for the funeral. No' long efter that he started takin' instruction for his vows.'

We both sipped our drinks in silence for a while and I thought of a line in a play, 'Suddenly the world shrinks and is colder.' And darker, too, I told myself as the young, mischievous face of Emile receded into solitude. Hugh tried to cheer us both up by recalling the fourth member of our Montreal quartet. 'Paul's doin' well, though. Back in Genoa.'

'With a business of his own?'

'But, certainly! And thrivin'. Married, too, of course, and a family of three at the last count. Moira and I had a wee holiday with them out there a couple o' years ago.'

'Good,' I said heartily and smiled – but felt guilty. Why had I not kept in touch with Paul and Emile? Why was it that Hugh continued to have a much greater talent for friends than I? Recalling what Moira had said of me earlier in the day I could only hope that she was right and that my damnable sense of detachment was crumbling at last. Sitting there with Hugh, though, in a large, comfortable living room which bore undisguised evidence of children in the house, I could summon up just one person with whom I'd kept in touch. Hugh had met him only once and briefly but knew a lot *of* him. I offered, 'I often hear from Otto Maier.'

'Otto! How did he make out?'

'Not very well.'

'Oh?' The tone of Hugh's voice indicated that if it was going to be sad he'd just as soon not hear about it.

'He and his girl friend were in a demonstration in Chicago.'

'They were intae the "flower power" weren't they? Hippies.'

'It was at the Democratic convention in 1968.'

'Oh, God,' Hugh groaned. 'A wish '68 had never happened – for *any*body.'

'They were batoned and gassed – like a lot of other people.'

'Aye. Still, he'll be recovered by now.'

'No.' I said. And I could feel the protective detachment building up again. Hardening. 'Otto was thrown in front of a police car which drove over him. Forward. . . and then in reverse. Thoroughly, in fact. Now he's in San Francisco teaching modern languages from a wheel-chair.'

Hugh stared at the floor shaking his head gently but did not say anything. For him and for me and people we knew of, there had never been a worse year than 1968. For so many hopeful causes, hope died severally. It died in March with Martin Luther King. It died in June with Robert Kennedy. In August it was crushed to death by Russian tanks in Prague. And, at the end of the year, it died absolutely at the Democratic convention in Chicago. In the letters I'd received from Otto since then he chose to ignore the obvious and still professed hope – at least for his own recovery. But even in that there were signs of resignation. Aloud, I said, 'He's taken up archery. He hopes to develop that.'

'A don't see how they can stop him.'

'No,' I agreed. 'They allow archery.'

My companion sighed and stretched his legs under the low table between us. 'Thank God *we* quit while we were ahead.'

I nodded. 'If only we'd known how lucky we were.'

Feeling that Moira was being left out of things, I made a point of helping her in the kitchen as she prepared an early dinner. And she took the opportunity to find out more about Barbara.

'She's an actress,' I said.

'Oh, that's interesting. Will I have seen her on television?'

'Only in commercials. She's a stage actress.'

'Where is she from?'

'Near Newcastle, originally.'

Moira busied herself for a few moments transferring contents between three pots. 'And do you plan to get married?'

'I do. But I don't know if she does.'

'Surely you've asked her!'

'There are complications.'

After a brief pause Moira suggested, 'Her career, I suppose.'

'No. Another man.'

As she bent to inspect the contents of the oven I could see disapproval competing with curiosity on her face. 'She's already married, then?'

'No. It's another sort of . . . attachment.' I couldn't bring myself to report that love might be involved.

But even if I had, it wouldn't have satisfied Moira. She was quite firm. 'Bill, if you're thinking of marriage there are plenty of girls who are not attached to anybody. Why make things awkward?'

'Well, to start with I'm too old or not rich enough for *girls* to be much interested. Barbara is the same age as me. But, more important, she's the first woman I've met who's both attractive and stimulating enough for me to spend the rest of my life with.'

'Ah, but that's her *job*, surely.'

'Oh, I like her job as well – and she's very good at it.'

'No, no . . .' Moira's attention was torn between the next stage of her meal and my evident need for enlightenment. 'I mean, actresses are *trained* to be attractive – and to stimulate. That's not *real*.'

Clifford had made much the same point. But he'd also said that, as an actress, Barbara was an imposter. Either way, it seemed unfair to actresses. While I indulged in this brief recollection Moira dived to rescue the dish at hazard and brought it safely to rest on the worktop. 'What is real,' I told her, 'is the independent spirit and vitality. You can't train people to have that.'

'But if there's another man, Bill . . .'

'Then I haven't a chance, eh?' I laughed. 'You must think I'm a born loser.'

'Not in the least!' She was mildly affronted that any levity should enter into the grim business of choosing a mate. 'But there's no use in making things . . .'

'Awkward?'

'Exactly. Marriage is not an easy business.' But she saw that I was not disposed to involve myself in a serious discussion. 'Hugh and I thought you'd marry a Scots girl.'

'I'm surprised Hugh thought I'd want to marry at all. But he seems to have settled down all right.'

'Not before time,' Moira said rather grimly.

'And I'm glad you're both happy now.'

'Oh, we still have our ups and down,' she insisted, 'but there's never any question of another woman.'

'I don't think there ever was any question of that.'

After an excellent dinner Hugh went off to work again but before he left he excavated my old notebooks from a cupboard in the hall. It was as a result of glancing through them again that I thought of a bold and probably idiotic plan. I decided to sleep on it, but in the morning it hadn't gone away, so I waited with growing impatience for my host to get back from Glasgow. Over breakfast I put it to him, just as a feasibility test; and also to obtain his help.

'Hugh!'

'Bill!' He parroted the exact inflection.

'I want to ask you about . . .'

'Can it wait till A finish ma food?' he interrupted sharply. For, of course, I'd forgotten that when he was eating he could think of nothing else – or strenuously preferred not to. He ate a maddeningly substantial breakfast before I came once more to the point.

'Are you off auto-pilot now?'

He smiled. 'Full manual control in gear.'

I leaned across the table. 'It's about the microfilm. The tribunal can't order a search warrant, but that doesn't stop somebody else having a search.'

'Breakin' in, ye mean? What dae you know about breakin' and enterin'?'

'Nothing. But I know someone who knows all there is to know. And he owes me a favour. What do you think?'

Hugh chuckled incredulously. 'It's the last thing A'd expect fae you.' But he could see that I was entirely serious and so pursued the idea. 'First, is it worth it? And A mean worth the chance o' gettin' caught.'

'Certainly. There's a lot at stake. Apart from fifteen million pounds of somebody else's money – my whole future could depend on it.'

'Okay. It's worth it.' Hugh slapped his open palm on the table. 'Second. Is what ye're lookin' for there – and can ye find it?'

'I've been in the office. I know the cabinet where the agent kept the *Niome* folder and it's likely he'd keep the microfilm in the same place. There, or with the full-scale drawings which are labelled.'

Hugh raised his hand from the table and indicated a touch-and-go situation. On balance, though, it was likely, so – 'Third. Who dae you know that can get ye in there. And can ye trust *him*?'

'Not if I tell him how much it's worth, no. But if I just tell him what he can get out of it, yes. His name's Tony Liddle.'

'I've heard the name. Is he in London?'

'You've read the name. No. He's here. That's where I hoped you would help. There was an item about him in the *Greenock Telegraph* at Christmas.'

'How do you know that?'

I cursed my lack of tact but had to press on with it. 'Well, I was over there at Christmas. I saw the item then.'

'Why did ye no' come to see us?'

'Oh, it was just a flying visit,' I lied, 'on business.'

'Uh-huh. So?'

'I thought if you called somebody at the *Telegraph* they would give you Tony's address or telephone number. You must have a contact down there.'

'Nae bother,' Hugh said with an assumed heartiness which, I knew, covered disappointment. 'At Christmas?'

'Yes. It was a story about a disco and/or gambling den.'

He got up and moved towards the telephone murmuring, 'Tony Liddle. I've definitely heard that name before.'

As Hugh got in touch with his friends in Greenock I reflected that he'd come across the name in exactly the same place which had reminded me of it – in one of my apprentice notebooks. Tony had long and well-documented experience in breaking and entering. As a youth he'd specialised in busting sub-Post Offices. Later he branched out into more profitable burglary. When he was twenty-one he got a fifteen-year prison sentence for killing his mother. I was sure that the lads in the *Telegraph* would have no difficulty at all in placing him. And I had little doubt that if I were able to meet him again he would agree to the job at the shipping agent's office in the Minories. What bothered me was that I'd no idea of the going rate for the job. And if it was more than I could afford . . . would Aage Jensen put up the money? Though he represented marine underwriters, the crimes they were used to paying for were much more respectable than this. In the event I did not have to tell Jensen beforehand, though I did have to enlist the cooperation of Sam Hanson.

EIGHT

For a street so near the Royal Mint the Minories was not particularly well lit nor well patrolled. Another advantage was that it was almost exclusively a business quarter. Very few people lived there and though it bustled all day it was deserted at night. The main disadvantage of the expedition was the fact that I had only the most superficial knowledge of the premises. I'd been quite unable to answer most of the pertinent questions Tony put to me. And there was no possibility of spending a day casing the place and observing the operation of the office block. Tony wanted to be back on a train for Glasgow before the cleaners arrived in the morning.

We got into the building an hour before it was likely to close for the night and at once put on overalls which he hoped would disguise us as maintenance men. Then I hid in the basement with the equipment while Tony, whose face was not known to anyone there, used the available time to move about quite freely inspecting various security devices. He even wandered into the agent's office on a spurious errand so that he could see what locks would have to be overcome and where their alarm was wired. Also, in full view of several people who passed him in the corridor, he removed and inspected the punch-card of the security rounds-man's clock on the floor where our interest lay. In fact, everything which nobody would believe a burglar might do, he did. When it came near knocking-off time he hid himself, quite separate from me. That, apart from avoiding discomfort, was to increase the chances of the other if one of us was caught before our mission was attempted. In that case, whoever remained free would go back to hiding until the offices were opened for the cleaners and then try just to snatch the goods and run.

The main plan, though, was that at 1.00 a.m. we'd meet
in the foyer – where there was no point in anyone patrolling –
and make our move together. That meant I had nine hours to
fill. I had suggested that until midnight would be long enough
but was assured that all workers split their time into two-hour
segments and the night-watchmen would come on duty at
six or eight o'clock. Therefore, one o'clock would fall in a lax
period.

So I had nine hours in which to reflect on the sheer stupidity
of what I was doing. Before long I regretted having spurned
Tony's suggestion that I bring a good book and a small torch.
Apparently that had been his practice in these situations.
He really was a quite remarkable man. Still very slight in
build and looking no more than twenty-five though already
in his mid-thirties, there was the impression of complete
fitness. He wore eye make-up but it was extremely subtle and
even so I was amazed that he had changed so little. The habitual
expression on his rather delicately featured face was still one of
polite interest and still behind that, in his pale eyes, there
glinted deep and effortless contempt. People did what Tony
wanted because he was dangerous. He was also efficient, and
quiet.

He had suggested that I look for a cupboard which housed
fire-fighting equipment. There, he felt, I was sure to be undis-
turbed unless there was a fire – in which case I'd *want* to be
disturbed. It also ensured that I had some comfort and was able
to doze on a pile of dry dousing-blankets for much of the long
wait. However, from about midnight on I sat ready to spring
and kept my watch under constant surveillance. At five to one
in the morning I pushed open the cupboard door and almost fell
out. My legs had stiffened alarmingly. It took several minutes
of frantic rubbing and knee-bending before I was able to climb
the stairs to the ground floor carrying the holdall which contained
Tony's tools and both our suit jackets.

He was already in the foyer, crouched behind the reception
desk. I laid the bag down beside him and he took out the
implements he needed. Then, having tucked the bag well under
the desk, we set off together up the service stairway. We

stopped at the floor where the office was and, outside the door, Tony indicated that I should lean against the wall and bend so that he could clamber onto my shoulders to cut the alarm cable which ran along the cornice of the ceiling. There was no visible sign of such a cable but there was no other place it could be. To cut it Tony bit deeply into the angle of the plasterwork with a fine arrow-head chisel then he dropped to the floor and quickly dusted up the fine sprinkle of powder which had fallen. When that was done he made no attempt to open the door but led me back to the stairway. We crept up to the top floor and to the end of the passage beyond and out of sight of the roundsman's punch-clock.

Again there was a long wait in the dark and I'd plenty of time to work out that the security man must start his round at the top of the building and work down. It hadn't occurred to me before but certainly it was sensible. If the watchman surprised intruders they, too, would try to escape downward and be caught by the man on duty at street level. Considering the amount I had already learned from Tony I was heartily glad that I had not attempted the break-in on my own.

Just after two o'clock we saw the indicator on the lift flicker and start to ascend. And sure enough the rather elderly guard came as far as his punch-clock and no further. He did not try any of the doors on his way to the clock at the other end of the corridor and, as soon as he'd registered there, went through to the stairway to reach the next floor down. We moved carefully onto our landing so that we could watch him emerge at successively lower stages until he was clear of the area where we wanted to go.

There was no difficulty in unlocking the office door. Tony gave his head a little shake of disgust that it yielded so quickly to his manipulation. Nor were there any problems in the office itself. The filing cabinets were even easier to open than the door and the sealed box containing the microfilm cassette was lodged neatly behind the retaining plate of the drawer devoted to the *Niome*. My impulse was just to pick up the box and leave but again my colleague insisted on a better procedure. The box was sealed around the sides with blue canvas tape. Tony carefully peeled it off for re-use and removed the cassette. He handed it to me then started looking around for an object of suitable size and equal weight to replace it in the box. He searched the waste-paper baskets at all the desks until he found a discarded typing ribbon cassette. It fitted and felt right so the lid was secured again with the sticky blue tape and replaced where I'd found it. But even then we didn't leave the office. We waited there until we were fairly sure the two o'clock round had been completed and both of the men on duty were back in their den by the back door.

Meanwhile, Tony told me that when he gave the word I was to go hell for leather down to the foyer, collect the bag then return to the basement and wait for him. But it was the audacity of his next move which I found most amazing about the whole operation. For, of course, I had not given any thought to how we would get *out* of the building. The heavy front doors were comprehensively locked and, like the back door and all the windows, wired with much more subtle alarms than Tony could deal with. So – right there in the agent's office – he phoned the police.

He waved me away before I had a chance to hear the conversation but later he told me that he'd posed as a public-minded citizen who'd noticed someone trying to break into the building. Probably before he'd hung up I'd reached the foyer where I scooped up the holdall then scurried down to my cupboard in the basement. Only a couple of minutes elapsed before Tony joined me. It was a bit of a crush and I was quickly aware of the sickly smell of whatever it was he put on his hair to hold it in the fashionable style. I reflected on the unjust circumstances which obliged Tony to be both effeminate and tough.

I gasped when I saw light suddenly appear under the door. Tony felt my jolt of fear and reassured me. Nobody had come into the basement. They'd just turned all available lights on. I asked him what was to be done and he told me we were waiting for the sound of the alarm. He was perfectly composed because he knew exactly the pattern of events he had set in train. The police that he had called would get in touch with their man on the beat. They would then alert the security guards in the building whose first reaction would be to turn on the lights. After that they would move everywhere together. When the policeman came to the door they would let him in. And when they opened the door to let him in, the alarm would sound. And that was exactly what happened, eventually. In retrospect it was quite amusing that, as we waited cramped and increasingly sweaty in the cupboard, we grew quite indignant that the police did not act more swiftly in protection of property.

When the signal finally came we headed up the single flight of stairs to discover the back door undefended. Tony opened it without trepidation because the alarm was already blaring away while the policeman and the watchmen started their search at the front. We walked quickly down the dark alleyway towards the Tower then circled back and away from the river. As we moved through the silent streets we were twice startled by what sounded like heavy machine-gun fire. The first time we broke into an involuntary dash but there was no sign of an ambush and rather shamefacedly I realised that the noise was no more than unmanned telex or teletype receivers clattering out messages from other time-zones. Before long, we emerged from behind Fenchurch Street station onto Leadenhall Street. Sam Hanson was waiting with the night-clerk at the entrance to my father's premises and had no hesitation in identifying us as engineers on a crucial repair contract.

Only when we were settled with stiff drinks in Hanson's office did I ask Tony what we would have done if the police had surrounded the building. He scoffed at the very idea. Nobody, he told me, was going to mobilise that kind of cover on the strength of a phone call from a busybody when there was no alert and no confirmation that anything was wrong. A leisurely 'look-see' was all the force would rise to – and that was what we got. Hanson was anxious to try the microfilm on the company's projection equipment and I gave it to him.

When he was gone I also handed over the two hundred pounds which was Tony Liddle's stipulated fee, including expenses. He accepted it with a smile and remarked that he had managed to get 'the rest o' the money' after all. I was puzzled and he

reminded me that many years before when he'd cheated me of
four hundred pounds I'd actually had six hundred pounds available. I nodded and recalled, too, that when I'd visited him in
Barlinnie prison he wanted to know how I'd wasted the remaining
two hundred he'd been generous enough to let me keep. Probably I was lucky he didn't claim interest on it. About an hour and
a half later when he had shaved and showered it was time for
Hanson to drive him to Euston for breakfast and the early train.
I watched him go with relief but also with admiration. Tony
Liddle was many things – many of them unpleasant and almost
all of them illegal – but he was not a hypocrite.

While I waited for Hanson to come back I too freshened up,
preparing for what was going to be a very tiring day in the
company boardroom where the projection equipment was set
up. Fortunately my father was out of the country and Hanson
had arranged things so that he and the resources of the company
were at the disposal of Jensen and myself. As soon as I decently
could I phoned Jensen, told him what I'd done and invited him
to spend the day at Colin Thompson Partners. If I'd thought
that, just once, I'd manage to startle him into an involuntary
exclamation I was disappointed. There was not a sound on the
line during the spiel and at the end of it he said with perfect
composure, 'Good. I'll be there at nine-thirty.'

Hanson and I had breakfast in an all-night restaurant which
catered to the needs of financial staff from various foreign
exchange dealers. It astonished me to learn that so many
people were night workers to the City and the World. Rather
light-headed from lack of sleep and intake of alcohol I suggested
Urbi et Orbi as an apt motto to place above the restaurant door.
Hanson just gave me a blank look so I did not mention that it
had been Hugh Gillespie's pleasant duty to stand at an open
window in Montreal and – with papal gestures – pronounce this
Easter blessing on the pedestrians of St Catherine East. Instead,
I asked, 'Did Tony Liddle tap you for any money before he left
you?'

'No. I thought you paid him.'

'Yes. Yes, I did. But that wouldn't stop him trying again.'

Hanson frowned at what he took as my ingratitude. 'I hope

you paid him enough. He's a guy that knows his job – and he delivers.'

'He certainly does, one way or another.'

Rasping his knife against the toast, my companion warned me, 'What he does in his own time is his own business' – which jumped several conversational hurdles at one leap. I'd overlooked two significant factors in seeming to criticise Tony. The first was that, despite Hanson's education and relaxed mid-Atlantic accent, he and Tony shared exactly the same background. The second arose because he'd misinterpreted my remark as a sneering reference to homosexual promiscuity. So – although I was effectively snubbed and the rest of our meal was completed in silence – I gained two more items of interest about the man who'd taken my job. He was a good judge of people like Tony but as bad a judge of me as he'd been of Jensen.

And Jensen arrived punctually at nine-thirty, concealing whatever exultation he might have felt that at last the mystery was going to be solved. The high and spacious boardroom had two windows which overlooked Leadenhall Street and was furnished in a style of old-fashioned luxury. But it was also equipped with all the modern devices of reference, information and communication that anyone could desire. Jensen walked into the room, looked all around and stopped at the head of the large oval table, rubbing his hands. Then, whether by devious tact or plain courtesy, he did exactly the right thing. Still smiling he turned to Hanson and said, 'I am very grateful for this opportunity. Where do you think we should begin?'

'I've wound the film to the engine systems diagrams,' Hanson said as he strode to the windows and drew the curtains. 'Before we go on to anything else we might as well clear up the trouble with the heating coils.'

'Fine,' the Dane nodded, 'for not only was there trouble on the voyage but Sandys took trouble to deny Bill's record of the events.'

I switched on the projector-light and a clear, line-representation of the auxiliary steam pipes was thrown on the large screen at the other end of the room. Included on it were all the control valves, the bulkhead junctions and a notation on each line which gave the diameter of the pipe. Hanson took up a pointer and positioned himself beside the screen. Jensen moved a chair from the table and set it outside the spill of light from the projector lamp. He sat and watched and listened while Hanson identified and traced with the pointer every line and connection on the diagram. Only once or twice did he interrupt his expert litany to have me clarify or confirm a dubious point. It was quite a performance from a man who had never seen that particular layout before. When he'd finished he turned to us and said, 'That's it. As far as I can see there's nothing wrong with it.'

'You are right,' Jensen murmured. 'There was nothing wrong with it – *then*.' He snapped open the catch of his briefcase and took out the diagrammatic sketches of the bulkhead connections I'd made following our inspection of the bow wreckage. Hanson and I spread these out on the table and painstakingly compared the pipes which actually led into the tank with those on the screen which had been designed to lead there. As we muttered to each other Jensen's intense stare shifted between us. He was entirely in our hands as far as this discussion went. For a long time there seemed to be no discrepancy whatever. Hanson lit a thin cigar to aid his concentration and the smoke drifted up through the unvarying beam of the projector in the shadowy boardroom. We examined a number of other diagrams before coming back to our first choice. I said, 'Surely there would be no need for two quite separate coil feeds; even in ice zones?'

'What?' grunted Hanson.

Jensen had been listening intently and at once reached for the bulky volume which set out Norske Veritas rules for all conceivable conditions.

While he searched the appropriate chapter I pointed out to Hanson an unmarked small-bore connection at some distance on the other side of the centre line from those we'd identified. 'That looks like a steam pipe.'

'Can't be. There's no return.'

'No,' Jensen announced. 'There is no requirement for another set of coils.'

'Let me think,' I said, and tried to bring into my mind a closely focussed image of what I'd been looking at when I drew the connection.

'There's no return,' Hanson repeated, alluding to the fact that the low pressure steam which is fed into the heating coils must also come back as hot water and normally the feed and return pipes are led close together.

'What did you think it was, Bill, when you saw it?' Jensen asked me.

'Well, if I'd seen it anywhere else I'd have said it was a high-pressure steam pipe.'

'Holy God!' exclaimed Hanson and ground out the stub of his cigar with triumphant verve. 'No wonder you all but blew the gauges.'

All three of us suddenly felt an urgent need to sit down and contemplate this incredible discovery. To a layman it would appear innocuous enough, but the difference in the heat produced by high pressure steam compared to the 'wet' steam for which standard coils are designed is dangerously wide. It was like pumping molten lead through a domestic water pipe. Also, the fact that there was no return indicated that there must have been some cross connecting inside the tank.

'But why didn't the overheating work?' Hanson asked himself aloud. 'That crude must have been giving off enough gas to get the ship airborne.'

And, curiously, it was Hanson's choice of that fanciful image which led directly to the answer. 'Air,' I said. 'There wasn't enough air in the mixture.' I stood up, certain of the fact. 'The oil was giving off so much gas there wasn't space for oxygen to fire or explode.'

'You're right, Bill,' Hanson said at once and glanced towards Jensen who was nodding careful agreement. 'The mix was too bloody *rich*!'

'Now,' I said, moving back to the projector, 'we have to find what else they built in – because whatever it was *it* worked.'

'Hold on. We'll have some coffee first.' He looked questioningly at Jensen. 'Okay?'

While we drank the coffee brought to us by Mrs Schuster, Jensen supplied an excellent reason why the first attempt should have been made while all the cargo was aboard. He explained, 'All of the cargo was insured. Not by my clients but by others. The plan was to collect on the ship *and* the cargo. In fact . . .' he gave a grim little shake of his head and sipped coffee far too weak for his taste, '. . . it will not surprise me to find that they also insured against accidental spillage and pollution.'

Hanson grunted, 'You've got to hand it to them.'

'So they hope,' the Dane replied grimly. 'But perhaps we can make it more difficult than they expect.' He went on, though, to report lack of success by his contact in the Liberian port where the illegal conversion had been carried out to Clifford's specifications. So far there was no evidence of who had done the work and it seemed unlikely that any would be found before the tribunal reconvened.

The brief period of relaxation did not refresh me. In fact when we resumed the search I found that my underlying exhaustion had seized the opportunity to assert itself. As we went frame by frame through the microfilm I became more and more drowsy. Finally Hanson suggested that I should go and lie down for a while on the couch in my father's office. I was glad to do so and fell asleep immediately. Then, it seemed, I was immediately wakened to go out and have lunch, but in fact two hours had elapsed.

During lunch we tried not to think of or talk about the task that faced us. I was glad to note, however, that Hanson's attitude to Jensen had certainly changed. Our morning's work together and their work in my absence had persuaded my father's partner that the tall, wary-eyed Dane was always worth listening to – very attentively indeed. And Jensen himself had gained confidence in the people he was dealing with. He talked about his father-in-law as a person and a close friend, quite separate from his role as master of the *Niome*. It surprised me to learn that the withdrawn, rather sullen Captain Meisling I'd known, though briefly, had a quite different personality within the family. By Jensen's account he'd been a fine athlete in his youth, volatile, adventurous and something of a hero to the not-much-younger man who'd married his daughter. Jensen smiled. 'That I should bring some stability into their family, you see.' But it was not long after that when Meisling's wife died and the Captain's ebullient nature changed. 'He lost his wife and I already had his daughter too soon. There was nothing to come back to ashore and only work at sea,' Jensen concluded. Neither Hanson nor I felt able to pursue the conversation but it did seem to me that we'd been told these things in a way to justify the efforts we were making. It was our fervent intention to prevent those whose greed had killed Meisling from profiting at his expense.

It was during that conversation at lunch that, for the first time, it occurred to me how real a person Jensen was. Before then I'd been too impressed by his intelligence to notice that he was a human being as well. Now it was possible for him to have other attributes, I could easily recall instances of his sly sense of humour. The picture of Irene Jensen driving the big Volvo also came into my mind and I connected that with how, in the flat, he'd looked at her and listened to her. Even when he'd been telling Hanson and me about Meisling there had been an odd tone in his voice when referring to the Captain's daughter. Somewhat to my surprise, I concluded what had been obvious: Jensen adored his young wife.

That afternoon in the boardroom – with sketches, photographs and notes all laid out on the long table – we completed the examination of the piping systems on the screen. And we grew increasingly depressed. As far as I could see, or remember, the remaining diagrams showed exactly the layout which had been in operation on the ship. Hanson switched off the projector and drew back the curtains. 'I think we've got to face the possibility,' he said, 'that the extra steam to the coils was it. There was no other method.'

I protested. 'But the explosions happened in exactly the area which was chosen for the first attempt.'

Hanson shrugged. 'Coincidence.'

We both started pacing up and down the room while Jensen remained motionless, standing at the table, leaning forward with his knuckles pressed lightly on the polished surface. I could not accept Hanson's defeatism. It would be altogether too unjust if a carefully prepared scheme to sink the ship had failed, yet a quite unplanned and accidental explosion had destroyed her. We continued pacing up and down the room and depression now was giving way to tension. When Mrs Schuster put her head around the door and quietly mentioned that she was going home, I was unreasonably annoyed at the interruption and Hanson very curt in acknowledging that certainly it was time to go home and there was nothing else we wanted her to do.

When she'd gone Hanson said to me, 'Well? It had to be an accident, huh?'

But before I was able to concede that point Jensen murmured, 'Sandys was dressed to go on deck when the explosion occurred.'

'That's right,' I said.

The Dane went on, 'Therefore Sandys knew it was going to happen. He caused it. There was no accident.'

Hanson sighed and moved to stand beside the Dane at the table. 'Okay! Now – what and *how*?'

There remained only the photographs of the wrecked bow which Jensen had bought from the salvors. We stared at them as though hypnotised while the Dane's lulling, slightly accented voice continued, 'It was the salvage of the bow, I think, which worried them most. They bought it back and paid to have it broken up as quickly as possible. So – whether it's possible to see it or not, the answer must be in these photographs. And it has nothing to do with the extra steam pipe or overheating the cargo.'

'Do you think they had prepared another way of doing it?' Hanson asked him.

'No. I think when the original plan didn't work, Sandys became desperate, and a little careless.'

'In what way?' I asked.

'Well,' Jensen returned to what struck him as a salient factor, 'he really should not have been dressed to go out on deck when the explosion happened. He must have known that. But of course, maybe he had to go out on deck to do what caused it; and had to be prepared for anything because he did not know what the result might be.'

'How does that help us?' Hanson wanted to know.

'It does not help us. At the moment,' Jensen replied. 'But it may *fit* if there is something else that we can see.'

The scene on the dockside came back to me and I pointed to one of the photographs. 'That's when we arrived. Remember, we had to wait until they pumped the water out of the shell.'

Jensen expelled his breath in a sudden gust. 'Why?'

'Well, we couldn't get down into the tank until they had pumped it out.'

'Yes,' the Dane slapped his open palms on the table. 'Yes! But why should there be water *in* the shell? When the water level fell in the dock why didn't the retained water in the tank run out?'

I was bewildered. 'Because all the valves and connections on the deck plate were closed or sealed.' I stared at him and was amazed at the sudden sparkle, almost like amusement, in his eyes.

'But *all* the valves should not have been closed.' He turned eagerly to Hanson. 'Don't you agree?' As the other engineer gave the question some concentrated thought Jensen moved away and slowly paced a complete circuit of the boardroom table. His lips were pressed together and he gave occasional sharp little nods. 'We did not need to go on the wreck at all. It was there while we watched it.' He came back to stand between us. 'What should have been open that was . . . ?'

I interrupted excitedly, 'The inert gas inlet and its vent! If they had been open – as they should have been – the water would have run out.'

Jensen gave several deep, pleased nods then backed slowly away from the table still nodding. 'Sandys prevented the inert gas reaching the tanks from which you had just discharged crude oil. The gas built up. Then, when he was ready, he went on deck to the remote controls of the valves and slammed the vent.'

I could see Hanson shared my immediate acceptance of these actions but he entered one small quibble. 'Why would he bother sealing off the vent?'

'No, no. He did not care about that – sealing the vent. He wanted the *spark* caused by slamming it.' Jensen spread his pale elegant hands, 'Maybe he had to try several times. Maybe he had to activate other remote control gear which connected through the deck. But finally he got the spark. That set off one tank which set off the others.'

The pattern suddenly fitted together. We knew the motive and the means and the operator of the whole intricate plot. We knew why and where. Above all, we knew *how*. There was no doubt in our minds. When Jensen went before the tribunal he would have not just a feasible theory but strong circumstantial evidence. Clifford was *not* going to get away with it after all.

NINE

When I got back to the flat on Lower Sloane Street after four days' absence I found it empty. Barbara was at the theatre, of course, but Clifford was gone completely. The porter told me he'd packed up and left early the previous day. The afflatus generated by our solving the problem evaporated. I had the feeling that, again, we were just too late. All along we'd been just one step behind Clifford and his employers. Stealing the microfilm had been a fairly drastic way of catching up, if not getting ahead. Yet, somehow he'd managed to top that as well. If, as I suspected, he'd flown out to Liberia, then by the time the inquiry acted upon Jensen's representation there would be nothing to find at the repair yard where the *Niome* conversion had been rigged. I called the Prince George to tell Jensen but there was no reply from his room.

Of course, the mere fact that Clifford had skipped the country might go a long way to casting doubt on his testimony. When the tribunal reconvened in four days' time, the chairman and assessors would surely take it amiss that one of the witnesses was not there to answer whatever supplementary questions they might wish to put to him. Cheered by the thought that Clifford had overreached himself for once, I prepared supper for Barbara and myself. I also gave some cheerful thought to the sleeping arrangements which might seem reasonable now that Clifford was out of the way. When the food was ready to be served it occurred to me that I should just move my gear into the bedroom they had shared as a sort of statement of intent. After some consideration, though, I rejected the idea as too presumptuous and put the stuff back in the drawers of the spare room. Barbara was not the sort of woman who'd welcome a fait accompli. It was now almost midnight and I called the Prince George again.

This time I got through to Jensen and told him the news. He did not take it well and suggested that he should come round to talk to me right away. I agreed without much enthusiasm. In the morning, I thought, would have been soon enough since I had plans for that night which ought to be put into operation without delay.

When Barbara got back she was very pleased to find me there and as we ate she told me that Clifford's decision had been very sudden. 'He told me he was needed urgently for this new job.'

'Did they contact him? Send a telegram – anything like that?' She shrugged wearily. 'I suppose they must have.'

'But you don't know that they did?'

She gave me a puzzled look. 'Well they must have told him or *he* wouldn't know, would he?'

Her perfectly reasonable response provided more difficulties for me. Soon I was going to have to tell Barbara what Clifford had done. Since the time she'd let me know what a great lover he was I'd avoided discussing him with her in case my jealousy should show. Much later she told me that a little show of jealousy would have suited her fine. At that moment, however, I was anxious to keep whatever I had against him on a professional level. Perhaps it would be better if somebody else told her. I mentioned that I was expecting Jensen. 'Then I'm for bed,' she declared and left me to play host. As I watched the bedroom door close I was aware of a comic conflict of interests. I wanted Jensen there so that he could tell her the truth and I did not want him there at all because he was fouling up my chance to get the new relationship established from the outset.

When he arrived, though, Jensen fouled up a lot more than that. First he punctured whatever hopes I'd had that Clifford's defection would count against him at the inquiry. 'No, no. They will think that an employer is so sure of his competence that they hire him before the inquiry is over. That will be in his favour. And that is what I want to talk to you about.'

'But what about your evidence? They must want to question him on that.'

'Of course, they may want to. But if he is not there they cannot. Which means that some of my evidence cannot be given.'

I was amazed. 'What?'

'On matters of fact, with proof, they would call him and he must appear. But what I can offer is merely a representation of possible events.'

'It's perfectly obvious.'

'Nevertheless. These boards of inquiry are very careful of their purpose. Even if I had cast-iron proof of what Sandys has done all *they* could do is deprive him of his sea-going certificate. Which now he does not need.'

'Then what the hell have we been struggling for?'

Jensen laced his pale fingers together. 'It is my intention that nobody should get a reward for what happened to Nils Meisling and the others; and the *Niome*.'

'Yes, of course.'

As I poured him a drink he went on to explain that whereas all the tribunal could do to an individual was deprive him of his ticket it also had the negotiable sanction of granting 'credence and weight' to the representations of other interested parties. And if it did so and the underwriters then took the insurance claimants to a civil court it was almost certain they'd win the judgment and the costs. Only foolhardy claimants, I gathered, would contest in such a situation. Jensen concluded, 'So you see the only danger of this new development is to you.'

I shook my head. 'I'm sorry. I don't see that at all.'

Jensen sipped the straight whisky and I could detect from the droop of his eyelids that he thought me unnecessarily obtuse. He restated the salient points. 'The inquiry is disposed to find somebody negligent. That would be sufficient cause for the disaster. If, for good reason, Sandys' testimony cannot be questioned then it stands as it is. Then, if they wish, his counsel can turn attention upon you. For you are there. And you cannot say that Sandys is lying because he *isn't* there. And there are many things you cannot explain because he isn't there.' Jensen drew his shoulders together and made a grimace. 'In that case the tribunal has a culprit or a scapegoat – and they don't mind which it is.'

I levered myself out of the uncomfortable Habitat armchair and stood irresolute with an empty glass in my hand. 'Clifford is a very cunning bastard.'

'For the amount of money he expects, cunning is no trouble. As to the bastardy . . .'

'How much do you think he stands to gain?'

The Dane pursed his lips, 'Ten per cent, split between himself and Dolby.'

'Yes. I'd forgotten. Dolby must have been in it too.'

'I have not forgotten. I think Sandys will take over a million pounds and Dolby less than five hundred thousand.'

'Let me get another drink.' I took his glass and poured another for each of us.

But Jensen had not completed his state-of-play assessment. 'As I have said, the inquiry would prefer to find negligence. And that means other causes could be neglected. However, if there's not enough to support negligence they must find another reason. That is what I provide. Then, instead of giving only some "weight and credence" to my evidence they could decide it likely that the ship was cast away.'

I handed him the drink. 'That would be much better.'

'Very much better.' He stared up at me, trying to calculate if the moment was right. And apparently it was. 'That is why I suggested that you should take a job with Norske Veritas.'

'That was some time ago.'

'Yes. And you did not respond. It's a pity that Sandys' reflexes are much quicker than yours. But you are not yet too late.'

I backed away from him, conscious once more of how completely he had foreseen all the ramifications of the affair long before any of them dawned on me. The annoying thing was that he did not find it at all remarkable that he had such insight. 'You think it would help if I took that job.'

'It would help if you had already taken it. You might have the same advantage as Sandys if you were out of the country now.'

'This job would be abroad, then?'

'No, no. The job would be in London but you would spend about a month in Copenhagen becoming familiar with our systems. The point is you would be away from the rest of the inquiry.'

I thought about it – but not primarily as a device to elude the tribunal. Increasingly, it had been impressed upon me that it was time I took up a more settled occupation. What I was being offered was an excellent position which might not be offered again. 'Yes,' I said. 'I think I would like to work for Norske Veritas.'

The Dane signalled his satisfaction by a single, gentle clap of his hands. 'Good. Then you must fly out to Copenhagen in the morning.' That was what he'd come to secure and now he rose to his feet.

I shook my head. 'No. I want to see the inquiry through. Perhaps I can be of use in your "representation".'

He tilted his head carefully to the side. 'Undoubtedly. But you should not.'

So pleased was I to hear this unequivocal recognition of my worth that I overlooked the cause of it. 'Why not?'

'Because to be of real use to me means you will be charged with a crime.'

'Surely it's not a crime to help one's friends!'

'Naw – but burglary is a crime. If I am to say exactly how we reached our conclusions then the microfilm must be produced – and I must also say how we obtained that.'

And, of course, he was right. His effort to get me out of the country had taken this into account as well. But my resolve to beat Clifford was still strong. 'I'm willing to face the charge,' I said.

Jensen seemed unhappy at the news. He sat down again and let his head droop. After a moment he pursued the consequences, keeping his eyes on the carpet to lessen my embarrassment. 'Bill, *I* am glad you are willing. And I am grateful. However, if you admitted the charge then Norske Veritas could not employ you. Apart from the crime there would be too much conflict with the other shipowners.'

'Yes. I see.'

'There is also the matter that you were not alone.'

I felt a sudden spasm of shame that I had forgotten Tony. If

I were truthful then I labelled him guilty in his absence. Certainly nobody was going to believe that I did the job on my own. The whole enterprise seemed to collapse around me. It was unfair. Breaking into that office in the Minories was probably the single most adventurous thing I'd ever done in my life; the only uncharacteristic action I'd ever taken. I recalled the sense of elation it had given me when Tony and I succeeded; which was heightened by that day-long slog of investigation in the boardroom. Again success. Now it was all reduced and made practically worthless by other considerations which had not even existed when I first called Tony Liddle and he agreed. I took a gulp of my drink and looked around the living-room of the flat which had taken on that frowzy early-morning look which all rooms have when the dawn is bright enough to challenge any artificial lights that are still on. I asked Jensen, 'What do you suggest?'

He stretched himself back in the chair and brought his hands together. 'It is possible,' he stated slowly, 'that I can avoid offering proof while still establishing a doubt. That might be enough. Or, I could use what we have but say the microfilm was sent to us. That we don't know who took it from the agent's office. That is, I could tell them a lie.'

'Yes! Why not say that?' The occasion of Jensen telling a lie was rare enough, in my view, to be entirely proper. 'You don't have to prove how you got the microfilm.'

'No. And there is a slight gain. The tribunal will want to know why the owner failed to offer the microfilm for examination. That would be in our favour.'

'Fine. Then let's say that.'

But still he seemed doubtful. 'The danger then is that your . . . "accomplice" will learn how valuable was the item he stole and he may cause trouble for everyone.'

'There's no danger of that,' I assured him. 'Tony could have asked for more money at the time and didn't. He was repaying a debt – in a way.' With some vitality restored I crossed to the window and drew the curtains back. Jensen got to his feet and stretched. It was impossible to tell whether or not he accepted my assurance but we agreed that we'd both attend the inquiry on Monday and that he'd offer the evidence of a microfilm which had come mysteriously into his possession.

Later in the morning – when I'd had some sleep – I phoned Tony Liddle's number but another man answered. He told me Tony was in the bath and asked me who I was and what was the personal matter I had to speak to Tony about. He had a Scottish, well-educated accent and, from his manner, I assumed he was a boyfriend of my 'accomplice'. I changed the purpose of my call to 'a business matter' and, reluctantly, he agreed to get Tony out of the bath. To him I explained the strategy we proposed with regard to the microfilm. He thought it a good idea and pointed out that he would have been glad to send the item to me if I could have brought myself to pay the postage as an extra. In the background I heard the other man ask, 'Is it photographs?' and I could imagine the sort of photographs he thought were at issue. I could also imagine that when Tony hung up there would be a long and mistakenly jealous argument about me. I replaced the receiver and shook my head over the quite unnecessary trouble I might have caused.

The new relationship with Barbara which I'd had in mind was not so easily settled. In fact it was not settled at all and provided a delayed action shock which I found difficult to cope with. Since the urge to seize the initiative had been thwarted by Jensen's visit – and by my own sense of the ridiculous – I decided to let a few days elapse in which the fact of Clifford's departure would become established and a different arrangement desirable. But there seemed little need for that breathing space because nothing changed at all. Barbara did not mope or unwontedly busy herself in cleaning or tidying the flat – one or both of which reactions I expected to see. She continued to be her cheerful, rather indolent, self; reading, watching television in the afternoons and hooting with laughter at some of her more inept colleagues who appeared in commercials. I'd never watched television in the afternoon before and I'd certainly never paid as much attention to commercials. These, I now learned, were the most entertaining part of the whole output. Apart from a number of 'voice-overs' Barbara appeared in a few of them herself, 'Always as a dim-wit or a dragon,' as she pointed out. In my opinion she was very effective and very funny. 'But you could be glamorous if you wanted to,' I told her.

'Only at a distance,' she said. 'That's why I stick to the stage.' She put a hand on each of her cheeks and pulled the skin back so that the lines were smoothed out. 'I'm one of the sunset brigade – have been since it was *noon*, for God's sake.' This was a reference to the fact that stage lighting is placed mainly at a low and constant angle. 'Just right for ageing film stars and ugly ducklings.'

'Ah, but ageing film stars never become swans,' I told her.

'Neither do ugly ducklings. They have to *start* as swans.'

My pitch was timed for Sunday when she would have the whole day free. And I started by taking breakfast to her in bed. To my relief she was awake, not dauntingly surprised and overall pleased. 'Bill, darling! That *is* kind. Thank you.'

When she'd propped herself up I laid the tray across her knees then sat on the bed. 'I thought we might go out somewhere today. All day.'

'Mmm. Lovely. Where?'

'Where would you like to go?'

'Somewhere warm.' She began eating with a great show of enthusiasm.

'Oh.'

She gave me an offhand glance. 'Well, it is cold outside, Bill. It's practically winter outside. You weren't thinking of a *pic*nic were you?'

'No. Of course not. I just can't think of a place where we could spend the whole day indoors.'

'How about *several* places indoors – all of them with bars.'

'A sort of pub-crawl?'

'Eventually, perhaps. We wouldn't have to crawl *at first*. And there are some very nice restaurants I haven't eaten at as well.'

I snapped off a piece of the crisply fried bacon on her plate and nibbled it. 'Don't you mind that Clifford has gone?'

'Mind? Yes. Certainly I mind.' She busied herself with slicing for a moment then chuckled, 'I also mind that my rent for this flat has suddenly doubled.'

'When did they do that?'

'No. Clifford's share. I'll have to pay the whole rent now.'

And thus, almost magically, the perfect opportunity presented itself. Though jubilant I managed to keep my voice on a business-like key. 'I meant to tell you, I've taken a permanent job in London. And I'll need accommodation. Couldn't *we* share the flat?'

She wiped her mouth and gave me a steady, amused look. 'That's a possibility,' she said. 'But wouldn't you be happier in a flat of your own? I mean, I can afford to pay the rent.'

'I'd like to stay here, with you.'

'Perhaps you'll change your mind.'

'No, I'm quite certain that . . .'

'Yes! Bill,' she interrupted quite sharply. 'We must think about it.' She turned her attention once more to her plate. 'Have you had breakfast yet?'

'No. I was just going to have it.'

'Fine.'

I got off the bed and went back to the kitchen severely chastened. The rather brusque reception of my offer was unsettling enough but I'd also detected a curious defensiveness in her response which was quite unlike her usual open and downright manner. Perhaps she just wasn't at her best first thing in the morning, though she looked the same as ever. As I set about preparing my breakfast the affectionate thought occurred to me that the big advantage of what Barbara called her 'scrubbed look' was that she woke up with the face she was going to keep all day.

On an impulse I phoned home to see what the situation was there. Mrs Benstead told me that both my parents were away – which was perfect. I told her I'd be bringing a friend down for lunch and probably dinner as well. She sounded quite pleased to hear it. No doubt the long business absences of my father and the frequent social absences of my mother left Mrs Benstead's excellent abilities under-used. I wondered what my parents would think of Barbara. My father would be guarded and affable and secretly wonder why I was bothering to get married at all. He'd also hope that any wife of mine would have high earning

power since I'd proved myself notably deficient in that area. And
he'd hope to God we didn't have any children. I was certain
Barbara would set his mind at ease on the subject, at least. My
mother would feel guilty about the daughters of her friends but
glad the girl was in the arts; though she would have preferred
a soprano rather than an actress. I grinned and crossed to the
bathroom door where I could hear the shower running. I tapped
on the door and shouted, 'Can you sing?'

'Right now?' the actress demanded.

'At all!'

And at once a hearty contralto started vying with the water
in a curiously punctuated version of *Always*. I took it as a
heartening choice but really it was no more than the throwback
to a repertory production of *Private Lives*. When she'd showered
and dressed I announced the excursion, 'We're going down to
Sussex.'

'By the sea?'

'The very same,' I assured her. 'At my home.'

'Oh.' She became markedly less receptive. 'I don't think it's
a good idea to go barging in on your parents.'

'My parents are elsewhere.'

'Good. I mean, that will avoid any awkwardness.' She
brightened. 'Yes, that's fine. All I know of Sussex is Brighton,
but there must be more to it than that.'

'Considerably more.'

'What a beautiful house!' she exclaimed when, eventually, we
reached it.

'Warm, too,' I said. 'With free booze.'

'Who could ask for anything more?' Barbara asked, then sang
it, '"Who could ask for anything more?"' On the train she had
delivered a number of these *sotto voce* audition pieces to the
astonishment of other passengers and to serve me right for
questioning her singing ability.

Mrs Benstead's husband met us at the station and Mrs
Benstead herself welcomed us, promised lunch in an hour and,
almost in the same breath, asked if we'd be staying the night.
Considering the fact that she would have to prepare the bed-

rooms, or bedroom, it was a perfectly reasonable question. It caught me unprepared, though, and Barbara laughed at my hesitation. She answered for both of us. 'No, I have a run-through in the morning.'

'Miss Cree is an actress,' I murmured to the housekeeper but I could see from her expression that the statement came nowhere near explaining why that might prove an obstacle to staying the night; or what a run-through might be. 'We both have to be back in London quite early in the morning,' I added.

After lunch we spent a very lazy time playing records and drinking. Occasionally I made an effort to turn the conversation towards more serious – and for me pressing – subjects but on each occasion Barbara chose to misinterpret my words, or put a tune to them, or just start a new subject of her own. She was very happy and relaxed. I brought out the photograph albums and found her genuinely interested in the record of my youth and the various photogenic occasions on which my father or my mother held centre stage. And she made a surprising remark.

'There are very few photographs of them together.'

The thought hadn't occurred to me but plainly it was true. 'No. They have very different interests.'

Her hand paused in turning a page, 'Apart from each other, you mean?'

I laughed uneasily. 'Well, there's nobody handy with a camera when they're spending time together. It must be the same with your . . .'

Barbara ignored the gaffe. 'I feel a song coming on,' she said, and marched to the piano where she accompanied herself in a heavily accented rendering of 'Cushie Butterfield'.

Before dinner we went for a short walk to stimulate an appetite and sober up a bit. Since her shoes weren't suitable for hill climbing it was really just a walk around the grounds of the house and parading up and down the driveway. Although many of the trees were autumnally pretty and the air was not really cold, the setting was not ideal for proposing marriage. Yet, that was when and where I did propose to Barbara. She stopped abruptly and drew the lapels of her coat together. I watched her face and noted her strange expression which was both pleased and, somehow, thwarted. 'I think we don't know each other well enough, Bill,' she said.

'Oh, surely we do!'

We were near the corner of the house and she crossed the narrow grass verge to lean with her back against the wall. Again she drew her coat closer around her in the way that reminded me of her nervousness on another occasion. I stepped closer to her and she grasped my hand. 'I think we're very fond of each other. And we do get on well together.'

'Isn't that a good start?'

She gave me a straight, candid look and pressed her lips into a slight grimace. 'It might be – if that was how it started. But that wasn't how it started.' Her demeanour suggested that more unpalatable information was imminent. I joined her in leaning against the wall so that we were side by side and both looking across the slope of the side lawn towards the kitchen garden. She went on, 'For some time past things haven't been going so well between Cliff and me. Seemed to be backing off.'

'Preparing to leave you?'

'Yes. I suppose so. But I knew he was still very concerned about me. When he came home this time – after the ship was sunk – he seemed to have made up his mind. Told me I was sure to find somebody else. In fact, he knew of somebody else he was going to invite to live in the flat.'

'Me,' I said and from the corner of my eye I could detect her nodding.

'He meant well.'

'Really.'

'And of course he was perfectly free to invite whoever he liked.'

'Or *dis*liked, for that matter,' I commented bitterly, remembering Clifford's unexpected visit, and first invitation, and his insistence that Barbara very much wanted to meet me. In fact a whole series of puzzling remarks and attitudes became suddenly clear. I smiled against the depressing weight of anger which now sank to my stomach. And all the time I'd thought that at least in one area I was stealing a march on him. 'So – I was set up.'

'Not by me.'

'No. You were perfectly honest from the start. The first thing you said to me was that Clifford had promised I'd be taller,' I said and imagined myself arriving as a mail-order parcel that didn't quite meet the specifications.

She refused to respond to my anger, well aware that however we'd met both of us had become glad of it. And certainly she had enough of her own to regret in the arrangements her lover had made. It was not until some time later that I was able to appreciate how difficult it must have been for her to confess to me that, regardless of his good intentions, Clifford thought her so lacking in attraction that he had to use tricks in order to obtain a suitable replacement. Eventually I would recall Barbara's remark on her difficulty in the adoption market – 'Tough trading situation. Buyer resistance. No takers.'

Right there, though, staring across the garden, I was preoccupied with my own injured feelings. 'Why did you have to tell me?'

'I didn't *have* to. I thought I should. Probably I would have just let things slide if we were only sharing the flat and maybe sleeping together.' She sighed and stretched her neck. 'In fact, before he left, Cliff told me not to worry – to let things go; and make sure you pay the rent.'

'How very predictable I must be.'

'Not predictable enough,' Barbara said and gave a rueful chuckle. 'I don't think Cliff ever imagined that you'd want to marry me. Nor did I.' She eased herself off the wall and, with her hands dug deep in her coat pockets, started walking towards the front door. I let her go in before I followed. And, as I did so, I thought of Clifford Sandys, the well-tanned, smiling, elusive victor of all our encounters – whether he attended them or not. Dinner was a subdued and guarded meal. We were very polite to each other and fell into the absurd trap of believing that the discovery of one unpleasant truth means that all truth dies. Even then I wasn't finished with flexing my stupidity. Before we left the table I said, 'Perhaps it would be better if I moved out of the flat.'

'Why not wait until the inquiry ends,' she suggested. 'That's the reason you thought you were there.'

Mr Benstead saw us off on the next train back to London. For most of that journey both Barbara and I pretended to doze.

TEN

Monday was a very dull wet morning and I soon regretted my decision to walk to Queen Anne's Gate as usual. A downpour started when I'd already passed Victoria but I dived back and down to the Circle Line for a one-stop journey. All the lights were on in the Prince George ballroom, imparting a soft romantic ambience – which clashed with the hard rows of seats marshalled across the floor and the long official table spotlit on the dais. Even through the two layers of glass on the roof one could hear the heavy drumming of rain. While we waited for all interested parties to assemble, two of the hotel's maintenance men brought in an easel which they placed close to the microphone at the witness's table.

I'd phoned Jensen when I got back from Sussex the previous night but there had been no reply. However, I saw from the agenda circulated by the inquiry secretary that he'd managed to claim the whole day to submit his representation for the insurers. The front rows of seats were taken up by the owner's counsel and his entourage on the right of the aisle and those for the underwriters on the left. The solicitor for Clifford and the others was further back, as was mine. Neither of our counsel was present. And, of course, Clifford wasn't there either. But his partner Dolby was. I spotted him sitting well back and in the corner of the room.

Just before the board members arrived Jensen walked down the aisle to his position near the witness's table. He carried a great mass of documents and was followed by an hotel porter carrying a bundle of very large stiffened cards which I took to be enlargements of photographs and other visual elements which would be placed on the easel to illustrate the argument.

I had to remind myself that Jensen, his counsel and I were the only people in the room who had any idea of the plot which was about to be revealed. Whereas it was quite unusual for insurers to complain at all, when they did so their complaint was about safety procedures which hadn't been well enough observed, or lack of some equipment which, notionally at least, could have saved the ship. Everyone else waiting for the proceedings to begin expected no more than a tale bemoaning neglect. And no doubt the owner's men were well briefed to cope with that. They would be quite *un*prepared to answer charges of collusion and fraud. The owner's distinguished and elderly counsel, Mr Edmund Ditton QC, would not welcome being made party to that.

The chairman opened the session, explained the intention of the day's business and called upon Jensen to begin. Jensen rose, left his pile of documents behind, moved very deliberately to the bare witness's table and placed upon it a single sheet of paper. The sheer simplicity of the action claimed everyone's attention at once. He sat at the table then adjusted the microphone to a suitable height. In a calm gentle voice he began, 'I wish to place before the board information and evidence which, the underwriters submit, may lead to no other conclusion than that the *Niome* was deliberately cast away in order to secure . . .' The gasp of astonishment which swept in a wave from the front row to the back could not have been louder or better orchestrated if it had been rehearsed. Jensen allowed it to break against the back wall before he completed his simple and damning sentence: '. . . in order to secure payment of the full insured value of the vessel.'

Ditton, the owner's senior counsel, half-rose to his feet as though hoping that by the time he was upright some justifiable objection might have occurred to him. Jensen turned his head with lazy politeness in that direction, knowing that there could be no objection. The underwriters were unquestionably interested parties whose main interest lay in collecting premiums. If nothing else, the loss of the *Niome* deprived them of income. Ditton sat down again. But he had an ally – and a personal friend – in the chairman of the board.

'That is a very serious charge, Mr Jensen.'

'Sir, I make no charge. I say I have information and evidence relevant to the purpose of this inquiry which I would like the board to consider.'

'You said more than that, Mr Jensen,' the chairman asserted comfortably. 'You mentioned a conclusion that had been reached.'

'No, sir. I said . . .' and here he referred to the single sheet of paper, though of course he knew the words by heart, '. . . I said, a conclusion *may* be reached – and so I hope it will be; by this inquiry.'

The chairman consulted his colleagues and they consulted the advisers who sat behind them. Meanwhile the sibilant undercurrent in the ballroom rose to a babble. My attention was taken by the huddle of figures around the owner's counsel and his agent. Then I wondered how Dolby had taken it and glanced across to where he'd been sitting. He was gone.

The chairman tapped for silence and spoke again, 'Mr Jensen, if there is a claim for insurance and if your principals are convinced the claim is fraudulent then that is a matter for the civil court, not for us.' He looked over Jensen's head to Jensen's counsel. 'Would you not agree, Mr Yates?'

Yates stood up. 'It may become a matter for the civil court, but Mr Jensen feels that . . .'

'What do you feel, Mr Jensen?' asked the chairman condescendingly.

'I feel I must protect this inquiry from any future ridicule.'

Another wave of audible astonishment lapped over the ballroom.

'"Ridicule"?' the chairman repeated the word in a dangerously quiet voice.

'Yes.' Jensen shrugged as though he feared his command of English was not equal to the occasion. 'If you say the loss of the vessel was due to negligence, or neglect, or some other accidental cause – then a civil court decides it was deliberately sunk for insurance . . . that will seem very strange, if not ridiculous.'

'You are in no position to anticipate what conclusion this inquiry will reach,' the chairman grated.

'And I do not, sir. But there is one conclusion it *cannot* reach unless you consider the evidence I wish to put before you.'

Jensen's counsel lowered his head to conceal a smile. Several other people in clear view of the chairman were not so discreet. He again consulted the experts who flanked him but there was really no doubt that Jensen had them square. And, wisely, his counsel had allowed him to state the matter in terms which even shipping correspondents would understand.

The chairman conceded. 'Very well, Mr Jensen. Please go on.'

The Dane started going through the points which we had discussed at such length. After just a few sentences I noticed the owner's agent easing along the row then hurrying out. There was nothing damaging in that. Even if the owner were entirely blameless he'd have to be informed immediately of the new disaster which threatened his chances of grabbing the jackpot. But there was little that his legal representatives could do in that first session except listen and watch very carefully for the smallest crack in Jensen's argument.

I saw them making notes at several stages of the exposition. Once the engineer member of the board insisted on clarification of the trouble with the heating coils and the fact that the trouble was reported ashore. I felt a little twist of anxiety when he also asked if the temperature of the crude had been taken at discharge. In all of his evidence Jensen did not refer to particular officers by name and so it was not apparent whether Clifford or I had been in charge at any given time. The board's engineer also took a very close interest in the illustrations which one by one Jensen set up on the easel. By that time the owner's agent had returned to the proceedings. Apart from having informed his master, I was certain he would have checked and found that the microfilm was missing from his office. As the Dane reached the reproduction of my sketches – greatly enlarged and clarified for display – he referred to the comparison with the original arrangement.

The board's engineer asked, 'Is that the arrangement we have already seen, Mr Jensen?'

'No, sir. I have made these comparisons with the shipbuilder's microfilm of their arrangement.'

The engineer demurred. 'Yes, yes. We have seen prints of that.'

'No. What you have seen is a misleading version of how these systems were altered. My sketches show how they were *actually* altered.'

The chairman intervened. 'Your contention is then that there are three versions of the same array of pipes?'

'Yes, sir.' And the Dane smiled to acknowledge that it was the lawyer not the engineer who was first to seize the crucial factor. 'There is the shipbuilder's version shown on microfilm, the owner's version which was offered to you for inspection – and the real version which –' he pointed to the sketch on the easel '– I have illustrated here.'

At last Ditton had a valid point of objection and rose to his feet with glowing and righteous indignation.

The chairman invited his comment. 'Yes, Mr Ditton?'

'We cannot, I think, allow this to proceed, Sir Iain. Mr Jensen alludes to "the owner's version" in identifying what I take to be the current working drawings of the ship which the board has already accepted as valid.'

The chairman nodded his agreement with this objection. Jensen, despite his earlier care not to pre-judge the issue, had stated a conclusion. In effect he'd claimed that the owner was directly involved and that he'd tried to mislead the board. Seeing how damaging the slip might be, Jensen acted quickly to forestall a termination of his evidence. 'Sir, I apologise to the board. When I say "the owner's version" I do, of course, mean what was offered as the current working drawings of the ship.'

The chairman tried not to smile at the way in which the Dane seemed to withdraw his objectionable remark yet rephrased the alternative to carry exactly the same accusation he'd made in the first place. 'Thank you, Mr Jensen. Please go on. And allow us to decide on the conclusions.'

But before he could go on to show the enlarged photographs of the wrecked bow, the board engineer had further questions about the sketches. 'Is this *your* version, then? Did you make these sketches, Mr Jensen?'

'No. They were made by the chief engineer, William Thompson.'

'Didn't he trust the drawings which were on the ship?'

'He did; while the ship was afloat,' Jensen retorted suavely. 'He made the sketches when all that was left was the bow.'

Although a little alarmed at hearing my name brought into this part of the inquiry I had to admire the way in which Jensen turned everything to suit his purpose.

And the engineer gave him a further opportunity by rather waggishly enquiring, 'Did Mr Thompson have a particular reason for this. Or does he just enjoy sketching wrecks?'

The Dane replied with chilling gravity, 'His reason, and mine, was an effort to discover why five men had died.'

The chairman gave his colleague a look of undisguised annoyance. There were no more interruptions as the photographs were presented and the anomalies pointed out. And it was only here that – however carefully phrased – the involvement of Clifford Sandys was made plain. I expected his solicitor to object but he didn't. And that suggested to me that if the owner was pushed into an untenable position then a way would be found to make Clifford bear all the blame. There were already signs of such a ploy as well as a promise to discredit Jensen when the owner's counsel asked for an extended lunch break. He mentioned several matters which he needed some time to prepare and all of them pointed to a vigorous fight-back in the afternoon.

During the lunch break Jensen seemed to spend all his time on the telephone so I ate alone. And I tried to figure out how, feasibly, they could make Clifford the sole villain. How could he get his hands on any money unless the owner got it from the insurers? As far as I could see there was no possible motive for him to engineer such a plot on his own. Of course other, though much smaller, ships had been sunk by single disaffected members of their crew. What motivated them was unpaid wages, revenge, malice, boredom or simple bloody-mindedness. But the scale and resources of these actions were puny compared to the planning which had gone towards disposing of the *Niome*.

The most conclusive indictment in this case was that work had been done and paid for to install piping, fittings and electrical connections which could have no other purpose than ensuring the destruction of the ship. It seemed to me that Jensen's case was irrefutable; but I reckoned without the subtle acuity of Mr Edmund Ditton QC, given even a few hours to arm himself.

As we were filing back into the ballroom I did manage to have a few words with Jensen. I congratulated him on his masterly handling of the morning's work.

He was far from complacent. 'The other side was taken by surprise. It will be different now.'

'What have you been doing?'

'Trying to reach our agent in Monrovia. Last week I passed on the name of the repair yard you found. He said he would check.'

'What did he find?'

'I don't know. And he's not in his office yet.'

As Jensen walked down the rows of seats I took my place at the back. But I could see the opposition watching him. They seemed to be confident, if not blatantly smug. As soon as the proceedings were reopened and the Dane was once more at the witness's table, the owner's senior counsel rose to question the evidence. Naturally he started with the business of the microfilm. He apologised to the board for the fact that it hadn't been made available for inspection because inspection was not possible without special equipment. And, in any case, the full-scale drawings which had been made available were identical with the original systems.

'Nevertheless,' the chairman said – as though he had been primed to say, 'the board would be grateful if you would now offer the material.'

Ditton came in on cue. 'Sir, I regret that we cannot. The microfilm was stolen from my client's office. It is now in Mr Jensen's possession.'

'Is that true, Mr Jensen?'

'Yes, sir. That is how I was able to make the comparisons I made this morning.'

The board members looked at each other and conferred briefly to agree on their understanding of the matter. The chairman stated it. 'You did not make that clear. We thought you were relying upon your knowledge as surveyor when the ship was being built.'

And certainly that was an assumption which he had cunningly allowed them to make. But now he confessed, 'No. I was the hull surveyor.'

Ditton moved smoothly into this credibility gap, 'Sir Iain, with the board's permission, there are some troublesome matters with regard to this microfilm which I would like to . . . clarify.'

'Please do.'

'Mr Jensen, how did the microfilm come into your possession?'

'It was sent to me.'

'By whom?'

'I don't know.'

Ditton allowed a pause to state the unlikelihood of that while he consulted a note. 'I believe you visited the Lindø shipyard quite recently.'

I gave a soft involuntary groan of apprehension. It had been too much to expect that the shipping agent would not go right to source.

But Jensen answered calmly enough, 'Yes. I did.'

'With what purpose?'

'To obtain the microfilm.'

'And you were unsuccessful.'

The Dane nodded.

'Because it had been passed on to its rightful owner. Then it was stolen.' Ditton smiled encouragingly. 'And shortly thereafter, Mr Jensen, it was sent by an unknown person to you.'

'That is correct.'

'On this secret visit to Lindø – when you tried to get your hands on the microfilm – did you go alone?'

'No. There was a . . . colleague with me.'

'You went as a representative of the underwriters, of course.'

'Of course. It was my duty to obtain any relevant material

which might be available,' Jensen stated, rallying somewhat.
Ditton gave an understanding nod. 'And that was the duty of
your colleague too.'

'I'm sorry, sir, I don't . . .'

'Your colleague, Mr Jensen! He must also be employed by
the insurers.'

'No. I was accompanied by William Thompson, the chief
engineer of the *Niome*.'

The chairman brusquely intervened. 'And what business was
it of his?'

Jensen held his ground. 'I asked him to come so that I could
have his expert assistance identifying the engine room systems
with which I was not familiar.'

But the damage was done and the senior counsel wasted no
time in pressing his advantage. 'Mr Jensen, in your illustrated
talk this morning you relied heavily on Mr Thompson's artistic
impressions of the wrecked bow. Now you tell us you were
very anxious to have his view of the original microfilm. Yet in
his own testimony to this board, Mr Thompson did not mention
either of these things.'

'He was not questioned about these things.'

Ditton conceded that small point. 'That's true. And of course
he had enough to answer for.'

My counsel was instantly on his feet. 'Chairman, that last
remark could be construed in a way that Mr Ditton cannot
intend,' he objected; though it was perfectly obvious that Mr
Ditton intended every ounce of it.

'We construe the remark as an observation that the chief
engineer was questioned at great length,' the chairman replied,
silkily obtuse. 'And he may now be questioned at even greater
length.'

I shrank lower in my seat. The whole structure was crumbling
again, but at least Ditton had finished his preliminary 'clarification'. He went on, with much less assurance, to question the
technical assertions which Jensen had made. But he didn't need
to be as sharp at that. He had already discredited the evidence
by implication. He had also discredited practically everything *I'd*
said. Jensen's perfectly reasonable claim that his investigations

required the assistance of an engineer began to look suspicious when the engineer he chose was one who, notionally at least, could cover his own negligence by the outrageous expedient of blaming the owner.

Nor did the owner's counsel miss the opportunity to raise the spectre of a personal vendetta on Jensen's part. It seemed that, almost by accident, he stumbled upon the fact that the lost master of the vessel was the Dane's father-in-law. When that came out I kept a careful watch on the faces of the board members. They made an effort to show that their judgment was not affected by the news. But the *effort* showed. Of course Jensen continued to be impressively unshakable. And he kept coming back to his best arguments – the microfilm and the photographs. He requested that suitable projection equipment be installed in the ballroom, preferably by the following morning and, to the dismay of some of the opposition side, the chairman agreed to have it done. The photographs which certainly explained the cause of the explosion did little to implicate the owner. He hadn't been there operating the valves for the inert gas system. That was the responsibility of the engineers he employed. In particular – Ditton was at pains to point out – it was the responsibility of the *chief* engineer.

That session of the inquiry ended earlier than usual because the chairman felt they could not usefully continue until they were able to view the particular frames of the microfilm on which much of Jensen's argument depended. The Dane and I immediately headed for the bar to take stock of our situation. I told him, 'Their sticking point is how you got the microfilm. What's on it won't make much impression unless we clear that up.'

Jensen shrugged. 'Perhaps.'

'Without doubt! They won't trust anything you say if they can't trust you on that.'

'There's nothing I can do about it now.'

'But *I* can. I can tell them that, without your knowledge, I stole it.'

The Dane was less than stirred by the nobility of the offer. Keeping his eye on the ball he murmured, 'That would do no good unless you also tell them that you sent it to me.'

'All right. I'll do that.'

'And Mr Ditton will recall that so much of our case depends on *your* sketches and *your* notes . . .' he sighed, '. . . and how can they trust a liar and a thief.' Abruptly, I leaned back in the corner seat. It was true. Strictly speaking – even roundly speaking – I was a liar and a thief. It would matter little to the tribunal that I was both in a good cause. 'Also,' he added, 'the fact remains that you could not have done the burglary on your own.'

'No, I couldn't.' That fact did remain though my impulse to do some good had overlooked it. There was Tony to consider.

'Excuse me,' said Jensen and got up to try the telephone again. Another consequence of telling the truth was the certainty that if the charge against the owner could not be proved the board would revert to their first preference of someone's negligence. And I would be the perfect candidate. With Clifford out of the way his counsel could shift all the blame upon me.

I looked around the crowded lounge. Most of the people were to some extent involved with the inquiry. As they enjoyed a drink they were also enjoying the suppressed excitement of a good scandal about to break. For the legal participants, attendance at a board of inquiry was something of a busman's holiday, with very good pay. There were no strict rules of evidence or procedure as in a proper trial in court and there was not even the slightest incentive or threat to their pride. None of them was going to win or lose. At the beginning when I'd explained the set up to Barbara she exclaimed, 'Then it's just like a charity performance! Practically no rehearsal and lovely notices for everyone.'

'Except me,' I groaned as I pressed myself even further back in the soft cushions to give the impression that I was sitting upright and confident. To my relief I saw Jensen returning through the crowd.

'Let us go outside,' he said. I got up trying to discern if his rather brusque suggestion meant there was more bad news or just a little good news for a change. His sleepy eyes gave nothing away.

Outside, the day had brightened a little although the skies

were still grey and there was a steady drizzle of rain. We strolled back along Queen Anne's Gate and crossed Birdcage Walk to enter the park past the forlorn little drinking fountain. Jensen had good news. He'd been able to contact the agent who told him there was a possibility of laying hands on the repair schedule drawings – if the bribe was big enough. These were the actual drawings used to install the destructive additions to the piping and wiring.

'That's wonderful!'

'It would be wonderful *if* we could get the drawings here on time, *if* they show what we expect them to show and *if* there is definite evidence to show the owner knew what was being done.'

I glanced at Jensen. He was striding along with his head carefully balanced to avoid jolting and his eyes gazing disinterestedly into the middle distance. In many ways he was an irritating man; much too apt at spotting failure in advance. I tried to match his cool tone. 'And *if* your clients can put up the money for the bribe.'

'My clients are experts in bribes. That's what insurance premiums are.'

'What!' I gurgled incredulously. 'Bribing who?'

'Bribing fate,' he explained. 'But I have told the man in Monrovia what we are willing to pay.'

We walked on along the water path towards the Buckingham Gate exit, stepping in single file around the large puddles caused by the morning's heavy rain. 'When will you know?' I asked.

'Some time this evening he will call me.'

'Fine. So, if he gets the drawings he can tell you what they show.'

Perversely it seemed, Jensen stymied that as well. 'No. He's an accountant, not an engineer. He would not know if he was holding the drawing the right way up.'

The sound of our footsteps on the gleaming tarmac began to beat like a countdown against the clock. There wasn't enough time to overcome all the obstacles which the Dane had so perceptively identified. And yet I felt heartened. Just this once, it seemed, we'd managed to get ahead of Clifford. If the drawings could be bought then he hadn't managed to block or destroy them. Here was one crucial loophole he'd left open. I smiled at the thought of his long and unsuccessful flight to Africa. But my satisfaction later proved ill-founded. The reason Clifford hadn't won this round was simply because he wasn't there. He was nowhere near Africa.

As we returned to the hotel along Birdcage Walk a solution to at least one of our problems suddenly occurred to me, but I did not mention it at once in case a lack of forethought allowed Jensen to demolish the plan. Obliquely, I suggested, 'There must be an international news agency in Monrovia.'

'Probably. But they are very discreet about shipping.'

'I wasn't thinking of their discretion, I was thinking of their equipment. They must have a wire service to transmit news photographs.'

There was no need to explain any further. 'Excellent!' said the Dane. 'But where could we receive them?'

'My father's office.'

I was astonished when my companion stopped, turned to face me and, very deliberately patted me once on the shoulder. It felt a great deal like receiving the accolade. That done, he increased his pace under the dripping branches until we reached the Prince George. But we were both elated by the knowledge that if the agent managed to get the drawings there was a machine which could scan them in Monrovia so that they would be redrawn at practically the same instant in London.

At the hotel Jensen went immediately to his room to await news from his agent and I called my father's office to clear the intended use of the transcriber. Maddeningly, both my father and Hanson were out of the country. The junior partner to whom I spoke was not at all sure if what I proposed was possible – or could be allowed. More irritating was the impression that he didn't entirely believe I was who I claimed to be. At last I demanded, 'Put me on to Mrs Schuster.' And since she certainly knew me, and the equipment was clearly within her domain, she at once agreed to help.

When all that was arranged I realised that I felt rather uncomfortable and very, very hungry. If things worked out well

there would be little point in going back to the flat. I called
Barbara then booked into the hotel to have a bath, a rest and a
good dinner.

Next morning in the ballroom Jensen and I were impatient for
the proceedings to start. He'd taken an early breakfast so that
he could supervise the setting up of the projection equipment
for the microfilm. The screen was secured on the wall to the
left and the projector on the witness's table so that the beam
lay across the room just in front of the dais. And the microfilm
was what the chairman decided he wanted to see first. As Jensen
went through the relevant frames I noticed the shipping agent in
urgent conversation with the owner's counsel and his assistant.
They seemed to pay little attention to the screen and as soon
as the projector was switched off we learned why.

The counsel rose to his feet and the chairman acknowledged
him. 'Mr Ditton?'

'Chairman, having considered the unfounded charges which
were made yesterday, and the allegations which appeared in
some newspapers this morning, my client has asked me to
advise the board that he claims the right to make representation
against the board. If the board permits, I will act for him in that
capacity.'

The three board members stared at the old lawyer with
identical stunned expressions.

I whispered to my counsel, 'What the hell does that mean?'

The young man grimaced. 'Roughly, the owner who was on
one side of the fence wants to be on the other side of the fence
as well. Ditton's accusing the Department of Trade, through the
inquiry, of slander.'

'Surely he doesn't believe that!'

'No, but it gives him a stranglehold on the chairman.'

And the chairman knew it, apparently, as he explained the
situation to his colleagues. It was only conjecture on my part
but, watching the three men on the dais, it seemed that it was
the non-legal experts who wanted to take the tougher line. The
engineer and the mariner became quite agitated as they pressed
their shared opinion on the unwilling chairman. And, it seemed,

they won, though the chairman tried to rationalise his decision
to continue with the inquiry. And he packed it with a neat punch
to the owner's weak spot. 'Mr Ditton, our business is largely
academic research. We are to discover, if we can, what caused
the *Niome* to sink. As to becoming a prosecutor of a special
interest as well as a defendant against negligence – we think
that your client is already a prosecutor, as an insurance claimant.
Is that not so?'

'I believe he is, chairman.'

'That seems enough matter to take up your attention, Mr
Ditton. And if it is to be pursued it must take up ours. Mr Jensen
will be allowed to advance the proper interests of *his* clients.'

'Translate,' I entreated my legal adviser.

'The chairman asked Ditton, which would the owner rather
have – no more press tittle-tattle or fifteen million pounds?'

Ditton had not the slightest hesitation. 'We shall be guided by
the board.'

I was able to translate that myself. And Jensen was able to
get on with his argument. He put up my sketches of the piping
and drew attention to the additional steam lines which had not
been on the original layout. 'This,' he said, 'was certainly the
cause of the overheating in the tanks.'

The engineer member of the tribunal who had very carefully
inspected the microfilm image now came down to have a closer
look at the sketch on the easel.

Ditton got to his feet again. 'Chairman, we have viewed the
magic lantern show with interest but the comparison Mr Jensen
hopes to make is no comparison at all. The microfilm is record
of fact. The chief engineer's sketches of a wreck which is now
broken up are no more than a vague memory of what might
have been there and fanciful conjecture of the purpose if it was
there. This cannot be depended upon.'

The engineer went back to the dais and prompted the chairman
who asked, 'Mr Jensen, do you vouch for the accuracy of these
sketches?'

'Yes, sir. I do.'

Ditton objected. 'Chairman, Mr Jensen has already told us
that he is a specialist in naval architecture and hulls. He is not

an expert in marine engineering and therefore not in a position
to vouch for the accuracy of what is shown there.'

This seemed an entirely valid point to the chairman. 'Well,
Mr Jensen?'

Jensen now came to the clincher. 'The reason I can vouch for
the accuracy of those sketches is that I have these drawings.'
He crossed quickly to his chair and picked up the large flat
package which contained the repair yard's drawings which had
been transmitted to my father's office late the previous night.
Opening the package as he went, the Dane walked all the way
across the floor, mounted the dais and laid the incontrovertible
evidence in front of the board's engineer. As all three members
of the tribunal started examining the drawings Jensen took the
opportunity to address Ditton in particular while seeming to give
a general explanation.

'These are drawings for work which was carried out on the
Niome at a Liberian repair yard. The work was scheduled and
paid for by North Cape Shipping's manager and the drawings bear
his initials on the approval stamp. They show the uncertificated
additions to the piping and electrical systems. And they confirm
what was found on the wreck of the bow.'

I could see the board engineer nodding. He was convinced.
The chairman then called Ditton, then the owner's agent, up to
the dais to satisfy themselves that what Jensen said was true.
Ditton could not conceal his embarrassment and the agent looked
as though he might snatch up the drawings and make off with
them. To let everyone consider their position the session then
broke prematurely for lunch.

As I walked out of the ballroom amid the babble of talk I felt
a glow of jubilation at our victory. Jensen remained with the
discordant group on the dais to make sure that no point of
interest would be overlooked. I'd almost finished eating when
he joined me. I stood up and shook his hand. 'Congratulations!
It was worth all the effort.'

'Thank you.' He sat down opposite me. 'I am very grateful to
you for your help.'

I smiled, 'Well, I was helping myself too. The inquiry can't go
for negligence now. I'm in the clear.'

'So far as negligence is concerned, yes.' He spoke with that soft deliberation I'd come to dread. 'They may still want to question you, though.'

'What for?'

'To find out if you were part of the plot. Somebody had to light the fuse. Why should it not be you?'

It was astounding how he always managed to find the worst possibilities with the greatest ease. Before my annoyance could increase, however, Edmund Ditton came to our table. He acknowledged each of us with a slight bow which was really just a nod, then spoke directly to Jensen. 'I have been in touch with my client and he asks me to tell you that he will now abandon his claim for payment of insurance by your clients.'

'I shall convey that to my clients,' said the Dane soberly.

Ditton added, 'You will receive written notification, of course.'

'This will be of interest to the inquiry,' my companion murmured.

The old lawyer gave a slight, smiling shrug. 'I will inform the chairman that we are withdrawing.'

'Will you inform the chairman *why*?' I asked, louder than was necessary. This weird understating of an issue which had caused me months of effort and travel and worry could not surely be disposed of so easily.

Ditton looked down at me as though he'd heard a noise but wasn't sure what had caused it. He was not disposed to answer my question or, for that matter, engage in any further discussion. 'Good afternoon, gentlemen,' he said and walked statelily away.

My companion, evidently amused by my expression of amazement and annoyance, smiled across the table. 'So – the job is over. I shall go home tomorrow.'

'But what about prosecuting Clifford, and the owner . . . surely they can't just get away with it?'

Jensen was unmoved. 'The underwriters employed me to save them fifteen million pounds. The money is safe. They have no further interest in the matter. And I have other things to do.'

When the board met the following morning they faced a dilemma. The next 'representation' they were to hear was one for compensation to some dependants of men killed in the explosion. That is, counsel representing the dependants made an outline of their case as interested parties to the board's eventual finding – whatever that might be. Normally such advance pleading was no more than a tedious formality from which the claimants could gain nothing but acknowledgement of the fact of their existence. This time it was different. The various counsel had listened with great interest – not to say bated breath – to Jensen's charge that the ship had been deliberately sunk. He had already fought the substantial part of their case for them. The board could not ignore the fact.

One after another the various lawyers rose to ask politely if the owner's counsel would, at a later date, be giving evidence to 'clarify' the purpose of the additional uncertified piping and wiring on the *Niome*. This was really as close as the procedure allowed them to get to their quarry. Time and again Edmund Ditton rose to state that he did not plan to clarify that purpose unless the board directed him to do so. But the chairman of the board knew that whereas he could direct Ditton to give such evidence such action would enable each of the opposing lawyers to tear him to shreds. If the board allowed that to happen they would do more to advance the intended civil actions for compensation than any litigant could wildly dream of, yet do nothing to further the ostensible aim of the board.

Just before lunch, having received a barrage of increasingly frantic advice from the Department of Trade officials, the chairman announced that he was adjourning the inquiry until some future unspecified date. Everyone in the ballroom knew that the date would depend on the outcome of the civil actions which would now be lodged against North Cape Shipping.

I walked out into the pale sunshine amused by the wrangle but confident that whatever happened in the courts had nothing to do with me. Once again I was mistaken; but the mistake didn't surface until I'd made valuable use of my illusory confidence.

ELEVEN

The suspension of the inquiry had a striking effect upon my state of mind. At last I was free of the *Niome* after almost a year of growing doubts and tension. Ahead there were no more interrogations and no further need to contest the pervasive suspicion which had hung over the survivors. I was out in the open, on dry land and unscathed. Also, I had a job. My month's initial training in Copenhagen was about to begin and by early December I would be back in London. All these factors contributed to a barely remembered light-heartedness. But – I was quick to realise – what contributed more was the fact that I'd beaten Clifford. Since the owner was not going to get the insurance money, Clifford was not going to get his share of it either. At long last I'd managed to get ahead of him. Certain of that, I could view my earlier reaction to Barbara as the stupidity it undoubtedly was.

In the final weeks of the inquiry her attitude had been unchanged. She still refused to believe that Clifford had done what I knew he had done. Several times I tried to explain things so that his involvement must be plain to any reasonable person. Barbara was not concerned with reason and took refuge in her confusion over the technical details I was at pains to clarify. She protested, 'Bill, you hardly know him. He's not that sort of person.'

'What sort of person is he?'

'He's like me. A person who had to make something out of nothing – and on his own. And he made it. Anybody that used to hard work isn't going to kill people for money.'

So – as Clifford himself had warned me – she was intensely loyal. But she did not blame me either and maintained her friendly, bright and amusing behaviour. On the Sunday after the final session in the Prince George I decided to try again. And I started by apologising for the petty selfishness which had caused the breach between us.

'I don't think it was selfishness,' she said. 'It was pride.'

'That's worse.'

'No. It's just stronger. *My* pride was in there too. Still is.'

I was immediately contrite again. 'Yes, of course.'

She laughed. 'Why is it wrong for you to have pride but okay if I have it?'

'Because I'm the one who's apologising.'

'And you've done that.' She gave me a mischievous wink across the breakfast table. 'So? What's your next line?'

'I'd like to go on living here with you.'

'Nobody's asking you to move. And?'

'I'd like to pay half of the rent until we get married.'

She pushed her plate to the centre of the table, and leaned forward on her folded arms. 'What if I don't want to get married?'

'To me? Or anyone?' I asked, striving to keep the tone practical and light.

'To anyone.'

'That's all right,' I smiled. 'As long as it's not just a grudge against me.'

'Bill, I never hold grudges.'

'Good. But what have you got against marriage?'

'Fidelity,' she said, keeping her amused gaze focussed on my eyes.

Involuntarily, I laughed.

Immediately she responded with a show of mock indignation. 'You think it wouldn't come up? Can you doubt that I get plenty of offers – and take quite a few of them?'

'I'd be surprised if you didn't,' I assured her.

'*Now* you'd be surprised if I didn't! As we are at the moment. But if we were married, though, you'd be horrified if I *did*.'

Behind the playfulness she was, as always, striving for honesty. So, while I kept the smile on my face, and even mimed giving the implicit question a lot of thought, I was in fact giving it a lot of thought. At last I said, 'You drive a hard bargain.'

She shrugged, 'I've had to put up with me for a long time.'

'And all I'm suggesting is that we share the burden.'

She leaned back from the table, breaking the defensive facade, and stared rather wistfully at the ribbed jersey of her dressing gown. 'The burden's bound to get lighter, as time goes on,' she said.

'Meanwhile,' I told her firmly, '*I'd* like to make you an offer. In fact, I have made you an offer – without strings.'

She smiled and stretched across the table to press my hand. 'My dear Bill, where would you *be* without strings?'

'In bed.'

She got to her feet. 'I was just going back to it.'

I finished my breakfast, brushed my teeth and joined her there. Some time later, when we were relaxing, I began to wonder if she had properly understood our conversation about marriage. Drawing her closer I murmured, 'I was serious, you know.'

'About what?'

'Barbara!'

'About getting married,' she hastily recalled.

'Right. And I think we should settle *when*, exactly.'

She nestled under my arm. 'Why do we have to settle it now?'

'Because I know that every time I mention it you'll say, "Why do we have to settle it now?"'

She chuckled and her body vibrated against me. 'I'm just trying to save you a lot of aggravation.'

'Don't bother. Now, tell me when would suit you.'

'When you get back from Copenhagen, I suppose.'

'Fine. Will you make the arrangements while I'm gone or shall I do it then?'

'Oh, Bill! Ar*range*ments!'

'I'll take care of everything when I get back,' I told her.

Before I left for Denmark we had another meeting with the playwright, Howard Murray. This arose from the chronic insecurity of actors and the fact that *What Every Woman Knows* was coming to the end of its run. The management wanted to make the house available for a good commercial Christmas show.

'Which means I'm looking for work again,' Barbara explained, 'so I'd better cultivate my geraniums.'

'He hasn't had time to write a play yet.'

'No. But it should be coming along and I have to know the strength of it before I try for other parts or turn any down.'

'When are you going to see him?'

'I'm not. I've invited him here.'

'When?' I asked, running through the likely excuses I could give for being elsewhere.

'I invited him to lunch on Thursday but he said he'd come *after* lunch.'

'Ah, yes. He doesn't like eating in public,' I reminded her.
'It's doubtful if he eats at all, if you ask me. Probably takes injections of formaldehyde.'

I shook my head at the memory of the charmless man. 'Is he really worth the trouble?'

'Do you think I'd bother if he wasn't?'

'Thursday,' I mused. 'That was when I . . .'

Barbara cut in sharply. 'That's when you'll be here, pretending you've just finished eating the marvellous lunch he missed.'

'I'm sorry you couldn't join us,' I told Murray. 'Barbara is an excellent cook.'

'One of those other things she's good at, no doubt.'

I glanced across the room at the lady. 'One of the *many* things.'

The playwright's eyes snapped from me to Barbara and back before he changed the subject. 'So much of my time recently has been taken up searching for a flat.'

'Where are you living at the moment?'

'An hotel in Hampstead. But one can't do much work in an hotel room.'

This puzzled me. 'Why not?'

Murray sniffed. 'Because the staff really prefer to have it to themselves. So they can spend the day not cleaning it.'

'Oh!' Barbara suddenly tuned in. 'The man in the flat two above us is moving out. Maybe you could get a hook on that before they advertise.'

Murray seemed to be interested and said he would open negotiations with the porter on his way out. Then the talk turned to theatre – what was opening; what was closing; and why. I gained many small but illuminating pieces of information. For example, that 'must close' warning advertisements really mean, 'Please God, keep us open.' Before long Barbara edged the conversation round to the play he was writing. She carefully avoided seeming to push, but her care was unnecessary.

'Miss Cree, I wouldn't be here unless I was prepared to tell you how it's going and when it's likely to be finished.'

'So – how's it going?'

'Very well.' He reached to the inside pocket of his neat business suit and produced a folded sheaf of papers. 'I've brought you the character run-down, plot outline and scene structure. Also . . .' he gave a grim little smile, '. . . an estimate of stage-time for each of the actors involved.'

Barbara chuckled admiringly as she accepted the papers. She immediately started to read through these arcane details.

'Stage-time?' I asked Murray.

He nodded. 'Actors will deny it up and down but they are acutely interested in how much time their character is actually on the stage in comparison with other characters.' He drew my attention to Barbara who had skipped over two pages, and added softly, 'Being on as the act curtains counts extra – and she is.'

I was astonished. 'And do you have to keep all that stuff in mind as well as the play?'

His straight black eyebrows rose fractionally, 'All that stuff is part of the play. Without the engineering you'd be as well with a monologue.'

'I'm an engineer,' I told him.

'I'm glad to hear it.'

It was difficult to tell if he was stating a fact or being sarcastic. 'Why aren't there any plays about ships?'

'There are. Eugene O'Neill wrote some – before he started attacking his family.'

Half way through the outline Barbara called encouragingly, 'It seems to be very economical.'

'Yes,' Murray agreed. 'I've worked with this management

before.' To me he said, 'Which is another advantage of good engineering. You can make things just as effective at half the cost.' Seeing that the actress was not yet ready to start discussing the play, he made a visible effort to enable our conversation to continue. 'Are you interested in the theatre, apart from Miss Cree?'

'Yes. But it seems I know very little about plays.'

'It's not necessary to know much about plays if you don't have to write them.'

'I did try to write a book, once.'

'One book, or you tried only once?'

His irritated precision was amusing. 'One book. And I tried *many* times.'

'But you've stopped trying now?'

'Completely,' I assured him.

'Good. There are too many books as it is.'

I smiled. 'But not too many plays?'

He shrugged. 'Too many of them as well. And I wouldn't be adding to the number if they didn't pay me in advance for doing it. What do they pay you to do?'

'I'm about to start as an engineering surveyor.'

'Have you lived in London a long time?'

'No, but I intend to. And somewhere quieter than this. Barbara and I are getting married in December and we plan to move out a bit.'

'I see.' It seemed to worry him and he was not a man to let politeness stand in the way of his peace of mind. 'Is Miss Cree pregnant?'

I gasped. 'No! No, *I'm* the one who wants to get married.'

He smiled and nodded. 'I ask because we hope to put this play on in the spring. A gravid leading-lady would bitch things up considerably.'

I couldn't help laughing at him. 'I imagine so!'

Barbara surfaced. 'Mr Murray, this is excellent.'

'Thank you,' he said. 'Now, I'll be happy to answer any questions you have about it.'

She had a lot of questions. While they became immersed in the possibilities and intentions I made coffee, then served it, then drank it, then listened. Before long I was lost by the technicalities and instead considered Murray himself. It seemed to me that, as he'd implied, he would be happier doing something else. Happier, but not better at it. Probably there was nothing he could do nearly as well as write plays. And thus trapped in his own fairly rare ability he grew resentful; and took it out on other people. My attention shifted to Barbara who harboured no resentment at all. As she leaned across the low table, talking or listening, her face was animated with childlike enthusiasm and her eyes shone with unguarded candour.

There is no doubt that it was this meeting which established the very productive relationship they were to enjoy. Soon, too, I began to value the acerbic civility of the reluctant playwright. And he proved enormously helpful to me. But our value to him was, essentially, that Barbara was exactly the right actress and person – in that order – to make all Mr Murray's geraniums burst into flower.

My first stop in Copenhagen was at the Jensens' flat. There I was given the news that the *Niome* saga was already well advanced into its next canto. The dependants of those lost on the vessel had, very shrewdly, realised that their best chance of success against the owner was to engage Aage Jensen in their alliance and have the matter pursued in the Danish courts. These, though not more efficient than the English courts, were certainly quicker. And the vessel had been lost in Danish waters. Jensen had agreed to be the prime mover on behalf of his wife who had lost her father in the disaster. Whereas she was not exactly a dependant she was her father's next of kin and heir.

'So,' Jensen said, twining his long fingers together, 'we want to know if you would be willing to give evidence.'

'It is not really for me,' his wife, Irene, added. 'But my father was the captain and a Dane and his case is likely to have most weight on behalf of the others.'

They could see I was not anxious to face further involvement in the interminable affair.

Jensen's wary eyes searched my face. 'Of course we can try
to leave you out but the defence will certainly bring in Sandys.
In fact they have already brought him in.'

'From Africa?'

'No. From Spain.'

And it was now I learned that Clifford's tale of a job in Africa
was just a blind. He'd gone to ground in Spain and opened a
bank account ready to receive his share of the insurance.

Jensen said, 'They must work closely with him to prepare
their side of it. As we should work closely with you.'

I sighed. 'Yes, yes, I can see that.' And there seemed to be
no alternative. 'All right. Count me in.'

The girlish Fru Jensen came quickly towards me, 'Thank you,
Bill.' She kissed me on the cheek. 'And while you are in the city
you must always be sure that you can come here whenever you
please.'

Her husband said, 'With your help there is little doubt that
we shall win.' He went into the hall to telephone whoever was
waiting to hear that he'd managed to convince me, and Irene
went back to the kitchen. Left alone I went to the window and
stared down the long sloping avenue of spiky lindens to the
centre of the city. Although it was still quite early in the afternoon
some lights had been switched on. The roads seemed very
black: in overdrawn contrast to the wide margins of snow
through which they ran. I craned my head a little to see the
thermometer set outside in the corner of the window embrasure.
The temperature was just below freezing and I was reminded
that it was almost a year since I'd last been there on Fredericksberg Alle. The snow seemed to be the same snow and I was
back where I began.

Although committed to this new goal I was far from convinced
of its worth. I turned to the room again and my glance took in
the photograph of Captain Meisling. He and the others who had
perished were beyond trouble and suspicion. They had stirred
little interest while they lived and nothing new would be discovered about them now they were dead. It was narrowly the
circumstances of their death which roused the endless activity;
the law, the greed, the enterprise and the revenge. Caught in

the middle were the survivors, the natural prey of anyone who could use them; for good or ill.

For a week all my activities at Norske Veritas were supervised by an officious young man who dutifully called me 'Chief' but obviously wondered why the company wanted to give coveted positions to foreigners. It was his job to guide me through all the formalities of the paper-work and to introduce me to the appropriate managers of the society's clients where 'new-building' was in progress. One of these was at an engineering works on the island of Funen, and this was to be my particular project.

Oddly, as soon as I was let out on my own I had the rather fanciful impression that I was being followed. The journey to Odense was accomplished by rail, then rail-ferry, then rail again. It took over three hours. On the first stage of the journey from the capital to the ferry port of Korsor I twice had the baffling experience of just failing to see somebody when I suddenly turned round; going to and coming back from the buffet car. Later, in Odense, the conviction that I was being shadowed grew more pronounced. It was difficult to identify any particular person because everyone was muffled up against the icy wind. But I did form the opinion that it must be my officious 'minder' from the head-office. It was ludicrous, but possible, that on instruction from our superiors or just off his own bat, he wanted to monitor my progress. The more I thought about his distrust and barely concealed disapproval of me the likelier it seemed. The only alternative was that somebody wanted to serve me with the Danish equivalent of a subpoena.

By the time I'd completed my survey of the diesel cylinder blocks and checked the various documents offered by the foundry of manufacture it was early evening and already quite dark. As I crunched over the packed snow in the small park which fronts the railway station it was difficult not to listen for footsteps keeping pace with mine. There were no such tell-tale signs and when I looked round there were only the receding shapes of people continuing in the other direction and merging into the dim grey background.

When the train reached Nyborg and rumbled smoothly into
the hold of the Storebaelt ferry I got out of the overheated
compartment and climbed the narrow metal stairway to the
upper deck, and the restaurant. I was very hungry. A few people
remained in their places on the train to eat sandwiches and drink
coffee from Thermos flasks, while others tried to doze as the
ferry ploughed on through the fourteen miles of open water
which separates Funen from Zealand.

The restaurant, which was warm and bright and crowded, put
the whole idea of a mysterious watcher out of my mind. By the
time I'd eaten a good meal my whole attitude to life had markedly
improved. I went out on deck to derive the full benefit of the
schnapps with which I'd finished off. The night air was sharp
but curiously still. I climbed up to a more secluded deck
where it was possible to get an uninterrupted view over the
stern and the broad white wake streaming away from us.
The area was lit by small lamps on stanchions widely spaced
around the guard rail. I'd been there only a few minutes when I
heard the footsteps I'd stopped expecting. I was leaning over
the rail and half turned to look behind me. The man walked
straight towards me and stopped only a few paces away. It
was Clifford.

The first idiotic thought which occurred to me was that he
was going to try and push me overboard. I turned fully round
so that my back was pressed against the top rail and my arms
hooked under it. In the uncertain light which illuminated only
one side of his face I saw him smile at the action.

'It won't come to that, Bill,' he said.

'It certainly won't,' I told him. 'Was it you who followed me
on the way over?'

He nodded. 'Sure.'

'Why?'

'I wanted to know what you were up to.' He pulled the zip of
his padded jerkin higher. 'But it seems you've got a job.'

'Yes. I'm working for Norske Veritas.'

'Very nice. Through your friend Jensen, I suppose.' He moved
to a position alongside me so that he leaned looking over the
stern while I held my stance facing in the other direction. 'Tell

me, what's he doing all this for? Why does he have to bother? And why are you into it again?'

'Why did *you* do what you did?'

'I was fed up with the sea.'

This seemed to me rather less than an adequate explanation so I tried him on what had been, for him, the more positive aspect. 'How much did you expect to get for it?

'One and a half million,' he said gravely.

'But what about Dolby?' I challenged him.

'Huh!' Clifford grunted dismissively. 'Dolby!'

'Didn't he help?'

'He helped to keep himself in a job, and earned promotion. That was all.'

'And you did it just for the money?'

'I hope you've got nothing against money, Bill, because I was going to offer you some.'

'*You* want to give me money!'

He hunched his shoulders. 'Well, not me personally, no.'

'The people who are paying you would like to offer me money.'

'On certain conditions, of course.'

'I'm not interested,' I said and started to move away. He grabbed my arm and pulled me back against the rail. 'Bill! How do you know, until you know how much it is?'

'I don't care how much it is.'

We were approaching Korsor and close enough to see individual lights around the harbour through a screen of fine snow which had started to fall. Since there was no wind the snow hung in the air, apparently motionless until you moved against it, and felt like wet cobwebs. The ferry reduced power as an identical boat passed us, heading outward, looking incongruously festive as it shovelled a path through the black water.

'How's Barbara?' Clifford asked, turning to slap his arms against his sides.

'Fine. We're getting married in a few weeks.'

He laughed and when he spoke his voice had assumed a new and buoyant tone. 'Oh? Are you? That might make a difference.'

'To what?

'To how much help you'd want to give Jensen and his wife.'

'Being married won't make any difference to that.'

He chuckled. 'No, Bill. You're missing the point.' He hitched his elbow onto the top rail and faced me. 'I'm suggesting you might have to choose between getting married and helping Jensen.'

I was still puzzled. 'Jensen is not going to interfere with my wedding.'

'Oh, no! *I* am.'

Quite loudly now over the narrowing gap of water we could hear the sound of the harbour; the garbled voice on the tannoy and the clanking locomotive getting into position to pull our train on the final stage to Copenhagen. What Clifford had in mind was very clear and I began to feel that slightly sick, defeated feeling again. 'How could you do that?' I asked, already knowing how.

'By coming back, Bill. By coming back to London. Coming back to Barbara.' His confidence advanced from the buoyant to the quietly exultant. 'She does miss me, doesn't she?'

Tempting me with money lost savour compared with the weapon I'd handed to him. I tried to sound indifferent. 'I don't think so. She can't miss you very much if she wants to marry *me*.'

He slapped his gloved hand against the stanchion, shaking the pattern of light which fell between us and sending a vibration through the rail at my back. 'Do you think for a minute she would have agreed to marry you if *I'd* still been there?'

The answer was 'No' but I didn't say it. I didn't have to say it. Instead, I murmured, 'Do as you please. It makes no difference to me.'

'It will when you think about it, Bill.' He started to move away. 'Think about it.' Moving swiftly towards the companionway he called over his shoulder. 'I'll know from the list of witnesses. They've got to tell us that.'

Feeling rather dazed, I followed him down and took my place in the train compartment which now seemed unbearably stuffy.

The more I thought about it during the next few days the more convinced I became that I should tell the Jensens that I'd changed my mind. Quite apart from the personal considerations, my initial reluctance to become involved again resurfaced as entirely reasonable. Irene Jensen had told me that the action wasn't being pursued for her sake but for the sake of the others. I didn't know the others. And even in Danish courts the case could drag on for another year, or more. Increasingly, I took a jaundiced view of what would be accomplished even if the Jensens were successful. Nobody would be punished for what they'd done. The only justice which was available was money. The owner's company could be forced to pay compensation to five families. The company could afford to do that – and probably had yet another insurance arrangement to cover just such an eventuality.

The puzzling facet was what Clifford would gain if I refused to volunteer my testimony. It was difficult to imagine that he acted out of unshaken loyalty to his paymasters. Much more likely, he'd foreseen that things might go wrong and, in the original deal, had negotiated an indemnity for himself. He was a meticulous planner, I knew. Perhaps he was being paid to maintain silence about his own part in the affair with a bonus if he managed to frustrate the legal consequences. Whatever it was, he must have been confident because he made no further effort in Copenhagen to follow or contact me.

I'd almost made up my mind to withdraw my offer of help to the dependants when it occurred to me that it might ease my conscience or strengthen my resolve if I knew where Barbara stood with regard to the threat Clifford had posed. I wrote to her but my letter contained less honesty than she deserved. Essentially it stated that I'd met Clifford and that he'd mentioned the possibility of his returning to London. Getting a little nearer the fact if not the truth I also mentioned that Clifford wanted to know how she thought about him.

While I was awaiting a reply to that letter I visited the Jensens to prepare the ground for my imminent change of heart. It was a wasted visit. The papers with my name prominent as witness had already been lodged. They'd done that as soon as I'd given my consent in the first place.

'What's wrong, Bill?' Jensen asked.

'I . . . I was wondering if these papers . . . Does your lawyer give a copy of the papers to the other side? The defendants?'

'Oh, yes! And they give us a list of their experts and witnesses.'

'I see.' A feeling of great weariness crept upon me. 'So? What happens now?'

'We each consider the position and a date is set for the hearing to begin.'

I groaned. 'Another hearing.'

'In Danish,' Jensen added with a mischievous intent which failed to amuse me. 'And there will be no ballroom or bar. No dancing or drinking at all.'

I said nothing and he interpreted my sudden loss of vitality to some uncertainty about my new job. My assurance that everything was going splendidly there and that I really enjoyed the work did not wholly convince him. But it was true. As I got used to the system I began to appreciate the excellence of the service which has given Norske Veritas such a fine reputation. I had only another week to go before taking up the secure position in London.

'I'll be sorry to leave Denmark,' I told him.

'Ah! But you will soon be back.'

'Really? Why is that?'

'For the court, I mean.'

'Yes,' I sighed. 'Yes, of course.'

Not until the day before I was due to leave did I receive a reply from Barbara. It was no more than a note saying she was looking forward to my return and adding that she had also had a letter from Clifford. My immediate thought was that I should phone her but the argument against that was the same argument which persuaded me to write in the first place. I wanted to avoid giving the opportunity for one of her sudden, on the spur of the moment, reactions. To me it was a very delicate situation which had to be negotiated. Whether mistakenly or not it seemed to me I had too much running against me to make a rash move – or even to appear worried about developments.

TWELVE

When I got back to the flat in London I made the mistake of telling Barbara everything. She did not take it well. It was difficult to judge which annoyed her more – that I should believe she would be putty in Clifford's hands, or that I was prepared to go back on my promise to Jensen. Nor did she find it particularly flattering to be considered merely as a stake in a male game of dares. She declared, 'I refuse to be a bribe.'

'But he didn't know that.'

'Obviously!' she retorted, bristling rather. 'But you should have known.'

'I couldn't be sure. You did tell me he was a marvellous lover.'

'So he was. And *was* is what he's going to stay.'

Thus, all my preparations for long and delicate negotiations were put to rout. Barbara sliced right to the bone. I'd begun as soon as I got back to the flat. Clifford, I learned, had beaten me to it by three or four days – and that should have warned me he was driven by more than a cash bonus. His more pressing need was revenge and, though he waited a good while for the perfect moment to spring it, the means had already been chosen and the groundwork was being laid even while I sought reassurance from Barbara that all was well. 'You didn't let him stay here, did you?'

'Sleep here, you mean? Certainly not. But he practically camped on the doorstep. And he came in a few times. Hoping I'd weaken, I suppose.'

'What did he say?'

She shrugged. 'That the job in Africa hadn't worked out. That he didn't know what to do but thought he might get something permanent in London.' She gave a hoot of laughter. 'Huh, permanent! Now that I have other plans he was going to do what I always wanted.' She pulled her slip off over her head and the shoulder straps looped and caught in her long hair. She tossed her head and shook the garment free. 'I told him he should have thought of that before.'

'Did you tell him we were going to get married?'

'Of course.'

'What did he say?'

'He didn't say anything. He laughed.'

I stretched my legs under the sheet and curled my toes. Clifford's laughter was something which made me uneasy – even reportedly. 'He's very confident,' I said.

She dragged back the bedclothes and more or less dropped full-length beside me. 'If you'd mentioned that when you wrote, I would have believed you.'

All the evidence of the tribunal had done nothing to shake her trust in Clifford's innocence on that score. Nor would she budge from that belief. However, Clifford boasting about the power of his balls was another matter. As soon as I gave her even the gist of the encounter on the Storebaelt ferry she was convinced. And, of course, by the time I told her she'd already had a visit from the man himself, apparently reeking of potency and very confident of using it; immediately, if necessary.

I eased my forearm under her waist. 'So – you sent him away and he won't be back.'

'He won't be back *here*,' she promised, coiling against me.

The playwright Murray had managed to get the flat in our block which Barbara told him about. He had just moved in when I got back from Denmark. I went upstairs to see if I could help and found that, naturally, he had his own system for settling down in a new home. He just left everything packed until he actually needed it. Since these were furnished flats, and fully equipped, it was not exactly a spartan decision, but it did strike me as notably strong-minded. 'I've moved around quite a bit,' he told me, 'and I assure you, the *necessity* method is the least wearing way to cope.'

I smiled. 'Yes. But it must take a long time before you finally get everything out.'

'Rarely do I get *every*thing out,' he told me. 'But what's still packed after three months is obviously unnecessary – so I just dump it.' He opened a cupboard which was piled high with large cardboard boxes. 'This stuff, for instance, is probably expendable.'

'Why do you move around so much?'

He gave me a brief, sharp look as he closed the cupboard and said, 'I have many things to do, in different places.'

'In theatres, you mean?'

'No. Nothing to do with theatres.'

This was puzzling but I let it go. 'How long do you plan to stay in London?'

'Until I get tired of the neighbours.'

I laughed and he smiled. No doubt he was pleased that he'd found someone to whom he could give an honest reply without also giving offence as a by-product. 'I expect they get tired of you, too.'

'No doubt. But they're usually more tolerant. So I get tired of them *first*.'

'Where did you come from originally?'

'Durham.' He indicated a chair, inviting me to sit down while he remained standing in the centre of the room.

'Oh, really! Barbara comes from up that way.'

'So I imagine. The accent shows through when she's angry.'

'And what did you do before you started writing?'

'Why do you want to know?'

It was annoying, yet a pertinent response. Why should he tell me anything if I did not have a reason for asking? But I had a reason. It was to find out if his experience might be of use to me. Carefully, I explained, 'I'd like to know if you had to make a complete break or if you just eased into writing in an academic way.'

'Huh!' he snorted contemptuously, reaching for a cigarette. 'It's impossible to *ease* into the theatre. And though there are a few academics who write successful fiction – there are no academics who write successful plays.'

'Oh! I didn't know that.'

He nodded as he thumbed his lighter. 'It's a much overlooked fact.'

'Have you any idea why?'

'I know *exactly* why. Simply, that it's much harder to bluff people in public than it is in private. And the reader is never asked to applaud.'

'So – you weren't a teacher.'

He sighed. 'Oh, dear! Do I look like a teacher?'

'No. But often you sound like one.' What he looked like was a rather weary fencing master in whom the practice of effective posture and elegant line were so inbred as to look natural.

'No. I was a miner.' He picked up an ashtray and placed it ready in the palm of his other hand. 'And in my case there was no *Miss Moffat* to push me into the light.'

This puzzled me for a moment, then I thought I saw the connection. 'Yes, you'd be a long way from nursery rhymes in a pit.'

He gave me an odd, bewildered look then burst out laughing in that loud, uninhibited way which had surprised me before. On this occasion, though, there seemed little justification for it. Fearing that I'd made a mistake I took some interest in his books. There were very few of them but I got up and looked at those there were. Besides two large dictionaries – one very old and one very new – there were two equally heavy volumes on contract law, a compendium of theatre stage-plans and a copy of *The Playwright at Work* by John van Druten. Having noted these titles, I remarked, 'I'd have thought you'd unpack the rest of your books as a priority.'

'Those are all the books I have,' he said.

I was astonished. 'What!'

'I'm not a *researcher*,' he severely informed me.

Baulked of that pleasant subject of conversation I returned to the question which had continued to nag at my attention. 'Apart from the theatre, do you do other work?' I hurried on to establish that this was a supplementary enquiry, already cleared for discussion. 'When you say you have things to do in different places . . . which obliges you to move about . . .'

'No. Not work. People. You see, I am much more concerned with people than plays.' He must have noticed that this came as a surprise to me for he smiled and nodded as though to insist upon it. 'Yes. And the people do not all live in the same place. And usually they are not as free to move as I am.' Having covered the minimum explanation, he stopped.

'I see.'

But I did not see. However, the occasion of this brief courtesy call did not seem a good time to pursue the matter. Nor did I make much progress in subsequent conversations with him. There was no easy way to get back to the subject. He was equally reticent about the reasons for his occasional absences from the flat. Sometimes it was only a few days, sometimes more than a week. He never explained why and so it was a long time before I could appreciate the real worth of Howard Murray.

The wedding was in the King's Road registry office with a reception at the hotel in Sloane Square. It was an event remarkably free of the suppressed rivalry, embarrassment or unease which usually attend weddings. The bride's family was non-existent. On the other hand, the bride's friends gave some of their best performances which projected well beyond the reception room. Howard Murray – resolutely eating nothing but drinking a lot – said, 'Probably you'll get a bill from Equity claiming for the use of their own clothes as costumes.' My side was strongly represented by my parents – Barbara whispered, 'At last, a photograph *together*' – and assorted relations but very few friends. Clearly it was thought by the Sussex set that young Thompson had gone out of his way to slight them by marrying an actress. The few of them who'd actually met her on our joint social calls had to admit that she was an amusing woman but, they told each other, that was scarcely a good excuse for marriage. Or a durable asset to their community. And since we'd made it plain that we had no intention of joining their community the lack of future threat allowed them to discover a large variety of pressing engagements which kept them away from London on the day.

Two people who did accept the invitation had been invited only after a great deal of thought; weighing rudeness against the past. I did not know how Sam Hanson and Hugh Gillespie would react to each other. When I explained my trepidation to Barbara I had to explain, also, that Hugh had spent years trying to reclaim the person he was in his youth by finding the person who'd shared it with him. That person was Sam Hanson. But when I found him in Montreal he was not at all the man Hugh remembered. He'd long before that burned all his bridges into the past and so I kept my discovery of him secret. Barbara approved of my good intention but thought it rather high-handed. 'Darling, protecting people from their illusions just allows them to think the illusions are real.'

'Yes. And in my opinion that's what Hugh needed at the time. God knows, it's what *I* needed at the time.'

She nodded briskly. 'Well, I think that time is safely past for both of you.'

So, Hugh and Sam were invited. And, in the event, I need not have worried. To my relief, the former bosom pals treated each other like polite strangers. Hugh's wife Moira remarked that the last time they'd seen Sam was at their own wedding. When I expressed surprise to Hugh that my long sustained subterfuge mattered so little he said, 'It's like you once told me, Bill – if ye wait long enough, nothing matters.'

Certainly Mrs Schuster's question did not seem to matter as I refilled her glass. She asked, 'Did you get that call from Glasgow?'

'Which call? When?'

'Oh, that's quite enough, thank you,' she protested when the wine reached the regulation level below the rim. 'It was some weeks ago. We told them you were in Copenhagen and gave them the Norske Veritas number.'

'Who, Mrs Schuster? Gave who?'

'I don't know. They didn't say.' She took a sip. 'It can't have been very important or you would have heard about it.'

But it was important. And I was to hear about it before very long.

At Christmas, Barbara and I went up to Scotland. I'd told her about Isa Mulvenny and she insisted on joining me for the party at the nursing home. Perhaps she detected the strength of affection I held for my former landlady and even through the bare outline of the circumstances I'd reported she felt a strong sense of empathy. Barbara – as I have continued to learn – had a great instinct for locating the *real* hinges on which peoples' lives depend and turn. They got on perfectly from the first instant. Isa was much as I'd seen her the previous year, though her speech was a little more slurred and the tremor in her fingers more pronounced. She was quite plainly delighted that I was married at last and kept glancing between Barbara's face and mine, smiling in a very knowing way. She asked where we'd spent our honeymoon and I said we'd come to spend it with her. Isa laughed and patted her lap approvingly. She insisted that we wheel her round the ward to meet everybody. It was as though she wanted it known that, contrary to their belief, her family was not dwindling but increasing. And at last she did have a sort of daughter-in-law who was beautifully dressed; and talked posh; and came to see her!

But Barbara was willing to do more than be charming and endlessly patient with the rambling stories of the old people there. She was prepared to *entertain*. And Matron was delighted to allow her. After lunch a space was cleared at one end of the large room and the piano uncovered. She was not a good pianist but she knew several old favourites by heart and started with a warm-up general sing-song. Then, leaning against the piano she recited in her warm compelling voice many familiar stirring pieces. I glanced round the attentive listening faces and saw several people moving their lips in sequence with the words she was speaking. It was when she embarked on some comic material and joined in the laughter she was provoking that I was shaken to realise how much she resembled a younger Isa Mulvenny. Her height and her hair were part of it, but more significant was the angle and the vulnerable expression as she turned her head with a broad smile just starting to fade. Long ago I'd seen Isa standing at a piano doing exactly that.

Having got her audience tuned in, Barbara started to

accompany herself through some fairly bawdy material. And they lapped it up. In particular she delivered a version of the old Scottish ballad 'Maggie Lauder' which left nothing to chance. The young nurses standing around the walls of the room were embarrassed but the old people laughed so much they threatened to topple themselves out of their chairs. When the hubbub and applause for that had died down it was request time. The first few titles called out were songs they'd already sung and forgotten. But I thought of another one and shouted to her, 'Can you sing "The Rose of Tralee"?' And she could. And she did. Beautifully. Like everyone in the audience I loved her for it and for the happiness of the whole day. I looked along the row of smiling faces to my old landlady. She was not merely mouthing the words, she was joining in and, however faintly, singing her own unforgettable favourite song. The unequal but sweet duet of Barbara's voice and hers brought tears to my eyes but I wouldn't have missed the occasion for the world. In spite of the callous disregard of her husband and her son, for whom she'd given everything, Isa Mulvenny was happy.

In the New Year I went back to work at the London bureau of Norske Veritas and found it very congenial indeed. The other staff members were pleasant and helpful and the organisation ran with effortless efficiency. There was plenty to keep my mind occupied. The trend towards more and more engine room automation set problems of safety and control which could be tackled only with the aid of computer simulation. This aspect of the job fascinated me.

My sense of well-being was increased towards the end of February. I received a letter from Aage Jensen informing me that, after a great deal of intricate manoeuvring, the dependants of those killed in the loss of the *Niome* agreed to settle out of court. I didn't know how much each family settled for, nor did I enquire. It was enough for me that I would be spared the necessity of attending a trial in Copenhagen. However, the settlement had the further effect of enabling the Department of Trade inquiry to resume its long suspended deliberations. I think it was news of that which brought into action the seventh and

final wave which was to sweep out from that now celebrated
explosion in the Baltic. And riding on that was a surface ripple
which left me floundering.

In March Barbara started rehearsals for Howard Murray's new
play. With special dispensation from Murray and the director, I
was allowed to attend the first reading. To my surprise, it was
held in the large upper room of a pub in Bayswater Road.
Apparently, it is only rarely that plays are rehearsed in theatres.
Necessity demands a wide expanse of cheap bare floor-space,
near a tube station, and a source of food, where heating is not
an extra cost. This last requirement is why upper rooms are
favoured. The heat, which somebody else is paying for, rises.
Even so, everyone kept their coats on and kept rewinding
scarves around their necks as they settled in the semi-circle of
chairs to read. Murray and the director were together facing
them and I was tucked into a corner by the piano with the
composer. The play was a small-scale musical with book and
lyrics by the playwright. It was intended to stage it first at
the Hampstead Theatre Club which had recently taken on the
valuable role as a 'try-out' venue for West End productions. In
that way the producer could find out if it was likely to make
money before he spent very much.
    On the strength of that first reading I would have advised the
producer to quit while he was ahead. It seemed to me a complete
shambles. Everybody was nervous and I couldn't hear a word
the actors were saying. From time to time the composer played
snatches of music but, clearly, was ignored by everyone. I
glanced at Murray. He sat with the script adamantly closed on
his lap, smoking one cigarette after another and staring at the
ceiling.
    In the taxi on the way back I asked how he thought it had
gone.
    'Same as always,' he murmured. 'Absolutely bloody.'
    'Surely they're not always as bad as that!'
    He nodded and sighed as he watched the sleet build up under
the taxi's windscreen wipers. 'Sometimes worse. Today nobody
wet themselves, wept or fainted.'

'Faint! Why do they faint?'

'From hunger, they *claim*.'

He then went on in a flat bleak voice to give me the play-wright's view of the first read-through ritual. 'It never varies. First, there is the obligatory *tête-à-tête* with the director while everyone is still coughing. He explains – sometimes in passionate detail – why the cast he has assembled is the best cast we could possibly engage.' Murray gave me a sidelong glance. 'He does this because he knows that there will be abundant evidence to the contrary once they start reading the play.'

I nodded. 'They didn't read very well, did they?'

Murray allowed himself a wintry little smile. 'Never do. It is not, of course, that bad readers are going to be bad actors. In fact many *good* readers are bad actors.'

I chuckled at this comprehensive exclusion of merit.

'The astonishing thing is, that although each of them came in clutching a much-handled copy of the play, they always give the impression that they've never seen this particular script before in their lives.'

'Yes!' I recalled. 'That was the impression.'

'It also surprises them that the pages are numbered consecutively . . .' he paused in an effort to make the system clearer, '. . . from the front towards the back.'

I laughed outright. From my brief observation of the event, this waspish comment was well-founded.

'Of course,' Murray concluded, 'there was an extra hazard at today's wake. With a musical, one has to have a composer.'

'Yes. But nobody sang.'

'God forbid,' the playwright intoned, 'that anyone should *sing* at the first rehearsal.'

Our attention was diverted by a series of slight jolts as the taxi jockeyed for position with other traffic skidding round Hyde Park Corner. When we'd gained the comparative safety of Knightsbridge I said, 'You must be very disappointed.'

He turned to me and raised his eyebrows questioningly. 'Why?'

'Well, considering how they read.'

'Bill, there would be no point in *having* rehearsals if actors could give a performance the first time they get together. It will be perfectly fine. Eventually.'

'Do you really think so?'

'Of course.'

'Then why didn't you tell them that?' I'd noted that at the end of the read-through he had not said a word to any of the cast – even Barbara.

'Just making sure my reach always exceeds their grasp.' He smiled grimly. 'Else, what's a first night for?'

When we got down to Sloane Square he stopped the taxi and took me to lunch. And during the meal he did not utter another word about the play, or rehearsals, or the theatre. Instead, he pursued a remark I'd made the very first time we'd met. I was flattered that he remembered it, and told him all I knew about the crucial age of twenty-seven. But more surprising than his memory was an attribute rare in persons who are good talkers – he was an even better listener. Without really being aware of it I soon branched away from the subject and started telling him about myself and how, for a long time, I'd rebelled against the pattern which had been set for me.

'But you've come to terms with it now,' he suggested.

'Yes. Now that I'm married and doing a job that I enjoy.'

'You're fortunate in both,' he said.

I smiled. 'Even though she's an actress?'

The playwright seemed pained to have the subject of theatre intrude upon the conversation. He made no response to the challenge. Instead, to my surprise, he asked, 'What happened to Mr Sandys?'

'Clifford Sandys?'

'Presumably.'

'How do you know about him?' I was aware that my voice was giving away more than I intended.

Murray affected not to notice my change of tone. 'The porter at the flats mentioned him.' He managed a strained little smile. 'And, apparently, the porter's wife thinks he'll be back.' He gave me a direct encouraging look through a drift of cigarette smoke. 'They both seem to have been much impressed by Mr Sandys.'

That was all the excuse I needed to lay bare the character,

actions and expectations of my former shipmate. And no doubt, under the playwright's expert prompting, I also revealed how much I'd come to fear Clifford's ability always to gain the upper hand. During this recital, Murray asked some odd, seemingly irrelevant, questions but there was no mistaking his deep interest in the whole affair.

THIRTEEN

Now that Barbara was rehearsing every day I was usually the first back to the flat and one evening as I turned the corner from the shortcut down Holbein Place I saw Tony Liddle waiting at the entrance.

'Hello, Bill. A thought it would be better tae see ye here than at yer office.'

'Yes,' I said, and my astonishment turned to concern over what he might want to see me *about*. 'Come on up.'

When I'd settled him with a drink he started coming to the point although it was some time before I saw it.

'It's about that wee job A did for ye in the city there.'

'What about it?'

'Ye remember ye phoned me efter that?' He paused but deduced that I could not remember and prompted me. 'Tae tell me ye were gonnae say the film was sent tae ye.'

'Oh, yes. That's right. And that's what we *did* say.'

'So A believe.' He took a gulp of his drink. 'Ye'll mind it was nae me ye spoke tae first.'

'No. Another man answered the phone.'

'Dougie. Douglas Tyrrel is his name.' Tony swallowed and his eyes wavered away from me. Now, apparently, he was coming to the hard part. 'He's a . . . he *was* a close friend o' mine.' He took a deep breath. 'At the time, anyway, we were pretty close and he was . . .'

'Jealous?' I asked.

Tony nodded, glad that I had taken responsibility for saying the word for it. 'So A had tae tell Dougie what ye were really phonin' aboot.'

'Surely he believed you?'

'Aye! Oh, aye. And later on A told him other things aboot who you were and yer father's business, and that.'

'I see.'

He looked anxiously up at me as I rose to pour myself a drink. 'Well, there's nothin' wrang in that, is there?' I hadn't been going to bother drinking until Barbara got in but as the conversation progressed there seemed to be a pressing need for it. I topped up Tony's glass as well.

'All that was more than six months ago,' I reminded him.

'So it was. But it didnae finish there.'

I sank back in my chair and sighed. 'No. I'm sure it didn't.'

'Ye see Dougie and me fell oot. An' he wanted tae . . . getback at me, y 'know.' I didn't know and shook my head. Tony ignored my ignorance. 'An' since you seemed tae be a friend o' mine you were the wan he picked on. Of course, he thought there might be money in it as well.'

'But why pick on me?'

Tony lowered his eyes. 'Well, A did sorta hint aboot you. Jokin'.'

A light began to beam on his tangled recital. 'So – it was he who called my father's office – when I was in Denmark?'

'No. That was me. A wanted tae warn ye.'

'About what? What was he going to do?'

Tony twisted uncomfortably in his chair, 'At the time A'd no idea what he wis gonnae dae. A jist wanted tae warn ye that he'd be waitin' for ye when ye got back.'

'But he wasn't.'

Tony nodded in contradiction. 'Oh, aye. He was waitin' all right. But it wisnae you he saw. There was somebody else hangin' about as well.'

I closed my eyes and banged my head back on the cushion. Suddenly I just did not want to hear any more; about Tony, or his jealous lover, or Clifford, or how I was involved, or the next crisis to be combatted. I felt a fierce sense of injustice. Surely, now that everything was going so well, Clifford could not still win! Tony watched me anxiously, trying to gauge the moment when he could continue with whatever it was – and too late – he'd come to say. Fortunately for both of us Barbara arrived and though she was exhausted I immediately gained strength from her.

Tony took her arrival as a signal to leave. He'd found it difficult enough with me even to hint about his relationship with Dougie. He baulked at the prospect of revealing it to my wife. Barbara was quite prepared to let him go. But she saw my anxiety and joined me in persuading him to stay. With very little explanation she took in the whole situation and fastened on the salient question. She too recalled how Clifford had laid siege to the flat in my absence.

She applied directly to Tony. 'What's happened that made you come here now?'

'Yesterday the polis were at me.'

'In Glasgow?' I asked.

He nodded. 'They were askin' aboot the job, ye know. As well as that there was a phone call fae Dougie. He said he'd made a deal wi' an English fella.'

'Clifford,' I informed Barbara.

'What did he want you to do?' she demanded.

'Give masel' up for it. Tell the London polis here aboot the whole thing. Especially that it was Bill's idea.'

'And?' I knew there was more than that. 'How much was Clifford offering?'

'No' enough,' Tony said. 'That's how I'm here tellin' you.'

'And what do you want Bill to do?'

'Well, he's got nae form, y'see. But if they got me for it A'd be out o' business for too long. A've got ma business tae consider.'

'You want Bill to say he did it on his own.'

'Aw, wi' advice fae me, maybe, but nae mair than that.'

In spite of herself, Barbara seemed amused. 'What business are you in, Mr Liddle?'

'A run a coupla discos.'

'With gambling on the side,' I added.

He didn't deny it and, now that he was on the unembarrassing subject of crime, appeared quite complacent as he glanced between us – waiting for a decision.

Barbara thought for a moment then turned to me accusingly, 'Is it true that you haven't got *any* form?'

Tony chuckled, glad to be dealing with such a level-headed woman.

I was much less sanguine. 'They'd never believe it.'

My accomplice dismissed such a petty objection. 'Of course they'll no' believe it! The thing is they cannae prove otherwise.'

Barbara ended the rival claims. 'If they could prove anything, Clifford wouldn't be offering money for a confession.'

That seemed a reasonable deduction so we decided to wait and see what happened.

And what happened was that I lost my job. Just how it was engineered never became clear. Perhaps Dougie was persuaded to tell the police what he knew and Clifford no doubt added the damaging questions which had come up at the inquiry. Tony had form, and the job in the Minories fitted the pattern. When all that had been established, and the suspended inquiry was once more in session, Norske Veritas was informed. With their own reputation and the susceptibilities of their owner clients to be considered they had no alternative but to let me go.

If nothing else I had to admire Clifford's timing. He had gone through all the fruitful options with a strict awareness of priorities. Depriving me of my job and ensuring that I'd be considered untrustworthy by any other employer was, as far as I could see, his last throw.

'So now you're both in the same boat,' Barbara remarked with unintentional irony.

'Yes. In a lifeboat again, but this time there's very little possibility of rescue.'

'Something's sure to turn up,' she said. 'Meanwhile, you can concentrate on my opening night.'

'I'll think of little else, I promise. But there's nothing I can do.'

'Talk to Howard. He must be worried sick.'

'Nonsense. He's perfectly composed. And offensively confident.'

'About the script, yes. But talk to him about how well we're going to *do* it. Actors are his Achilles heel.'

This seemed to me a ridiculous contention, though fairly amusing. To Howard it was neither. When I went upstairs to see him he agreed with Barbara. 'Yes. One always imagines that with the best will in the world they will somehow go berserk when they get their hands on the reins. Once they're out there on the stage nobody can touch them, or stop them, or change them.'

'But they'll say the words you wrote.'

He threw up his hands despairingly. 'Oh! If saying the words were all!' He shook his head. 'No. It's not the words that matter. It's what actors *do* and feel – or seem to feel. It's actors living for the watchers that matters.'

I smiled. 'Barbara will live as fully as she possibly can.'

'Yes, Barbara certainly will. If I were wise I'd have kept her on from curtain-up to curtain-down.' He turned suddenly to me and in his unsettling, direct way said, 'And if *you* are wise you'll not try to change her.'

'What makes you think I'd want to change her?'

'Self-preservation,' he said grimly. 'Now that you've lost your sense of security, don't try to shake hers.'

'You mean because I've lost my job?'

'Yes. And you can't blame *that* on Clifford Sandys.'

'But I do! He is directly responsible.'

'Really?' It was impossible to believe his surprise was genuine. He waved me to a chair and poured me a drink. 'How was he able to do that?'

Of course I told him exactly how. There was something rather eerie about the way Murray was able to extract information. He now gave me the impression that he had a whole repertoire of well-tried ploys. And now, too, I was able to see some pattern in the occasional questions. They were posed not to clarify my feelings but to establish facts. Once or twice they even revealed facts I'd not been aware I knew.

After a couple of preview performances – to which the critics were not invited – the opening night of *Be Your Age* proved that, as Murray had predicted, everything was perfectly fine. Since the piece was, essentially, a vehicle for Barbara the main credit for the success went to her. And she deserved it. As the middle-aged anthropologist bent on saving some of London's new 'darling dodos' from extinction she crackled with vitality. In particular, her delivery of the main theme number got prolonged applause. I wished that Murray had broken his vow of abstinence to attend. As it was, though, his lines and lyrics were presence enough. A delighted audience watched Barbara lean against the piano to deliver the message with all the authority and style of a younger, thinner Sophie Tucker. She sang:

> For all unequal battles
> Of which history prattles
> The saddest, I opine
> Is fighting Time
>
> Be it Faust or that girl in Shangri-La
> There's always the devil to pay
> When you face yourself as you really are
> And you're facing Dorian Gray
>
> So, before some fanatic
> Stabs your portrait in the attic –
> Why not? –
> Let Time be your friend.
>
> Although a little mellow
> He's an understanding fellow
> If you fight him, what's to win?
> Losing pounds or a chin
> Lifting this, grafting that
> It's a grind shifting fat
> And think of the money you spend –
>
> Why not? –

And this time the audience joined in with her:

Let Time be your friend.

But the unexpected warmth of their response became, in Barbara's hands, an immediate part of the act. She advanced a few paces and addressed them in a very direct manner.

Don't stand still while he strolls on ahead
Standing still is a way to be dead

The people you're with back there are fooling
(And here we get to the core)
If all of you know damn well you're fooling
W$_{HO-ARE-YOU-DOING-IT-FOR}$?
Other dodos have learned
That you can't buck the trend
So – why not? –

And here everyone chorussed once more:

Let Time be your friend!

In the cramped dressing rooms afterwards, and in the papers the following morning, there was little doubt that *Be Your Age* would soon transfer from Hampstead to one of the smaller theatres in the West End.

While the publicity for *Be Your Age* increased, I tried hard to get another job. For a time both Barbara and I seemed to spend the day on interviews – I went out to seek them, she stayed in the flat to give them. Now and then a journalist would arrive at the street door while I was still at home. On those occasions I quickly went upstairs to spend the time with Howard Murray.

'Why don't they want to interview you?' I asked him.

'They *do*,' he assured me. 'But I always refuse. And my agent has instructions not to tell them where I may be found.'

'Perhaps Barbara will blurt it out.'

'They won't ask her about me.' He smiled complacently. 'Short of murder or a sex scandal – if you won't talk to journalists, you don't exist.'

And that did seem to be the case. In the various press and television interviews which arose from *Be Your Age*, the name of its author was never mentioned. Apparently that was how he wanted it. But then, suddenly, he changed his mind. He decided he would give an interview. And for some curious reason – which he chose not to explain – he wanted me to go with him to Manchester for the occasion.

'Why Manchester?'

'That is where the journalist lives. Please come with me, Bill. It'll only take a few hours all round.'

I shrugged. 'Okay. If you want. I'm doing nothing else. But I thought journalists were supposed to come to you.'

He smiled, 'They do when it's something *they* want. But this lady is a very special journalist.'

My assumption was that the interview had little to do with the theatre but was part of his 'other work'. I felt a slight tingle of excitement to be let in on it. As we flew up to Manchester he told me her name was Dorothy Castle and asked if that meant anything to me. It didn't. He also mentioned that she was a freelance journalist who worked as a part-time researcher for Granada television. 'And she's a militant feminist,' he added, 'so remember the manuscript.'

'What manuscript?'

'Abbreviated manuscript, "Ms".'

I had not flown to Manchester before, so the unfinished look of the airport surprised me. But the ceiling decorations of the main hall were impressive. 'The roof seems to be crowded with stalactites.'

Murray glanced overhead. 'They strike me,' he said, 'like an array of vast, used condoms.' And that really was more accurate.

Ms Castle probably held her post at Granada because she lived so near the studios in the Quays area, though on the Salford side of the river. She had a ground-floor flat in a small Victorian terrace. We heard her typewriter rattling away as Murray knocked on the door. To me he said, 'I'll introduce you as my agent.' No doubt he'd delayed telling me that until it was too late for me to argue.

Dorothy Castle was a short, very neat-looking woman in her

late twenties. She had intense brown eyes and moved her head in a jerky challenging fashion. Her dark hair was tied back in a very businesslike style. And she got down to business right away. My amazement grew as the playwright lied to her with perfect conviction. He told her he was born in Manchester and gave an address. She told him, 'All those houses were demolished years ago.'

Murray's face took on an expression of regret. 'Oh, really?'

He also told her that we were making a number of stops on our way north to fix up touring dates for the play; that his next play would have a strong feminist theme; that he'd admired several pieces she'd written and that he might be looking for a researcher to work on a television series which was being discussed. He turned to me, 'Of course that's still at an early stage, isn't it, Bill?'

I nodded and thought, whatever it is Murray wants from the meeting must be important to make him adopt this ingratiating pose so alien to his normal behaviour. But as the interview progressed I could detect no sign of the ulterior purpose. Apart from telling the journalist what she wanted to hear, he gave her several interesting opinions and a number of excellent quotes. When the playwright began to worry about his next appointment Ms Castle offered to make us some tea. He accepted and while we drank the tea from thick mugs, he idly questioned her about her own career. And now the young woman came into her own. It was my impression that she was dissatisfied with her life but attacked it with spirit. When Murray remarked on a photograph she told us it was of her son. 'That was taken a couple of years ago. He's ten now.'

Murray picked it up admiringly, 'And have you brought the boy up on your own?'

'Oh, yes!' she said grimly. 'Ever since his father deserted us.'

With sympathetic attention on the woman, Murray passed me the photograph. He asked her, 'How long ago was that?'

'When Dennis was about eighteen months old.'

'No doubt you were glad to get rid of the man.' He offered her a cigarette and lit it for her.

'I was at the time, but not now.' She inhaled deeply. 'If my

husband could be found I sure as hell wouldn't be playing around
with freelance stuff and part-time jobs. I could really get ahead
with my career.'

'Maybe he wouldn't be willing to allow that.'

'Allow!' She gave a grunt of scorn. 'Huh! He'd have no choice,
believe me.' She shook her head decisively. 'He'd have no choice
whatever.'

It was at this point that Murray decided he really must get on
to his fictional engagement. Ms Castle asked me if we wanted
to see the copy before publication. I gave the playwright a
questioning glance. 'No, no, no,' he said. 'I'm perfectly safe in
your hands. But I think Bill would like a copy of the published
piece for his records.'

'Of course,' she said. 'What's your address, Mr Thompson?'
I gave her my address and she promised she'd personally send
me the material.

As soon as we got out of the house I demanded to know what
the whole charade was for. But all he would say was, 'Insurance,'
and paraphrased, '"A smile as small as hers might be, Precisely
our necessity."'

Back in London, I resumed my search for work. Now that I was
married my idea was to find another engineering position in the
city. There were quite a number of good opportunities for
mechanical engineers but – not surprisingly – few for marine
engineers. My application to become a surveyor for Lloyds was
very rapidly turned down. No doubt the efficient grapevine
had already spread the news which Norske Veritas had acted
upon. But perhaps they were just waiting for the publication
of the Department of Trade report on the *Niome*. I became
increasingly depressed and Barbara began to worry about my
future. It was a hazard she hadn't bargained for and had little
resources to cope with. She could be wonderfully encouraging
of things she understood and of the people she worked with.
I was something of an alien. And an alien, moreover, who was
impervious to plain common sense. To her it was obvious that
if I was so anxious to have a job I should ask my father for
one.

I was adamant. 'No. I've spent my life fighting my way free of my father.'

'So that you could do what?'

'Be myself. Stand on my own feet.'

'And – how does it feel?' she drawled.

'Fine! It feels fine.'

'Good. Then you're not bothered about anything.'

'I'll find another job, don't worry.'

'My darling, I am *not* worrying. There must be other things you can do apart from working.'

'What, for example?'

'Writing. You said you once thought of writing. And look at the material you've got! A full-blown disaster at sea – all to yourself! Make use of it instead of moaning about the trouble it's brought you.'

'I am *not* moaning.'

'Sorry darling. It just seems to me you are not making best use of your time.' Then, to my great irritation, she moved away singing, '"Why not, let Time be your friend?"'

I threw a book at her. And she threw it right back. Also, a cushion. My wife was not a lady who bore anger or tantrums stoically. Her inclination was to join in so that we *both* got some benefit. But she also knew when to keep quiet or, rather, what to keep quiet about. There was never any mention now of our moving out to the quiet house in Richmond which she'd dreamed of long before her great success in Murray's play. What with an assured long run, recording contract and other lucrative offers, there was no problem about being able to afford the move. She could afford it. And that's what stopped her. What she could afford on her own she saw as posing a threat to me and feared it would undermine my confidence. Unfortunately, she was right. In retrospect I'd like to be able to say that it would not have mattered. But, even now, I know that it would have.

And the long stretch of unfilled time dragged on. Eventually I started to consider that I'd be better going back to sea for a while. There, after all, is where marine engineers belong. Of course, I did not tell Barbara of the plan. And it was just as well I didn't for no sooner had I started to make tentative advances in that direction than the inquiry report was published. To my amazement it contained censure of my actions. It was fairly oblique censure, to be sure, and dealt with a certain laxness they'd detected. They suggested that I had not been as diligent as could be hoped for in familiarising myself with the machinery over which I had complete supervision. They expressed regret that I had not pursued the matter of temperature gauge failures. And they noted that I had acted precipitately after the explosion.

On the overriding question of the ship being deliberately sunk, they were becomingly vague but gave 'weight and credence' to the idea that by some means unknown the ship was intentionally set at hazard. The certification inspectors were chided for not making more thorough inspections and the owner was rapped on the fingers for not maintaining updated machinery drawings. On my interpretation, they were saying that if somebody plants an immense bomb on a ship then the inspectors should spot it before it explodes. If they do not spot it, however, then the persons who planted the bomb should submit for approval a wiring diagram which shows how the device is going to be set off. The report concluded with a note that the owner had dropped his claim for insurance. No doubt this was intended as a condemnation but it read like approval for a public-spirited gesture.

Although the board had not deprived me of my chief's ticket they might as well have done. I was shocked, and my depression found new depths to explore. The only companies who would employ me at sea now were companies I wouldn't work for. As soon as he'd had time to read the report my father judged the moment ripe to offer me a berth in Leadenhall Street. And I accepted. There was nowhere else to go.

So it was that at thirty-eight I found myself bound to the desk which had been waiting for me since I was sixteen. But just the desk. The actual post which was to have been mine was filled by Sam Hanson. In effect, I became his assistant though in surface dealings we were treated as equals. At first I thought I'd never get over the humiliation of having to go into my father's business after all. But gradually I realised that whatever it was that I'd fought against didn't fight back. I could still remember my former attitude and determination and plans to succeed on my own terms, but memory isn't feeling. I couldn't feel it. And, upon discovering that area of numbness, I discovered other areas connected to it. Pretty soon I started to think of my work as a fairly agreeable chore.

With a good job and a good salary and a destination for every working day there seemed to be little cause for bitterness. Yet I kept one core of bitterness abundantly fed. At a moment's notice I could summon up Clifford Sandys. He was to blame for it all. He was the never-failing, stimulating goad. The fact that he was still out there – scheming, manipulating, twisting sure-footedly along devious paths – reassured me. I still wanted to get my own back on him. It was possible that he'd return to London. I promised myself I'd be ready for him.

Barbara said, 'For God's sake forget about Clifford.'

'There's a limit to what I can forget.'

'But he doesn't matter now.'

'To you,' I pointed out. 'But he matters to me.'

And, indeed, I was haunted by the image of him. The silhouette of his face intruded upon my picture of the *Niome* in blazing ruin. Frequently, I was startled awake by the odd way in which only half of his face was illuminated when he appeared on the deck of the Storebaelt ferry. In the lifeboat, at the table in the ballroom, on the ferry – he was smiling. When I became oppressed with these memories I cheered myself by thinking that he had exhausted all the possibilities of spoiling my life. And, I told myself, at least I'd never have to see him again in person. As usual, this proved too optimistic by far.

I was amazed at how quickly time passed when I started to work for Colin Thompson Partners. The job was not nearly so interesting as I'd had at Norske Veritas, but there were compensations. First, there was the removal of guilt. During all the years when I'd been at sea it had never occurred to me that I felt guilty about refusing to work for my father, yet as soon as I did so there was an immediate sense of relief. A more important compensation was that I could turn most of my attention away from work altogether. Barbara's influence was strong in this change of focus. Her world was so completely different from mine. It was lighter, more colourful and filled, it seemed, with gallant free-booters. Moreover, on the high seas of theatre even disaster is, eventually, hilarious. But most important of all, there was Barbara herself. To me she was a constant marvel and once she saw that I was content enough with my work she really started to enjoy her own success.

When the play's three-week run at Hampstead ended there was a break while the producers waited for a West End theatre to become available. So, for a few months when she had neither rehearsal nor performance to worry about, she became the model housewife. She got up to make my breakfast and saw me off for the unvarying nine-till-five stint. Then she cleaned and polished the flat. Then she spent the afternoon shopping before hurrying back to prepare dinner for me. After the first couple of weeks of that, when I got home there was a surprise. She was smartly dressed – which was remarkable enough – but what jolted me was that she was wearing make-up.

'Are you going out?' I asked. 'I mean, are *we* going out?'

'Neither of us – as far as I know.' She wrapped me in an investigative embrace, kissed me, then stood back to gauge my reaction. 'Well?'

'What?' I'd learned to be wary of her more effusive moods.

'Well, how does it feel to be molested by a glamorous wife?'

'Very pleasant.'

'*Pleas*ant! You must be sickening . . . for something. Let me check your blood pressure.' And she did so – though not in the orthodox fashion, or place.

'Barbara! Why have you deserted Oxfam, and why are you wearing make-up?'

As she poured me a drink she explained. 'The trouble is, people around here know who I am now.'

'Oh? And who are you now?'

'I'm the star of *Be Your Age*, and they say, "By God, she looks it."'

I laughed and accepted the glass she was offering me. I held it up to note there was an extra large amount of whisky in it. 'What have you cooked for the very first time today?'

'Drink!' she commanded, and poured herself an equal tot.

Gradually it emerged that she had realised after several encounters while out shopping that people were identifying her with her role in the play. Several press articles had made exactly that point. But the character she played was more than ten years older than Barbara. So she had taken defensive action. And the effect was very flattering. She looked much younger than her real age, and very smart indeed. This seemed to invalidate her argument and I put it to her, 'So how will they know who you are if you look like *that*?'

'I'll carry a banner,' she said.

But her new image was necessary, too, for promotion of the play. Often the truculent photographers who accompanied the interviewers expressed disbelief that any subject could be as ill-prepared for their cameras as Barbara. They took it as part of the Bolshie conspiracy they suffer daily or, at best, as a personal slight. In future, Miss Cree would always be photogenic, even though she was horrified at the price of day-wear cosmetics.

Another advantage of the break was the opportunity to spend some time with the Gillespies in Helensburgh. Hugh had an accumulation of free days left over from the previous year and we persuaded him to take them all together at the end of May. I, of course, could take time off whenever I wanted it, but I had to clear it with Hanson. He saw no problem. In fact, he said, 'No problem.' It was a favourite expression of his. He seemed slightly incredulous, though, when I told him how I was going to spend the holiday. 'What do you want to see Hughie about?'

'I don't want to see him *about* anything. He's a friend of mine.'

'Sure. He's a friend of mine, too, but . . .'

'But what?'

Whatever he was going to say, he decided against it. Instead, he did his shrug and chuckle. 'Well, the last time you went up there things seemed to get out of hand.'

'This time,' I assured him, 'I won't bring back any gay burglars.'

To my astonishment, his expression immediately hardened and he stated almost belligerently, 'The "gay" I don't mind.'

Evidently he thought I already knew that and was just taunting him. But I had not known and, as I walked out of his office, I marvelled how it had never once occurred to me that the disaffection between Hugh and Sam Hanson years earlier might have arisen from such an obvious incompatibility. And now, too, I recalled how defensive Hanson had been of whatever it could be assumed Tony Liddle did in his own time.

It was Hanson's recalling the outcome of my previous visit which led me to wonder how Tony Liddle was getting on. While Barbara and Moira were happily engaged on another expedition, Hugh and I were in Glasgow and I suggested that we should call on him. The response to this was almost like an echo. Hugh demanded, 'What dae ye want tae see him aboot?'

'He's a friend of mine,' I repeated.

'He's a chancer.'

'And a chancer,' I conceded. 'Still, he was a great help to me.'

After considerable difficulty with the latest one-way system we found the address on the South Side. The building had recently been cleaned and the tawny sandstone reflected the evening sunlight but, as seems inevitable in Glasgow, the pavement of the entire street was cracked, uneven and broken. Glasgow city council must have enormous stockpiles of faulty paving slabs rejected by the rest of the United Kingdom.

Tony greeted us warmly enough, yet did not quite conceal the fact that he was nervous and uneasy. I introduced Hugh. They smiled and shook hands but Tony's expression became more strained. That was when the first glimmer of a patently absurd thought occurred to me. I put it out of my mind while we chatted about mutual interests. The police had not followed up their enquiries, I was glad to learn, and the disco down in Greenock was thriving. Certainly the furnishings of the flat seemed to confirm what Tony himself asserted. 'Everythin's goin' great.' He then suggested that we should all go out and have a drink. I told him I was perfectly comfortable right there and Hugh mentioned that he'd be driving. Tony nodded and remarked, 'A'm learnin' tae drive – at last.'

Remembering the trouble we'd had getting there, Hugh said, 'Ye'll have a job passin' yer test in Glasgow.'

Tony said, 'Better here than London. Their traffic's murder. The last time A drove there . . .' He stopped abruptly.

My absurd thought grew less absurd. 'In London?' I asked. 'Have you been down recently?'

'Oh, aye. A go doon there now and then. Tae see friends, y'know.'

I chose to misinterpret the verbal tic as a statement and asked, 'That *I* know?'

Tony just couldn't be bothered explaining what he'd meant or concealing what I might guess. 'Aye. A see Sam occasionally.'

Hugh visibly started in his chair. 'Sam Hanson?'

Tony nodded, 'It's him was givin' me the drivin' lesson.'

One or two more puzzling things fell into place. Hanson had probably told Tony about Hugh. But, apparently, this chance meeting with him was not what had caused the unease. The real reason for it arrived just as we were about to leave and any slight malice of which I might have been guilty was amply repaid. We heard the outer door slam and Douglas Tyrrel walked into the room. He was the same Douglas Tyrrel whose jealousy had cost me my job at Norske Veritas. He and Tony were back together again.

In the car returning to Helensburgh both Hugh and I were uncommonly silent. At last he said, 'A would never have believed it about Sam.'

'I think that was the trouble,' I told him. But my own preoccupation was not so readily disposed of. The sheer injustice of the situation we had discovered infuriated me. And whereas the Sam Hanson connection was not mentioned when we got home, I felt free to give Barbara and Moira an indignant report as innocent bystander and chief casualty of a lover's tiff. Naturally, Barbara wanted to hear the full background as well as the consequences so I told the whole story of Tony Liddle when I'd known him as an apprentice. This brought up the whole business of my Greenock notebooks again and Hugh dug them out for my wife to read. She sat up in bed reading them until late into the night and I was asleep before she finished.

The following morning as we prepared to go down for breakfast, her enthusiasm was total. Obviously I was flattered, but
not entirely convinced. On other occasions I'd heard her coo
over mediocre performances of her friends – that is, to the
friends who'd *given* the mediocre performances. She was just a
great encourager. However, her enthusiasm continued throughout breakfast and that was more convincing because she was a
devoted eater as well. I explained to her that this was the
material I'd once spent a year trying to form into a novel, with
no success whatever. There was no way in which the fragments
and disparate characters could be brought together. I appealed
to Hugh for confirmation of this, since he'd been at my elbow
during the effort.

He nodded. 'Right enough, Barbara. There's nothin tae con-
nect them.'

Nevertheless, Barbara insisted that we take the notebooks
back to London with us.

By the time the play re-opened, amid an extra flurry of publicity,
Howard Murray was already commissioned by another management to provide a new play. And right at the outset of the deal
he'd stipulated that he'd want Barbara to take the lead in it. The
new producer was more than willing to give him that assurance
and the lady herself was delighted.

'Howard, really? Another geranium so soon! You must be
using marvellous fertiliser.'

'Yes,' he informed her, 'it's a stimulating compost called Cree.'

'Oh, put that to *mus*ic!' she exclaimed, then dashed off to
yet another celebratory occasion at which she'd be asked to
sing for her supper. She always gave them 'Let Time Be Your
Friend', though mischievously aware that the bulk of her
audience had no such intention. They were fighting it all the
way.

The sparkle and glitter of these events was marred for me
by the fact that among the telegrams of congratulation there had
been one from Clifford Sandys. He was in New York, apparently,
but it would have been too much to expect he'd remain ignorant
of Barbara's well-trumpeted success. And not for a moment did

I imagine that he'd got in touch again just for old times' sake. Everything Clifford did, he did with a purpose. But it was to be almost a year before that purpose came to light.

FOURTEEN

That first year of *Be Your Age* started well for Barbara and me
– then, almost imperceptibly, deteriorated. The basic trouble
was that we didn't have enough time together. Time was *not*
our friend. Our relationship had been built up during the period
when she was rehearsing – and thus at work when I was
working, or during the extended break – when she was at home
day and night. There had also been a spell when she was
performing – but then *I* had not been working. Neither of us
was really prepared for a long run in the theatre which had no
clear end in view. I was away all day and she was away for most
of the night. And even at that she never tired of going on from
the theatre to parties. The whole thing became insistently, and
sometimes acutely, unsatisfactory for both of us.

Very often I spent the evening in Murray's flat. When I told
him of my woes he was less than sympathetic. 'Is it just the lack
of fucking opportunity?' he asked.

For a moment I thought this merely qualified the word 'opportunity' but his cool, clinical gaze insisted on the verb. I said,
'Well, since you put it so delicately, yes. But not only that.'

He brushed away whatever else it might be. 'Surely you can
find a temporary replacement?'

'I don't *want* to find a temporary replacement!' I assured him,
then somewhat incongruously added, 'And anyway we don't
know how long this bloody play of yours is going to run.'

He laughed, 'Several temporary replacements, then. There's
a Broadway production to consider as well. If we can get the
Americans to take a British leading lady.' He was referring to
the fraught situation between branches of the actors' union in
the West End and Broadway. Whereas American producers

often wanted to produce hit London shows, they did *not* want
to import the London cast. They had many fine and strenuously
vocal actors of their own demanding the work. However, the
playwright has a veto on casting and if Murray kept turning
down Broadway names the way would be open for Barbara to
repeat her success on the other side of the Atlantic. But I was
not thinking about any of that.

I gulped. 'New York?'

'Yes. We've started negotiating.' Noting my strained expression he asked, 'What have you got against New York?'

I told him of my fears that Clifford might pounce there. This
seemed to him a more serious and worthy subject. 'Ah, the
elusive Mr Sandys. If he does reappear I'd be interested to
know when, and why.'

'What is it that interests you about him?'

'His sheer gall,' Murray replied.

Some months later, following the news that Barbara would
probably be leaving the London production to open the show in
New York, we heard again from Clifford. Barbara showed me
the letter. The expensively printed letterhead was that of the
Association of Theatrical Press Agents and Managers on West
47th Street, but it was signed by Clifford. In brisk terms he
advanced the virtues of the service he was willing to provide as
a personal manager. He hoped that she would talk the matter
over with her agent and proposed to come and see her personally. The whole thing was very businesslike. I tossed the page
onto the coffee table between us. 'And what are you going to
do?' I asked.

'I'll talk it over with my agent.'

It was very late at night and both of us were tired. I'd fallen
asleep in the chair waiting for her to get back from the theatre.
Now I got to my feet, slightly cramped, and offered to pour her
another drink. She shook her head. As I poured myself another
I felt totally depressed. There was just no fighting Clifford. And
his timing was faultless as ever. Obviously he'd spent a while
planning how he might cash in on Barbara's sudden fame. And
he'd found the ideal way. It had become increasingly clear that
she did need a manager. If she were going to work in New York

it would be essential. Her agent would tell her that. As I slumped once more in the chair I said, 'No doubt you'll be his only client.'

She didn't answer.

'Barbara, it's perfectly obvious that he's set this up just to fleece you.'

'I think he'd make a very good manager,' she said. 'He has enterprise. And drive.' She finished her drink. 'And he'd always be there.'

'So – you've made up your mind.'

'We'll see what he says. He may be able to do quite a lot for me.'

'Oh, yes! And we do know what he does best.'

She laid her empty glass on the table and went to bed. I waited up a lot longer and got thoroughly drunk.

The evening when Clifford came back to the flat is particularly memorable for me. The alarming thing was his paying a surprise visit to the theatre first. Barbara phoned me to say he was there and that she'd be bringing him back after the show. To her it seemed entirely natural that a manager taking on a new client would want to see the performance. She had no patience with my angrily expressed suspicions and warnings and when I began to lose coherence she hung up. The sick feeling in my chest increased. If Clifford had not won so often in the past perhaps the sickness would not have grown almost to a state of panic. But he *had* won, all along the line; and now that the relationship between Barbara and myself was far from satisfactory I was ill-prepared for a showdown. In that state of mind I phoned Murray in the flat upstairs. There was no reply. Robbed of his support my craven reaction was to declare 'no contest'. I put on my coat and prepared to quit the arena.

When the lift door opened it revealed the playwright, dressed to go out and on his way down. 'I've been calling you,' I said. 'Didn't you hear the phone?'

He reached past me to set the lift in motion again. 'Yes, I heard it.'

'Then why the hell didn't you answer it?'

'Because it could have been a waste of my time.'

'Christ! Don't let me waste your time.'

As we stepped out into the entrance hall he asked, 'What's wrong?'

'Your "elusive Mr Sandys" has appeared. In fact, he's coming back with Barbara tonight.'

Murray stopped. 'Why?'

'He wants to set himself up as her personal manager in New York.'

'Ah, then it would *not* have been a waste of my time.' And with that he took my arm, wheeled me round and urged me back into the lift again.

'I thought you were going out.'

'This is more important.' When the doors opened at my floor he said, 'I've got to make a telephone call. I'll be down again shortly.'

But in fact when he came down again he was only a few minutes ahead of our guest. I asked him, 'What are you going to do?'

He said, 'I'm going to help you, and hinder Mr Sandys.'

'I think it's too late now.'

'But I started some time ago.'

I was amazed. 'Really?'

'Oh, yes. I started the first time you mentioned him to me.' We were interrupted by the arrival of Barbara and Clifford.

And he looked very prosperous indeed. He was heavily tanned, seemed much broader and a lot more relaxed. And he'd had his teeth capped. After the introductions it became clear that this former shipmate of mine was now something of an expert in theatre business and had persuaded my wife that he should be her personal manager – starting in New York. It was then that the playwright launched his first depth-charge. 'Oh, dear,' he said.

Barbara asked, 'What is it, Howard?'

'Bad news. I'm afraid your New York début is off. This time.'

'Oh no!'

The playwright nodded his head sadly.

'Why's that?' Clifford wanted to know.

Murray spread his hands resignedly, 'The thugs in the Guild

have teamed up with Equity and together they've forced my hand.'

'Bastards!' said my wife calmly.

Clifford, however, was not prepared to accept it. He leaned forward in his chair, resting his forearms on his knees, and delivered the crucial point to Murray. 'In that case, you'll have to use your veto.'

'I've already used it on several occasions.'

Barbara readily confirmed this. 'Yes. He has. There's a limit to the number of times he can say no.'

Clifford insisted, 'I think if you held out they'd have to agree.'

'Perhaps,' said Murray, smiling, 'but circumstances have changed.'

'When did you find out?' Barbara asked.

'They phoned me earlier this evening,' Murray lied.

I felt everything was moving a bit too fast for me. Obviously, the decision had been made earlier that evening, but they hadn't called Murray. He had called them, and withdrawn his objection to an American leading lady. He'd done that as soon as I'd told him where Clifford hoped to operate. It seemed to me a very satisfying counter-attack though, of course, I was sorry it meant disappointment for Barbara. I was sitting beside her on the couch and put my arm round her waist. Howard Murray and Clifford were facing each other across the room. And Clifford did not take kindly to being thwarted. 'What circumstances, Mr Murray?'

'Mmm?' the playwright gave the impression of trying to recall the point.

'You said circumstances had changed. What circumstances?' Though Clifford himself was the change in circumstances Murray had in mind, he readily invented another reason. 'It's the new play I'm writing for Barbara. The producer of that naturally wants her here to do it.'

'I'm looking forward to it,' Barbara said. 'But I don't see that three months in New York would make all that difference.'

'None at all,' Clifford asserted. 'In fact it would be a bonus.'

'For the producer, or Barbara, or you?' asked the playwright. His mild, apologetic manner was gone completely.

Clifford at once leaned back in his chair and took a new sighting on this stranger who'd turned into an adversary. 'Me?' he asked mildly. 'What could be in it for me?'

My wife, unaware of the tensions, explained, 'I think Howard meant that I won't need a Broadway manager if I'm not going to New York.'

'You still need a manager – even here in London.'

Barbara shook her head doubtfully. 'I don't think so. Not really.' She turned to me. 'What do you think, Bill?'

'Not at all,' I said firmly. 'Your agent can do all that's required over here.'

Clifford's smile was as threatening as ever. 'Even so, I think I'll stay in London for a while.'

'Why not?' Murray said, and reached for a cigarette. 'That'll give you an opportunity to visit your wife.'

Barbara's body stiffened against my arm and I too jolted with surprise. She exclaimed, 'His *wife*!'

The playwright nodded as he replaced his lighter in his top pocket. 'Yes. And his son, of course.'

I was staring at Clifford and for the first time I saw his composure shaken. He gripped the arms of the chair and his eyes were locked on the fine spiral of smoke which curled up from Murray's cigarette. At last, and far too late to have any hope of convincing us, he said, 'I haven't got a wife. What do you mean?'

'I mean Dorothy. Surely you remember Dorothy?' Murray made a gesture in my direction. 'She wrote to Bill recently.' I nodded, marvelling at Murray's pre-planning. He went on, 'Bill and I met her in Manchester.'

Barbara asked me, 'Did you?'

And though it was only at that moment I knew who I'd met, I stated evenly, 'Yes. She's a journalist.' To Clifford I added, 'And she's very anxious to get in touch with you.'

He lunged to his feet, then, aware of the way in which Barbara was looking at him, he turned away from her and moved round the back of the chair. As he did so, his voice was trying desperately to be calm. 'I don't know what you're talking about.'

The playwright went implacably on. 'We're talking about the

girl you married in 1967 and the child you deserted while he was
still an infant.'

Nothing could have been better calculated to alienate Barbara.
She leaned forward. Clifford still avoided her eyes. She sought
more details from the source. 'Are you sure of this, Howard?'

'Absolutely sure.' He then related that after little more than
a year of marriage Clifford prepared his getaway by leaving the
reputable shipping company he'd sailed with in favour of a
thoroughly *dis*reputable one, where there were very few questions asked and no answers given. To my amazement, the dates
– many of which I'd supplied – tallied exactly with those which
Dorothy Castle mentioned. Clifford's first assignment from his
new employer was a convenient distance away in west Africa
where he'd supervised the lethal alterations on the *Niome*.

Midway through this recital our quarry showed signs of bolting
but the undisguised authority in Murray's voice stopped him at
the door. 'Wait, Mr Sandys. You haven't heard the offer.'

Clifford turned. 'Offer?'

'Yes. You see, we didn't tell Dorothy where you were.'

'Why not?' Barbara enquired indignantly.

The playwright then neatly excluded me from the consequences of our Manchester visit. 'Because,' he explained, 'I
wouldn't wish an unhappy marriage on anyone.' Barbara slumped
back against my arm. 'And, I suppose, it's none of my business.'

Clifford rallied at that, 'Right! Damn right, it's none of your
business.' He strode back into the room to confront the playwright.

Murray urbanely ignored the threat. 'However, I may meet
Ms Castle again and it would make me feel easier if I honestly
could not tell her where you were – even if I wanted to.'

Clifford looked down at him and nodded slowly. 'So – the offer
is that you'll keep quiet if I get lost again?'

'Yes,' Murray said firmly. 'And I think we *all* wish you would.'

Clifford looked first at Barbara then at me and on both faces
he read the same message. Getting lost was the best thing he
could do. 'Okay,' he nodded again to Murray, but now decisively.
'Okay, I'll go. But just tell me, *why* have you done all this spying
and tracking? What the hell is in it for you?'

'It needn't concern you,' said the playwright. And Clifford left us.

Many times after that I asked myself the same question and got an equally unsatisfactory answer. The playwright was anxious, though, to reduce the scale of my amazement at his coup. He pointed out that, given the sort of person we were dealing with, it would have been strange if there had *not* been 'something negotiable' in Clifford's past. And, given his nature, there must have been aggrieved females. 'It was likely that I'd find a couple of bastards, or at least one girl willing to cry "rape". Instead, I found a deserted wife who'd no intention of letting him off with divorce, because of her career – and their son.'

'But how were you able to find the wife?' I asked. 'She'd been trying to find Clifford for years, with no success.'

Murray pointed out, 'Sandys was trying to hide. His wife wasn't. I started at the point she hoped to reach.'

As he told it, all of this was perfectly clear but it did not explain why he'd wanted to pursue these enquiries. In Barbara's opinion Howard Murray was just protecting an investment which happened to be her. But that didn't really fit the circumstances. And I had the impression he would have done as much for persons quite separate from his own interests. Recalling his many mysterious absences from the flat it seemed to me likely that the banishment of Clifford and the restoration of my peace of mind was only one among a number of personal conflicts where he involved himself – probably with equally heartening results. Murray's conclusive intervention in my affairs reminded me of a poem by Edwin Arlington Robinson and my grateful imagination saw the playwright as a particularly tough version of 'the man Flammonde'.

Barbara would have nothing more to do with Clifford but she did devote a lot more attention to me. We talked very sensibly about what was going wrong between us and though she identified the problem exactly as I had done – she proposed a solution. 'You ought to have a job that allows us to be together during the day.'

I smiled, 'Sure. Something with a permanent night-shift.'

'But not *all* of the night,' she specified.

'That might be difficult to arrange.'

Then she played her ace. 'Not if you worked at home.'

'Weaving baskets. That sort of thing?'

'No. Writing.'

'Barbara! I've told you I tried that.' And I'd no intention of going through the fruitless discussion of it again so I got out of bed and headed for the shower.

When I got back that evening the first thing I saw was all my Greenock notebooks paraded the length of the coffee table. With no preamble whatever Barbara thrust a drink into my hand, pushed me onto the couch and started her sales pitch. 'You have here,' she said, 'some valuable material.'

'Which won't make a novel,' I firmly pointed out.

'So? Don't *make* a novel. Make a collection of stories – and get the hell out of the third person!'

'What?' I was incredulous at this effrontery, but also amused. 'Be*cause* . . .' she pinned me back, '. . . I have found the link you need.'

'I'd be glad to know what it is after all this time.'

'*You* are the link. You've got to be in all six of the stories.'

'Barbara,' I explained patiently, 'if the material has any interest it's in those six characters. Nobody would have any interest in me. And, anyway, I can't write in the first person.'

'Then you'll have to learn,' my wife decided. 'Ask Howard. He does it all the time.'

This was absurd. 'He writes plays.'

'Right! And plays are stories in which everybody says "I". The only characters in plays who use the third person usually turn out to be crazy. It's an infallible sign.'

'I laughed. 'Well, I'm not crazy,' I said. 'But I am hungry.'

'Food!' she declaimed with a fine show of artistic fervour. 'I offer him a career and all he can think of is food.'

On the following Sunday – when she had the whole day to bustle in – Barbara gave me the fruits of further inventive thought. And now she was on first-name terms with the memorable prisoners in my notebooks. Also, she had the format and title of the book I should write. She told me, 'We'll call it

"Apprentice". And instead of having six stories we'll have five. One for each year of your time.'

That did strike me as neat. 'Which five?' I asked.

She reeled them off in her own order of preference, 'Dosser Farr, Elsie, Delia Liddle, Turk Thomas and Lord Sweatrag.'

The person she'd cut was a favourite of mine. 'What have you got against Miss Douglas, the music teacher?'

'She needs shaking till her teeth rattle,' Barbara told me. 'Apart from that she has no problem and no story.'

I had to smile at this callous view, but, in the months that followed the discussion, I was easily drawn in by my wife's obsessive belief in my ability. And I did start practising in the style of a first person narrator. It was an embarrassing exercise. After what seemed a long while the results started to improve and I could read them aloud to myself without squirming.

Assured of some progress, Barbara now revealed the next part of her strategy. 'I'm convinced you'd get on much faster if you didn't have to fight against the noise of that traffic.'

I sighed. 'Ah! I see.'

'What? Darling, what do you mean?'

'I mean that apparently I've been thinking, now would be a good time for us to make our long delayed move to Richmond.'

She kept a straight face and even managed some astonishment. 'How odd you should say that! Do you know, I've been thinking exactly the same thing.'

Of course she had. But now the move would be for my sake. So, when she'd completed her second full year of *Be Your Age* in the West End she left the production and devoted all her energy to this converted coach-house at West Temple Sheen.

I continued to work for Colin Thompson Partners in Leadenhall Street and twice daily took the grinding journey which began and ended at an extremity of the District Line. That tiresome shuttling did a lot to shake me out of the rut. Barbara never knew what a staunch ally she had in the Underground. But even at work things were changing. My father announced that he was going to retire at the end of 1979 and though he would maintain

financial control of the company it was to be run thereafter by
Sam Hanson. The news was yet another bleak milestone in my
relationship with my father. It didn't do much for my relationship
with Sam Hanson either. In the new year, having moved into
the larger office, he fired two of the junior engineers. He also
fired Mrs Schuster for no better reason than her faultless
knowledge of how things used to be done. When he heard of it,
my father objected strongly to that. But the damage was done.
Once Mrs Schuster found out she wasn't wanted, nothing would
persuade her to stay. Hanson then set the guidelines for our
future association. There was no question now of considering
me as an equal – even on the surface. Hanson was top man and
intended to run a tight ship. There were to be no more casual
days off and I, like everybody else on the staff, must complete
an accurate weekly project sheet. This would show exactly how
every hour was spent and allow realistic costing to be made. All in
all, the agreeable haven showed signs of becoming an up-market
sweatshop.

It is likely that, even so, I would have got used to the new
order and complied with its requirements, if a quite separate
event hadn't affected me so deeply. On 11th March 1980 I
received a telegram which informed me that Isa Mulvenny had
died that morning. I phoned the Matron at the nursing home,
asking her to call me when she knew the funeral arrangements.
Barbara wanted to go as well but I dissuaded her. The family
would resent my presence enough without the attendance of my
wife. The time they chose for the burial was fairly early in the
morning so I decided to travel up overnight on the train. And,
because I did not have a suitable dark suit, I wore my old
uniform.

It's strange what triggers the changes in people's lives. Mine
changed because, standing at that ill-attended graveside, there
came to me an urgent need to repay a debt. With all my heart,
I wanted more people to remember Isa Mulvenny. It just was
not enough that she should be swallowed up and forgotten within
fifteen minutes on a blustery cold morning. That was not enough
for her. In the train going back the same day, I was filled with
remorse that in all the notes and character sketches I'd written

about my time in Greenock – I'd said nothing about her. And
she was where it all began. My career in engineering began
when she took me in at the age of sixteen and treated me like
a son. And it was going to end with her death.

Still dressed in my uniform, I switched onto the Circle Line
at Euston and tried not to think of what I was doing but only to
feel the unreasonable imperative. It was very late in the afternoon and Hanson was preparing to go home. He looked up
sharply and something about my appearance seemed to startle
him. 'What's up, Bill?'

'My time's up. I'm resigning. Today. *Now.*'

'You can't do that. We need three months' notice.'

'Then you'll have to whistle for it because I'm not coming
back to this place again.'

Within three weeks I'd written a long, complete story called
'Portrait of Isa Mulvenny'. And there wasn't the slightest
difficulty about expressing myself in the first person. That done,
I abandoned yet another of the existing characters to make room
for the new piece. Then I set about completing the other four
stories to maintain the format Barbara had suggested. And of
course she was delighted that, at last, I was writing. Besides,
for all of that summer, our whole days were spent together in
a quiet house tucked behind a defensive hedge on a leafy narrow
street. It was a world away from Greenock and just as far
from the blaze of the sinking *Niome* or its drawn-out, painful
aftermath.

Barbara said, 'Isn't it amazing how you've changed.'

'In what way?'

'Well, you've become so . . . *positive*. And suddenly you have
no trouble writing. What happened to all the obstacles?'

'There was really only one obstacle,' I told her. 'I *wanted* to
write for myself. But now I *must* do it – for Isa Mulvenny, and
for you.'

Barbara seemed much affected by that. She was about to say
something, then suddenly turned and walked out into the garden.
I smiled. Now that the book was finished I was trying to devise
a way of introducing myself to the reader. 'Be honest,' my wife

had warned me. 'Don't try to bluff them.' With that excellent advice in mind, I resumed typing the preface to *Apprentice* – and the beginning, at last, to a life of my own making.

TOM GALLACHER

APPRENTICE

In this perceptive and powerful set of linked short stories, Bill Thompson is the Apprentice, working in the Clyde shipyards in the 1950s. An innocent abroad, he is at first mystified by his proud and private fellows. They are stubborn, unsophisticated and in many ways ignorant. But Bill has just what they need: he has an education.

Apprentice is the first of the Bill Thompson trilogy.

'A first and marvellous collection . . . a subtle exploration of the great divide between the way people see themselves and the way other people see them, and the false judgements, pain, humour and confusion that follow'

The Bookseller

'All the stories have neat, sting-in-the-tail endings that are never contrived'

Daily Telegraph

'He captures the strain of tragic eccentricity in the people of his lively stories'

The Irish Times

'Sympathetic but unsentimental . . . it is readable and has staying power'

Time Out

sceptre

WILLIAM McILVANNEY

THE BIG MAN

The Big Man is Dan Scoular, a working-class legend of physical prowess, fighting for his heritage – a decaying community in a small Ayrshire town – fighting to keep it afloat and intact.

'Inspiring and harshly funny. As in Orwell at his fiercest best, McIlvanney's outrage is all the more potent for being tranquil. Grand fiction that reads as truly as fact, (which says), "this is where we've been and this where we really are"'
David Hughes in the Mail On Sunday

'A vivid transcription of a small town and the people who live there . . . Wry, funny, tender, largely unsentimental and very readable'
Henry Stanhope in The Times

'Confirms his reputation as the most incisive observer of working-class Scottish life'
Rob Brown in the Guardian

'A novel of great power and microscopic observations . . . Ambitious material, handled with sharpness and poignancy and full of memorable moments and images'
Isabel Quigley in the Financial Times

'A prose of growing assurance, with vivid and memorable results'
Douglas Dunn, Whitbread Book of the Year Winner in the Glasgow Herald

sceptre

Current and forthcoming titles from Sceptre

TOM GALLACHER

**APPRENTICE
JOURNEYMAN**

WILLIAM McILVANNEY

**THE BIG MAN
DOCHERTY**

RONALD FRAME

SANDMOUTH PEOPLE

MELVYN BRAGG

THE MAID OF BUTTERMERE

BOOKS OF DISTINCTION